Also by Anna Schmidt

★ COWBOYS & HARVEY GIRLS ★

PATHFINDER

ANNA SCHMIDT

sourcebooks
casablanca

Published by Sourcebooks Casablanca, an imprint of Sourcebooks
P. O. Box 4410, Naperville, Illinois 60567-4410
(630) 961-3900
sourcebooks.com

Printed and bound in Canada.
MBP 10 9 8 7 6 5 4 3 2 1

WANTED:

Young women, 18–30 years of age, of good moral character, attractive and intelligent, as waitresses in

HARVEY EATING HOUSES ON THE SANTA FE RAILROAD.

Wages $17.50 a month with room and board. Liberal tips customary. Experience not necessary.

Write Fred Harvey, Union Depot, Kansas City, Missouri

Chapter 1

Juniper, New Mexico, Winter 1903

"MISS ELLIOTT! A MOMENT PLEASE." AIDAN CAMPBELL, manager of the Palace Hotel, hurried toward Emma. They had worked together for several years now in the Harvey Corporation, and Emma took pride in knowing he held her in high esteem. That respect came in spite of the fact that they had shared a brief romantic relationship, one Emma had broken off. Since that time, Aidan had been overly formal in his dealings with her.

Aidan handed her a telegram he'd clearly just received. "Read this," he said. Given his smile and obvious excitement, Emma had to assume this was good news.

MY DEAR FRIEND CAPT MAX WINSLOW AND COMPANY COMING TO JUNIPER STOP ARRIVING TODAY BY PRIVATE TRAIN STOP MAKE THEM WELCOME STOP

It was signed Ford Harvey. Ford was the son of the company's founder, Fred Harvey, and the heir apparent to the empire of hotels and restaurants his father had built.

"Well," Emma said, handing the telegram back to Aidan. "One does not say no to Mr. Harvey or his son, but really, Aidan, a military company here in the hotel? The other guests will surely wonder what brought this about."

Aidan's eyes bulged. "You have no idea who Captain Max Winslow is?"

"Should I?"

In his excitement, Aidan dropped all hint of formality. "Emma, he is a famous former army hero as well as part owner and star of the Last Frontier Wild West Show—a show that is coming here to Juniper for the winter. It's bound to be a boon to business."

Emma chewed her lower lip. Housing and feeding a bunch of soldiers was one thing. In her opinion, doing the same for a troupe of theater people would be far more challenging. According to everything she'd heard or read, such people could be quite rowdy, and their moral standards were questionable as well.

"How many are in this group?" She hoped raising the practicalities of the relatively small number of rooms available in the hotel measured against the number of performers might give Aidan pause.

"Only Captain Max, his leading lady, and the troupe's manager will stay here. The roustabouts, livestock handlers, and other members of the cast and crew will have their own quarters on the grounds."

"The grounds?"

"The area the town council has leased to them for setting up the show just outside town."

"None of that was covered in Mr. Harvey's telegram," she noted.

Aidan sighed. "Are you so busy managing the dining room and counter and playing mother hen to the girls you haven't time to read the paper?"

"The *girls* are young women we rely upon to maintain the high standard of decorum and service for which we are known," she reminded him. "They are the face of this and every other Harvey establishment." She pressed her palms over the starched front of her pristine white apron as she stared at the tips of her perfectly polished black shoes. She rarely challenged Aidan in this way. He was, after all, her superior. "I apologize. It's just that…"

"We'll make it all work out, Emma," he said, lowering his voice. "We always do. Alert your staff, and I'll see to getting rooms set up." He glanced once again at the telegram. "No time given, so we need to get ready." He motioned to his assistant at the front desk before turning back to Emma. "I'll reserve a table for the captain and his costar and manager to use whenever they choose. You should appoint your very best waitress to serve them." He started toward the desk and hesitated. "Better yet, *you* should serve them. No one better." He hurried away.

Emma bristled. She already pulled double duty as the manager of the dining room and more casual counter service as well as housemother to the waitresses. Harvey Girls always lived on-site, in this case on the top floor of the hotel. They were expected to set an example of ladylike manners and morals as well as abide by strict rules and curfews. There was always at least one who thought she could ignore the rules, meaning Emma had the added role of disciplinarian. She had her hands full already, and now Aidan expected her to wait on these show people in the bargain?

Fortunately, she had established the practice of meeting with all the waitresses just after the morning breakfast crowd at the counter thinned and before the dining room opened for lunch. They were waiting now in the dining room. Emma mentally counted heads as they lined up so she could make sure their uniforms—a black dress covered by a bibbed white apron—were spotless and their shoes polished.

Trula Goodwin was missing.

Emma sighed and glanced at Trula's roommate, Sarah.

"She's got another of her headaches, Miss Elliott," Sarah murmured. Two other girls rolled their eyes.

"And did this headache come upon her around two this morning by chance?" She saw Sarah's eyes widen in surprise. "Perhaps as she was creeping up the kitchen stairs, past my door?"

"It was…later," Sarah stammered.

Emma had discovered that letting these young women know she was aware of infractions of the rules worked miracles in terms of making them think twice before crossing that line. Still, Trula continued to test the boundaries, and Emma had given her enough warnings.

She tapped her pencil against her lower lip, pondering how best to handle the situation. In the distance, a train whistle sounded—the 9:05 freight train. She would give Trula until noon tomorrow to pack her things and decide her destination. Of course, that would leave them shorthanded at a time when that was the last thing she needed. But they would manage.

She forced a smile and faced the girls. "Ladies, we have some special guests arriving perhaps as soon as later today. My understanding is that they will be with us for some time. Has anyone heard of a Captain Max Winslow?"

The girls gasped in unison, and their eyes widened with excitement.

"He's the one on the posters all over town," one girl announced as others turned to one another with animated smiles.

"I saw his show when I was in training in Kansas City. He is gorgeous," a second waitress said.

Emma cleared her throat to regain their full attention. "Apparently, the entire company will winter here in Juniper, although only the captain and two others will be staying here in the hotel. The point is, Captain Winslow is a personal friend of Mr. Ford Harvey, so we all need to be at our——"

A tap on the closed double glass doors interrupted her lecture. Emma turned as the door opened halfway and possibly the best-looking man she had ever seen in her life stepped into the room. Behind her, she heard the girls whispering and giggling nervously.

"I apologize, sir, but the dining room does not start serving until…"

He removed his hat to reveal thick waves of black hair, a face tanned golden, deep-set eyes beneath the ridge of his forehead, and a nose that might have seen a fight or two. He moved toward her.

"Max Winslow, ma'am." His eyes were gray, almost silver, and he was standing close enough that she could not help but notice the fan of thick black lashes that framed them.

"It's miss," she said, her voice a raspy whisper. Behind her, a few of her girls tittered and were shushed by others. "Miss Elliott," she added primly, finding her full voice.

"Well, Miss Elliott, I'm mighty pleased to meet you. I stopped at the front desk, but no one was there, and I heard you talking to these fine ladies and…"

"Your train is here?"

"Ah, that answers the question of whether or not we're expected. I don't take the train if I can help it. I came on horseback. Diablo's tied up right outside there. The others will be along later tonight after they tear down from our last performance and load everything and everyone on the train."

Several of the girls broke ranks and hurried to the window to look outside. "He's gigantic," one of them murmured.

"He's marvelous," another added.

Emma wondered if they meant the captain or the horse. She gathered herself and looked up at him—at least six feet of him with broad shoulders that filled the cotton chambray shirt he wore, a shirt stained with perspiration and dust from his journey. "I'll go find Mr. Campbell, the hotel manager," she said. "I'm sure he has a room ready for you and—"

"No need to fuss, Miss Elliott." He stepped toward the girls at the window. "If you ladies could direct me to the livery, I'll get Diablo settled and then come back." He flashed a smile, and Emma thought at least two of her waitresses might swoon. This was getting out of hand.

She cleared her throat. "The livery is just to the other side of the railway station," she said and, with a sweep of her hand, indicated the door. "I can have Tommy, our bellboy, take care of that for you if you like."

Once again, she had his full attention, and that smile was now aimed exclusively at her. "I reckon I'd best take care of it. Diablo can be a little touchy when it comes to who handles him." He had reached the dining room doors. He swept back the hair that had fallen over his forehead and tugged on his hat before tipping two fingers to the wide brim. "Ladies," he said, glancing at the group of waitresses. "Miss Elliott," he added with a slight bow.

And then he was gone. As soon as the doors clicked shut, the girls started to babble like a brook sprung from its winter bonds.

"He's even better-looking than his posters," one girl said.

"He's downright adorable," another sighed.

"I heard him and Rebel Reba are sweethearts," a third chimed in.

Emma couldn't help herself. "Who on earth is Rebel Reba?" she asked.

The girls froze and stared at her, much the same way Aidan had when she hadn't known who the captain was.

"She's the captain's costar," one explained.

"She's as good as he is with a six-shooter," another added.

"And she's beautiful besides." Trula stepped in from the kitchen, tying the sash of her apron as she joined the others.

Emma ignored her. "Let's get back to business, ladies. The captain and his party will have this table available at all times," she instructed as she pointed to a round table near the double doors. "They are not to be disturbed by staff or other guests." She saw Trula grin. The table she'd indicated was one Trula served.

"Mr. Campbell has asked that I serve our special guests," Emma added, and Trula's smile faded. "In the meantime, we have our regulars from the train due to arrive soon, so that will be all. Prepare your stations. We have a busy day ahead." The girls turned away. "Trula, my office, please."

∞

As Max rode slowly down the street, past the railway station, he saw Ed Brunswick, the show's advance man, tacking up posters announcing the *Last Frontier Wild West Show, the Only Authentic Portrayal of the American West.* Max raised a hand in greeting to Ed, who grinned and pointed to the latest poster. The sign covered a good part of the side wall of the local mercantile, and its vivid color portrayed Max on Diablo, the horse reared on hind legs as Max waved his hat in the air.

The truth was it was all an act. Max hated what his life had become—what the West had become. With the driving of the native populations onto reservations and the floods of settlers and now tourists, everything had changed. That rugged, independent, free-spirited land he'd known as a younger man was pocked now with towns like Juniper and cattle and sheep ranches—some huge and others smaller—all fenced off with barbed wire. Any hint of what the open range had been had all but disappeared. The life Max had planned—a ranch of several thousand acres on open land—seemed as improbable as the idea years earlier that the vast herds of bison roaming that open prairie would be all but eradicated. But the bison were pretty much gone, and so was Max's dream of living out his days on the raw frontier.

After finishing his service with the army, he'd bummed around, trying to find work, but his skills as a scout and pathfinder were no longer in demand. The coming of the railroad had changed all that. He'd been dead broke and prone to drowning his sorrows in a pint of rye whiskey when the Last Frontier Wild West Show had come to Montana. He'd heard they were hiring men to set up tents and care for livestock while playing extras. After signing on with the company, he realized how much he hated the phony way life on the range was being portrayed. One night, fortified by whiskey, he'd gone to the show's owner and laid out his complaints.

To his surprise, Bert Gordon had not only listened, he'd offered to let Max come on board as the show's advisor, giving him free rein to restructure the acts to make them more authentic. "We're up against the big guns—Buffalo Bill Cody, for one," Bert had told him. "We need an edge. You give me that, and I'll make you a full partner, Max Winslow."

And Max had done exactly that. He'd stopped

drinking altogether, spending all his time figuring out how best to show people—especially youngsters— what the West had once been in a way that was both entertaining and educational. One of Gordon's instructions had been that Max would need to find roles for all current performers.

"These folks have stayed with me in spite of offers from those bigger outfits," he had explained. "Loyalty like that deserves loyalty in return."

Over time, Max had come to think of the rest of the company as family, and they had urged him to take on a role himself. So three years after first walking into Gordon's office, here he was—Captain Max Winslow, American hero and the star of the show. He was uncomfortable with the title. Sure, he'd done his part to serve his country and to protect others, but he would not count himself a hero.

He shook his head at the strange ways life can turn and led Diablo into the shadowy interior of the blacksmith shop. The smithy looked up, wiped his hands on a stained rag, and stepped forward. He was grinning, and Max had learned that usually meant he'd been recognized. It looked like Ed's hard work passing out handbills to the locals had paid off.

"You're the captain," the blacksmith said.

"Well, hopefully, even with everything at peace, the country still has more than one captain," Max replied with a grin. He extended his hand. "Max Winslow," he said by way of introduction.

"Mick Preston. You need a place for Diablo there?"

Max's horse was almost as famous as he was—some days, maybe more. One of the highlights of the show was when Max put the stallion through its tricks—counting, running a gauntlet of barrels, playing dead. "You've seen the show?"

Mick nodded. "Caught it up in Columbia last summer." He walked toward an empty stall at the back of the shop. "Diablo will be fine here. You can count on that."

The horse had a sixth sense about people, and Max saw that he'd accepted the blacksmith without question. "Much obliged," he said as he bent to unbuckle the saddle and remove it. "I'll keep this with me at the hotel."

"Good idea," Mick said as he admired the fine leather and silver decorations that studded the saddle. He pulled a stub of a pencil from behind one ear and picked up a scrap of paper to write some figures and total them. "Board, feed..." He handed the paper to Max. "How's that?"

Max barely glanced at the figure, one he guessed was either too low or exaggerated. He'd seen both and figured in the end they tended to balance out. "Looks fine, and how about I throw in tickets for the show for you and your family?"

"That'd be swell," the blacksmith said. His grin beneath his light-brown mustache revealed a missing tooth. "You're staying at the hotel, are you?"

"That's the plan."

"Lucky man. Surrounded by all them pretty girls. On the other hand, you can look, but don't touch. Fred Harvey has rules when it comes to his girls."

"So I've heard." Max led Diablo into the stall and hung the blanket over the railing. He slid a grooming brush over the ebony coat. If he were human, Max thought, Diablo would be smiling about now. He slid a hand down the muzzle and detached the hackamore, hung it on a peg, then picked up his saddle. "Thanks for everything, Mick."

The blacksmith lifted a pair of heavy iron tongs and a horseshoe and returned to the fire. "It'll be a welcome distraction having you folks around," he said and jabbed the horseshoe into the fire.

As he headed back to the hotel, Max could hear the steady ring of metal on metal as the blacksmith went about his work. A freight train was just leaving the station. On the covered portico outside the entrance to the hotel, he saw one of the Harvey Girls talking to a man dressed in a suit.

Miss Elliott.

In the years of traveling with the show, he'd stayed or dined at Harvey establishments all across the West, and he'd flirted with his fair share of the uniformly pretty, uniformly untouchable girls he'd met along the way. But there was something different about Miss Elliott. It was the smile, he realized. He knew that smile. It was a performer's smile, one that didn't quite reach the eyes, that didn't come from somewhere deep inside. A smile that hid something—sadness or loneliness maybe. Either way, he knew that smile because it was the same one he gave the cheering audience throughout every performance.

∞

Aidan received word that the train carrying the Wild West show and its cast would finally arrive late that night. The dining room would have closed, but Aidan insisted Emma have her staff in full uniform line up along the platform at the railway station to welcome the troupe.

She assured him everyone would be in place, except for Trula Goodwin.

During their meeting in her office, Emma had gone over the long list of Trula's infractions. She'd reminded the young woman how many times she'd been warned and told her she was no longer suitable for the Harvey organization. If she had expected hysterics and tears, she was mistaken. Trula had stood silently by the door, her eyes locked on Emma's face, her lip curled with disdain.

"Will there be anything else?" she asked when Emma finished.

"Not at the moment. Let me know your destination by tonight, and I'll arrange for your ticket."

Trula had smiled. "And if I decide to stay in Juniper?"

"That's your choice. Just understand you are no longer employed here."

∞

"I had to dismiss Trula Goodwin," Emma informed Aidan.

"Now? You chose now to leave us short-staffed?"

Emma knew Aidan was aware of Trula's transgressions. She also knew under any other circumstances he would be praising her for taking action. "We'll be fine, Aidan," she said. "Trust me."

He glanced at the other waitresses. "Once our

guests arrive," he said, "I want the Harvey Girls to escort them from here to the hotel, make them feel welcome, assure them anything they want is—"

"We're not servants," she reminded him. "And these show people are not royalty."

"I simply want us to make a good first impression."

Emma saw that for the half-truth it was. Recently, Aidan had been talking about applying for a position in Kansas City, headquarters for the Harvey Company. It would be a promotion—one he deserved—but kowtowing to a bunch of actors? "Aidan, I doubt impressing these people will do anything to—"

"You read the telegram. Captain Winslow is Ford Harvey's good friend. If I do things right, he might put in a good word for me. Maybe for you as well. Think of it, Emma. We could work together in a larger market." He left the dining room, giving instructions to other staff members as he crossed the lobby to his office behind the reception desk.

Although the dining room was busier than usual for both lunch and supper, Captain Winslow was not among the guests served. In fact, Emma had not seen him at all since he'd left earlier in the day to stable his horse. Of course, she had thought about him. How could she help it when her waitresses spent every spare minute peeking out the windows or whispering and giggling behind their hands? She reprimanded them with a look, but one time when she'd glanced toward the door, she'd caught a glimpse of a wide-brimmed black Stetson, and her pulse had quickened. She silently chastised herself for the disappointment she felt when Seymour Gilmore, a wealthy rancher from the area, entered the dining room and hung his black hat on the coat rack near the door.

Nerves, she thought. After all, this was important for everyone, and she especially wanted things to go well for Aidan. They'd been through a lot together, and despite breaking off any romantic attachment with him, she believed Aidan deserved to achieve his dreams.

So she lined up with her staff and made one last check of the waitresses before hearing the whistle blow and the distant chug of the train moving closer. Suddenly, Aidan changed his mind about the lineup for the reception, deciding to arrange the waitresses in two straight lines, before handing Tommy a bouquet of flowers.

"For Miss Reba," he explained when Tommy gave him a mystified smile. "The train will make a brief stop here for those members of the company staying at the hotel. Then it will move on to the show grounds and remain on a side track there for the duration of their stay."

Emma took the position Aidan assigned her at one end of a welcome committee made up of Aidan, the other managers from the hotel, and the mayor. She smiled at her waitresses, enjoying watching them primp a bit as they leaned forward to watch the train make the curve that would bring it into the station. They deserved this as much as Aidan did. As Harvey employees, they were paid well, made good tips, and received free room and board in the bargain. But after a while, the work could become tiresome— always smiling in spite of the heat, heavy trays, spills in need of clearing, or the complaints of customers who seemed determined to break them. How often had she lain awake nights, hearing the distant rumble of a passing train and wondering if she had made the right decision all those years earlier. She was glad they would have this distraction for the next several weeks.

"Good evening, Miss Elliott. Looks like Mr. Campbell has rolled out the welcome mat."

She had not seen or heard Captain Winslow approach. On top of that, he was such a presence that she took half a step back and bumped into the rough wooden wall of the station, nearly losing her balance. The captain touched her shoulder, steadying her.

"I apologize. I didn't mean to startle you."

Just then the train rumbled into place, and a cheer went up from inside the passenger cars lined up behind the locomotive. All along the platform, the show people leaned out the windows, chattering to one another about this new stop on their tour. A tall, slender woman dressed in a royal-blue velvet gown and a hat rivaling the size of one of Mr. Harvey's famous coffee urns descended the metal stairs of the first car and accepted the help of the conductor and Aidan, who had immediately moved forward to greet her. She had a dazzling smile, and she lifted her skirt just enough to expose a hint of her ankle before turning her attention to the crowd before her. It was obvious she was searching for someone.

"Maxie!" she shouted and waved at the captain.

Of course.

"That's Rebel Reba," he said as he took a gentle hold on Emma's elbow and steered her forward. "Come on. I'll introduce you."

Emma decided she was acting every bit as silly as her waitresses, the way she blushed and ducked her head as Captain Winslow led her across the platform to greet the woman. She pulled her arm free and signaled Tommy, who stepped forward with the flowers.

"Oh, how lovely," the actress trilled. "And from such a handsome delivery boy," she added, pinching Tommy's cheek. Tommy looked as if he might pass out if he didn't first explode with embarrassment.

And then the actress set her sights on the captain.

"Maxwell," she murmured, stepping in front of Emma as she wagged a finger at him. "Naughty boy, going off on your own that way. Bert was frantic." She tapped her cheek lightly, signaling her expectation of a kiss.

Captain Winslow ignored her and turned to Emma. "Reba, I'd like you to meet Miss Elliott. She's in charge of these lovely ladies who have come out tonight, in spite of the late hour, to welcome the company to Juniper." He swept a hand toward the waitresses.

Emma saw a hint of a frown furrow the actress's smooth brow, but her smile never wavered. "Well, aren't you girls sweet," she said, ignoring Emma as she placed one hand in the crook of the captain's elbow while clutching the oversized bouquet in the other. She allowed her gaze to sweep over the line of Harvey Girls. "Maxwell, I see I may have some competition here," she teased. "I must say Mr. Harvey and his son do have an eye for fresh young faces."

Aidan cleared his throat. "Good evening," he said. "I am Aidan Campbell, manager of the Palace Hotel.

And this is Mayor Frank Tucker, Miss…I'm afraid I do not know your surname."

"Charmed," she cooed. "And it's just Miss Reba, all right? I mean, we're all going to be such good friends." She released her hold on the captain, handed the flowers to one of the waitresses, and offered her free gloved hand as if she expected the two men to kiss her ring.

To Emma's amusement, Frank grabbed it and started pumping up and down as if trying to get water. "Welcome to our little community, ma'am. You just let me or Mr. Campbell here know if there's anything—anything at all—you might need to make your stay more comfortable."

"Well, I—" The actress tried extracting her hand, but the mayor caught it between both of his and continued speaking.

"You see, I own the mercantile over there, and anything we don't already have in stock, I'll order for you. Just say the word."

Again, Aidan cleared his throat. Frank glanced at him and then at his grip on Miss Reba. He patted her hand and released her. "Anything at all," he repeated.

Aidan turned to Emma and nodded toward the flowers. "Perhaps you could have one of your girls arrange those in a vase and bring it to Miss Reba's room, Miss Elliott."

He pronounced *vase* as "vahs," Emma noted with amusement.

"In the meantime," he continued, turning his attention back to the actress, "you must be exhausted after your travels. Allow me to escort you to the hotel." He offered his arm. "I've arranged for our very best room for you," he added. "There's a wonderful view of the mountains and…"

His voice faded as he escorted Miss Reba across the street and up the path to the hotel entrance.

Emma examined the feeling that engulfed her. Jealousy? No. Whatever she had once felt for Aidan was over. This was more like irritation. As usual, Aidan had left her to deal with everything—making sure Miss Reba's trunks got delivered and the flowers were arranged and anything else that might be required.

"Maxwell!"

She turned to the sound of a booming voice coming from a squat little bandy-legged man who was rushing down the platform, dodging between carts loaded with luggage. He had the stub of a cigar clenched between his teeth, and he was wearing a bowler hat, a bold checkered suit, and a bright-yellow bow tie.

"Bertie!" Captain Winslow grinned and moved toward the other man. The two of them clasped hands and talked over top of one another.

"Quite a nice place for our winter—" the captain said.

"If Reba wasn't so goldarned good with a gun, I might shoot her myself," the other man fumed. "The things that woman demands."

"What now?" The captain sounded anything but amused.

Emma busied herself directing her staff back to the hotel with instructions to get the flowers in water and delivered as soon as possible.

"Miss Elliott!"

She turned at the sound of her name and saw

Captain Winslow hurrying to catch up with her, the other man close behind. She waited for them, her Harvey Girl smile firmly in place.

"Miss Elliott, may I present Bert Gordon, my partner and manager of our little show. He'll be joining Miss Reba and me for meals. Bert, this is…" He hesitated, obviously looking for her first name.

"Emma Elliott," she replied. "Welcome to Juniper, Mr. Gordon."

"It's just Bert," he replied, removing the cigar and tossing it aside. "I don't stand on ceremony, miss."

She liked him immediately. "Or perhaps Bertie?" she teased.

He made a face. "Max here likes giving people names. I guess I ought to count my blessings he came up with that one for me. Some in the company weren't so lucky."

"They are terms of endearment," the captain protested.

"Well, endearment or not, you're the only one who gets away with calling our leading lady 'Reebs.'"

Emma smothered a smile, imagining how the actress might bristle at that.

The captain shrugged. "You need help with getting everything unloaded and set up out at the grounds?" he asked Bert.

"Naw. I got this. You see Miss Emma here safely back to the hotel. Tell the desk clerk I'll be checking in later." He grinned at Emma. "Real nice to make your acquaintance, Miss Emma. I have a feeling we're going to get along just fine."

"My pleasure, Mr. Bert. I'll look forward to seeing

you for breakfast tomorrow. There is nothing like a cup of Harvey coffee to get your day started off right."

"Better make that two cups. Tomorrow's likely to be a long day." He tipped his bowler to her and then headed back down the platform where he boarded the train and signaled the conductor to move on.

Suddenly, Emma realized she and Captain Winslow were alone. "Well, I should get back," she said.

"Since we're headed to the same place, do you mind if I walk with you?"

"That would be..." *Wonderful*, she almost said. "That would be all right," she amended.

The distance from the station to the hotel had always seemed to Emma to be no more than a city block, and yet on this evening, it felt much longer. The captain walked beside her, matching his stride to hers, his hands clasped behind his back. As they rounded the end of the station, she spotted a large poster advertising the show. The illustration showed him mounted on his horse.

"Not much of a likeness," Captain Winslow muttered when he noticed her glancing at the poster.

"I think—"

"I mean Diablo is a lot better-looking than that," he added with a grin.

She laughed. The truth was she was grateful he had found a way to break the silence. They covered the rest of their walk in short order, and once they entered the lobby, Emma turned to him. "Well, have a good evening, Captain."

"How about Maxwell or just Max?" he asked and then hurried to add, "I mean, you seem to be okay with Mr. Bert and Miss Reba. We're all going to be staying in the hotel, and Mr. Campbell tells me you'll be serving us at meals. Folks like us—show people—are pretty informal and friendly."

"The Harveys have their rules when it comes to staff and guests."

He grinned. "The Harveys don't have to know. Not when we're both off duty." He didn't wait for her to respond. Instead, he tipped two fingers to the brim of his hat and headed for the stairs up to the guest rooms. "I take my coffee with a lot of cream," he said.

"And Mr. Bert?" For some reason, she was reluctant to have him go.

"Black, like his mood will be at that hour."

"And Miss Reba?"

He rolled his eyes. "Reebs doesn't show her face until noon, which will account for Bertie's foul mood. Good night, Emmie."

Emmie.

"Good night, Max," she murmured as she watched him take the stairs two at a time.

Chapter 2

THE NEXT MORNING, EMMA HAD JUST FINISHED CHECK-
ing to be sure everything was ready for the arrival of
the late morning train when the double doors to the
dining room opened and Aidan ushered Max and Bert
to the table reserved for them. Although normally
the dining room was only open for lunch and supper,
with breakfast served at the more informal counter in
the lobby, she understood Aidan saw this as a special
circumstance.

He nodded to her, then set the cups for beverage
service to the two men. It was a Harvey tradition that
when a patron arrived, the waitress took the order for
a beverage and then, depending on that order, placed
the cup upright, turned down, tilted or off its saucer
completely to indicate to the girl charged with serving
beverages if the guest wanted coffee, tea, or milk.

Aidan shot Emma an apologetic smile as he left
the dining room, closing the doors behind him. He
was acknowledging this was unusual and added to her
workload, but his look said this was something special.
She checked the bow in her hair and her apron for

perfection, loaded a tray with a silver coffee pitcher and a smaller pitcher of cream, and approached the table.

"Good morning, gentlemen," she said. They looked up from the menus Aidan had left them. Bert mumbled a greeting and returned to studying the menu. He looked tired and out of sorts, his suit rumpled and his bow tie askew. Emma was pretty sure he'd had no sleep. Max smiled at her and looked as if he'd slept well and hadn't a care in the world.

She poured coffee—a full cup for Bert and precisely three-quarters full for the captain, leaving room for cream.

"Ah, Bertie, Miss Emma is not just a pretty face but a mind reader as well," he said as he added a generous splash of cream to his cup.

Emma laughed. "You gave me the orders last night," she reminded him.

"That I did, and as you can see, Bert's mood matches his choice." He picked up his menu and glanced at it. "What do you recommend?" Setting the menu aside, he picked up his coffee cup and took a swallow.

"The orange pancakes are a specialty," she replied, her focus on his hand—the tanned skin and long fingers. She swallowed and forced herself to turn to the show's manager, who was already refilling his cup from the server she'd set between them on the table.

"Eggs over easy," Bert said, "bacon—burnt to a crisp—biscuits…do you have honey?"

"We do indeed," she said. Having received Bert's order, she had no choice but to turn back to Max. "And for you, sir?"

"I'll have the same plus an order of those pancakes you mentioned." He glanced around at the empty tables. "Kind of slow this morning," he noted.

Before Emma could explain, Bert chimed in. "The dining room doesn't open for breakfast, but I asked Mr. Campbell if we could have somewhere more private than the counter. We've got stuff we need to talk about, Max."

Maxwell looked up at Emma. "We're making extra work for you?"

"Not at all," she assured him. She picked up the coffeepot and cream pitcher. "I'll just refill these and place your orders," she said.

In all her years working for the Harvey Company, she could not think of a single time when a customer had given the slightest consideration to how his actions or demands might inconvenience the staff. Of course, it was the Harvey way to accommodate even the most bizarre requests if possible, and providing a private venue for a business meeting was hardly out of the ordinary. Still, he had noticed. She liked that.

She gave the kitchen staff the order and refilled the creamer. Stepping around the corner to the counter, she held the coffeepot under the spigot of the larger urn. Through the glass panes of the closed dining room doors, she could see the two men, their heads bent close as they talked. She thought about the way Max had looked up at her, his smile, and how those deep-set gray eyes—eyes the color of storm clouds coming over the mountains—had captured her gaze in return. She found it almost impossible to look away, to get on about her business, to—

"Ouch!" She cried out as the hot coffee overflowed and splashed onto her hand. She dropped the coffee-pot and watched as the hot brown liquid found a path across the tile floor.

Sarah, who was working the counter alone now that Trula had been dismissed, rushed to her aid. "Are you hurt, Miss Elliott?"

"I'll be fine. Get a towel so I can clean up this mess, and then see to your customers." She knew she sounded brusque and regretted it. "Thank you, Sarah," she said more gently when the girl returned with two freshly laundered towels. She handed one to Emma and used the other to wipe the floor.

"Did you hear about Trula?" Sarah asked.

"What about her?"

"She's working for Miss Reba as her personal assistant," Sarah whispered.

"How on earth did that happen?" Emma tried not to encourage gossip among her staff, but if this meant Trula would be staying in the hotel—as a guest—that could be a problem.

"Trula was in the lobby when Miss Reba arrived last night," Sarah replied. "Miss Reba was telling Mr. Campbell how her 'girl' had left the show at their last performance and she was in need of a replacement. You know Trula—she saw opportunity knocking and threw open the door. Just stepped up and introduced herself and said she'd like the job."

"That I did, and Miss Reba has requested her break-fast served in her room—suite." Trula stood behind them, a piece of paper in her hand. "She'll have tea with lemon, two soft-boiled eggs, a slice of unbuttered toast, and a dish of fresh berries with cream." She handed the list to Emma and turned to go.

"Very well," Emma replied. "But you can wait and deliver the order yourself, Trula. This won't take long."

Trula smiled triumphantly. "Miss Reba expects her meal to be delivered by staff. She says I am no longer a waitress. She says I have come up in the world and should not lower myself to menial tasks." And with that, she turned and left, taking the lobby staircase rather than the stairs in the kitchen used by staff.

Before changing her coffee-stained apron for a fresh one, Emma handed the order to George Keller, the hotel chef, who had clearly overheard the encounter.

"She's gotten a bit uppity overnight," he muttered as he added a plate of pancakes to the large silver tray holding the order for Max and Bert.

"I'll ask Tommy to deliver the order," Emma said as, with great care, she filled a fresh pot with coffee and added that and the creamer to the heavy tray.

Expertly, she lifted it, balancing it on the flat of one palm and returning to the dining room.

Max was on his feet the minute she came through the swinging doors that connected the dining room to the kitchen. "Let me help with that," he said, relieving her of the tray before she could object. And then he started doling out the dishes—plates filled with eggs and bacon and piping hot biscuits.

"Really, Captain Winslow," Emma protested, "you must allow us to do our jobs. Mr. Harvey—"

"—is not here," he noted again as he handed her the empty tray, his fingers brushing hers in the transfer.

"Still." She set the tray aside and refilled their coffee cups, leaving the coffee server and the cream. "Will there be anything more?" she asked.

Bert had already devoured one egg and half a biscuit. His mouth was full as he glanced up at her and gave her a genuine smile. "Good grub," he managed to say as he reached for his coffee. "Best coffee I ever had."

Max laughed. "Miss Elliott, I would say you have one very satisfied customer."

"I'll leave you to enjoy your meals and conduct your business," she said, and once she'd removed the tray, she took up her position just outside the kitchen door, across the large room from the two men but available should they need anything.

She observed them as they ate and talked. The topic seemed quite serious. Bert often gestured dramatically with both hands, once nearly toppling the small vase of wildflowers that was a feature on every table. He appeared to be quite upset while Max remained calm, leaning back after finishing his meal and stretching out his long legs as he cradled his coffee cup in both hands and listened intently to what his table partner was saying.

Several times he looked past Bert, glancing at Emma. The first couple of times he simply smiled, but as the discussion went on and she remained at her post, his expression changed to a frown. Finally he stood, said something to Bert, and started toward her. He was smiling again, but there was a question behind that smile.

"There's no need for you to stand guard, Emmie."

She bristled. "I am not standing guard, Captain. I

am simply attending to my duties. As long as you and Mr. Gordon are guests in this dining room, I have a responsibility to—"

"Okay. That's ridiculous, but if that's the way things are done around here—"

"It is the Harvey way. Was there something more you or Mr. Gordon needed, or may I clear your dishes and give you more room for conducting your business?"

"And then you'll leave? Get on with your day?"

"If that's what will make you most comfortable," she replied.

He released a sigh of pure frustration. "You know, Emmie, one of the things I think might be most wrong with today's world is too many rules about how things get done."

"And yet my job requires me to follow a certain protocol."

He studied her for a moment, then grinned, stepped aside, and with a sweeping bow invited her to step forward. "Follow your protocol then, Emmie. I'm not here to cause trouble."

∞

Max returned to his place at the table and watched as Emma cleared their dishes, refilled their coffee cups, then carried the heavy tray back to the kitchen as if it weighed no more than a single plate. What was it about this woman that had drawn him to her from the moment he'd first walked into that dining room? She was hardly the first female to catch his eye, but Emma

Elliott had not only caught his eye. Somehow, she had captured his curiosity.

There was something about her—an aura of self-confidence and dignity. And while she was slim and petite in stature, he had the feeling she could hold her own in any situation that required a quick mind. Her hair was light brown, with highlights that caught the sun streaming through the dining room windows. And her eyes—those wide hazel eyes—sparkled with intelligence. Yes, Emma Elliott was a woman worth getting to know.

Bert was going on about the usual problems central to keeping a show like theirs afloat—problems that all came down to money.

"And then there's Reba," Bert was saying.

"What about her?"

"She's hired a new 'assistant' and expects us to pay for the girl."

"We haven't been here half a day, and Reba's been asleep for most of that," Max said. "How on earth…?"

Bert shrugged. "Some girl in the lobby last night, one of the waitresses here they'd let go. Apparently, Reba was sweet-talking the hotel manager about needing someone and this girl—"

"A girl who'd been let go from her duties here at the hotel?"

"That's what I heard."

"That could be trouble if she's got an ax to grind, and I assume she does. And you know Reba."

"Not as well as you do," Bert said, a reminder that there had been a time when Max and Reba were more than just costars.

"That's the past," Max grumbled.

"For you maybe. Not for her."

And that was at the root of a lot of the trouble the show had gone through lately. Reba's emotions ran the gamut from teary pleadings for them to reunite to threats to leave the show, something she knew they couldn't afford. Reba was almost as popular as Max was, in some cases more so, especially with the men who bought tickets. And she brought a lot to the show—sharpshooting skills as good as any man's, not to mention the ability to create half a dozen believable characters for the various vignettes that made up the program.

"Just be nice to her," Bert was saying, an old refrain he delivered at least once a day.

"I am nice. Trouble is she wants more than nice."

Bert sighed and stared out the window at the passing traffic—wagons, men on horseback, women hurrying to the shops. "Cheer up. We're here for the next several weeks. Maybe some good-lookin' cowboy will come along and sweep her off her feet."

He stood, and the minute he did, Emma appeared.

Max watched her approach the table, her smile at the ready.

"Add our meals to my room bill, sweetheart," Bert said, then blushed as he hurried to add, "Sorry, miss. Old habits." He retrieved his bowler and opened the door leading to the lobby. "Max, I'll see you later over at the showgrounds?"

"Yeah." Max leaned back and picked up his coffee cup as Emma walked back to her post. "Could I ask you something?"

She stopped walking but hesitated before turning around. "All right," she said, coming back to the table.

"Sit," he invited, indicating the chair Bert had vacated.

"I…"

"Here's the thing, Emmie. The show—meaning my business and livelihood and that of a few dozen other folks—is kind of at a crossroads. Some of the performers think I've been too stubborn about how I present things. The show lacks glamour and romance according to them."

"I can't see how I—"

"I value the opinions of everyday folks—people who might buy a ticket. How long have you lived in Juniper?"

"I started working here four years ago."

"And before that?"

"I've been with the Harvey Company for a little over eight years now, working first in Kansas City and then here."

"And did you grow up in these parts?"

She remained standing, her hands resting on the back of the chair. Her expression told him his question might be more complicated than he might think. "No, I grew up in Nebraska."

"Okay, but you've lived out here for nearly a decade, long enough to have maybe seen what this part of the country used to be. So tell me what you think folks around these parts expect from a show like ours."

"Really, Captain—"

He quirked an eyebrow, and she blushed before correcting herself.

"Really, Maxwell, I do not see how I might possibly—"

"You see, my idea is to remind people of what the West once was. Open range, buffalo roaming the plains, a frontier—unknown, undiscovered, with endless possibilities for adventure and people who might not all look the same but who shared the same hopes and dreams."

She edged onto the chair. "I think that sounds wonderful," she said. "Who wouldn't love such a presentation?"

"According to Bert and others, people prefer fantasy to reality. The other shows give them that—train robberies and attacks by native peoples on settlers and such."

"I can't think how I might be of any help to you."

"Come out to the showgrounds. Let me show you around, maybe watch a rehearsal, and give me your honest opinion."

She stood, smoothing creases from her apron. "I have responsibilities. I can't just take off."

"We often rehearse at night. You could come by after the dining room closes."

"Speaking of the dining room," she said, "we are due to open soon, and there's a good deal of preparatory work to be done." She retrieved a tray from a nearby station and began loading it with the coffee service on his table.

"That's not an answer, Emmie." Max added his cup and saucer to the tray and stood.

"I...I'll think about it," she finally said.

"Well, that's good enough—for now." He grinned.

She frowned. "Please understand that my duties here do not end with the closing of the dining room. I am also responsible for the waitresses. They have a curfew, and something could come up that requires my attention."

Max studied her for a moment. She was still young and yet carried her responsibilities like a far more mature woman. He respected that. At the same time, he couldn't help wondering if the burden of her job left any time for her to enjoy life. As someone who had spent a good part of his youth and early adulthood dealing with circumstances that left little time for pleasure, he was determined to bring pleasure to others and to find what enjoyment he could in his work and life. He wasn't entirely sure why, but he felt he and this woman had a lot in common. She was obviously intelligent, someone who might understand what he was trying to do. And based on the brief conversations they'd had, she was also a straight shooter. Emma Elliott would give him her honest opinion.

"Tell you what, Emmie. I understand Sunday is a day off for you and your girls. How about after church we take a ride out to where we're setting up the show, and I'll give you a tour."

"I suppose that would be all right," she replied after chewing her lower lip and glancing around as if expecting someone to object. Then she straightened. "At the moment, however…"

Max grabbed his hat. "I'm going," he said, heading for the door just as half a dozen identically dressed Harvey Girls entered the dining room from the kitchen. They stopped dead in their tracks when they saw him, glancing from him to their supervisor and back again. "Ladies," he said with a grin. As he shut the door, he heard Emma clap her hands three times and instruct the girls to get to work.

Emma Elliott took her work seriously. Max respected that. Traveling around the country the way he did, it wasn't often he had the opportunity to get to know those he met on more than a surface level. Staying here in Juniper for the next several weeks would mean he'd have time to make deeper connections than usual. And the idea of deepening his friendship with Emma pleased—and surprised—him.

⌘

For the remainder of the day, the dining room and counter kept Emma shuttling between the two, making sure her waitresses kept pace. Word had spread of the arrival of the show people, and the locals were curious. The female guests were disappointed when they learned the handsome Captain Winslow had already come and gone for the day. The railroad workers and cowhands who frequented the lunch counter groaned when told the vivacious Rebel Reba rarely made any public appearance before midafternoon.

Finally, after the last of the travelers boarded their trains and the hotel guests left for the shops or an excursion through the countryside, Emma moved through the dining room, kitchen, and lunch counter, congratulating everyone on a job well done. Once the waitresses had hurried upstairs to change out of their uniforms and into more relaxed clothing for the evening, Emma headed to her office where a mountain of paperwork awaited her. She sighed and pulled the first file from the stack. It was the schedule of train arrivals and departures, and it brought back memories of a time when she had viewed such a schedule as thrilling and filled with possibilities.

When she first joined the Harvey Company, it had been the idea of travel that had driven her to strike out on her own. She'd dreamed of seeing the West, especially the national park called Yellowstone. She'd read articles and seen grainy photographs of the wonders of the park, and one day she aimed to see it all for herself. But while the promise of travel was real, the opportunities were not, especially once she had accepted the position as house manager for the Harvey Girls in Juniper. For the last three years, work had consumed her.

Someday, she thought as she tackled the work schedule for her staff.

"Miss Elliott? Do you have a moment?" Aidan stuck his head around the door. His formality clearly indicated this was a business matter.

"Of course. Come in."

He pushed the door open and waited while Miss Reba swept past him and into Emma's cramped and cluttered office. She glanced around and finally settled her gaze on the lone extra chair, which was stacked with freshly laundered, starched, and folded linens. She arched a penciled eyebrow at Emma.

"Let me move these," Aidan said as he scooped up the pile and looked around for some place to set them.

"Here," Emma said, taking them from him and

setting them on a counter just outside her office. As she closed the door, Aidan swiped at the seat of the chair with a handkerchief and invited the actress to sit before taking a position standing next to her. Emma returned to her place behind the desk. "How can I be of service?" she asked, directing the question to the woman seated before her.

"I have come to clear the air, Miss Elliott," she announced. "And to make sure you understand that Trula Goodwin no longer works for you, no longer takes direction from you. She works for me now, and as my personal assistant, she also speaks for me. Do you understand?"

Aidan twitched nervously, his eyes wide with questions Emma wasn't about to answer, even if she knew what those questions were. Instead, she folded her hands on top of her desk and cleared her throat. "Is there something specific that has upset you?" she asked, thinking at the same moment that as she had predicted, Trula was already causing problems.

Reba released a huff of exasperation. "It is my understanding that when she came to the kitchen this morning—on my direction—she was treated rudely, specifically by you."

Emma leaned forward and locked eyes with the actress. "You are correct in pointing out the fact that Miss Goodwin has changed employment—and employers. And because all of that has come about lit-erally overnight as it were, it's understandable that she may be a bit confused when it comes to protocol—yours and that of the Harvey Company."

Reba glanced up at Aidan, who seemed suddenly

fascinated by the tips of his shoes and did not meet her gaze.

"Furthermore," Emma continued, "it is true that Miss Goodwin and I came to a parting of ways that was less than amicable. In time, she will see that it was for the best, but until such time arrives, may I suggest that requests for any of our hotel services go through Mr. Campbell, and he can relay them to the appropriate manager." She stood. "Following that protocol should alleviate any confusion Miss Goodwin may have regarding her duties." She smiled. "Is there anything else I can do to make sure your stay with us is as comfortable and enjoyable as possible?"

"You are dismissing me? Me?" Reba sputtered as she rose to her feet and glared at Emma. "Do you have the slightest idea who I am, Miss Elliott?"

"Yes, I do. You are a guest at a Harvey House and as such entitled to the very best service we can offer, the same excellent service anyone who stays or dines with us receives."

Aidan cleared his throat and stepped forward. "Well now, Miss Reba, it seems that we have found the perfect solution."

"I hardly see how—"

"The proposal Miss Elliott has made gives me the great privilege of being at your disposal day and night. I am at your service." He gave her a half bow.

Reba turned her back to Emma and placed her hand on Aidan's cheek. "Day or night, Mr. Campbell? That may be an offer I will find difficult to refuse."

Aidan blushed until his face turned nearly as ruddy as the dark red fingerless gloves Miss Reba wore.

When he saw Emma watching this little scene, he gathered himself and glared at her. "Thank you, Miss Elliott. I'm sure you have work you need to do," he added.

For a moment, Emma wondered if she was going to have to remind him they were standing in her office. She moved around the desk. "Miss Reba, we are honored to have you here," she said. "And I assure you everyone on the staff is dedicated to making sure your stay with us is memorable."

Clearly, the actress responded well to compliments. "Thank you, my dear. Perhaps Miss Goodwin over-reacted. The young are prone to that, don't you agree? They can be quite dramatic." She clasped Emma's hand between hers. "I'm sure you and I will be great friends before this is all over."

Emma had her doubts, but she held her smile. "I hope so. And now if you both will excuse me…"

Aidan held the door for Miss Reba, and after she had gone on her way, he glanced back at Emma. "Thank you," he said softly before shutting the door with a click.

Emma returned to her desk and sat staring at the new schedule for a long moment. The cast of the Wild West show had not been in town twenty-four hours yet and already she had the feeling it was going to be a challenging—and exhausting—stay. Knowing that, she got to work. The more paperwork she could manage to complete before the next crisis arose the better.

Chapter 3

MAX WAS HELPING THE CREW PITCH HAY FOR THE livestock when he saw a buggy coming up the dusty road that led to the showgrounds. It was nearly four, and apparently Reba had finally decided to join the rest of the cast for rehearsal. As usual, she was dressed in red—her signature color. This time instead of the fancier gowns she favored, she was wearing a tan split riding skirt, a bright-red blouse trimmed with black fringe, silver-studded boots, and a soft-brimmed hat held in place by a narrow leather strap she'd tightened just under her chin.

She was not alone. A girl of perhaps eighteen held a parasol over Reba, protecting her from the desert sun. The girl wore a plain calico dress and sunbonnet. She looked like someone straight off the prairie. Reba's idea, no doubt. She'd gone through a string of girls she called her personal assistants, dressing each of them in cast-off costumes she deemed suitable for whatever the day's schedule might bring.

Max stabbed his pitchfork into a pile of hay and strode forward to greet his costar. "Miss Reba," he said, offering her a hand down from the buggy. He glanced toward the driver—the bellboy from the hotel. "Tommy, right?"

The kid ducked his head and grinned. "Yes, sir."

Max dug a coin from his pocket and handed it to him. "I'll see that the ladies get back to the hotel, Tommy. Thank you."

Once Tommy turned the buggy back toward town, Max gave his attention to the latest personal assistant. "I don't think I've had the pleasure, Miss—"

"This is Trula, Captain," Reba interrupted, clearly seeing no need for a more formal introduction. "Trula, my dressing tent is just over there. My trunks should be inside. Go unpack my costumes and make sure they are properly brushed and hung."

"Yes, Miss Reba," the girl murmured, but she was looking at Max.

It was a look he knew well. As the show crossed the country, she was hardly the first to bat her lashes at him and give him a smile that held a hint of boldness, of invitation.

"Trula!" Reba glared at the girl and pointed to the dressing tent.

"Yes, miss." Trula gathered her skirts and hurried away.

Max chuckled. "You know, Reba, you might want to consider hiring a more mature woman, a motherly type. Might stick around longer."

"Perhaps you think that woman who runs the dining room would suit," Reba replied.

"Why, Reebs, what a good idea," Max said. He laughed as he dodged the slap she aimed at his shoulder.

The two of them headed for the corral where Diablo and Reba's white mare, Angel, waited. Both animals were already saddled and ready for them to mount up for a rehearsal of the latest trick riding and shooting act Max had developed. They led their mounts to the open field the crew had marked off with posts and ropes. To either side of the oval performance area, the men were building bleachers that would hold the throngs of spectators attending the first show a week from Saturday. Bert had reported strong ticket sales for that opening performance, and Max knew that giving those folks a great show ensured others lining up to buy a ticket. Usually, they didn't have to worry about ticket sales on a long-term basis. Their schedule was a maximum of two days and nights in any one place before moving on. That ensured the bleachers were filled for every show. But they had set up winter quarters in Juniper, meaning weeks in the same place. It would be important to keep the show fresh so people would come back more than once.

"You stay here, and I'll start from the other end," he told Reba, who had strapped on her gun belt and was checking to be sure the twin pearl-handled six-shooters were loaded. She nodded. "Then we'll start the dance, you moving clockwise and me…"

She sighed. "The opposite way. I've got it, Max. This sun is brutal. Can we just get this over with?"

Max nodded and mounted Diablo. As he rode to the opposite end of the oval, he checked to be sure the targets were in place. He and Reba would ride in opposite directions, alternately firing at the targets, competing to see who could come closer to hitting the bull's-eye. On the sidelines, cowboys kept score, posting the results on large boards the audience could see. Gradually, the speed with which they rode and shot would increase until they were galloping full out in opposite directions, firing as they rode.

When he reached his position, he gave Reba a wave, and they started the rehearsal. The piece required expert marksmanship and riding, and Max knew he had a winning act when the other performers and the crew slowly stopped what they were doing and gathered to watch, cheering each shot that hit its mark.

Max let out a shout and pressed Diablo to full speed. It wasn't the same, but at times like this, he recalled the thrill of the hunt, the danger of the life he'd led as a scout and military man on the frontier. For one brief moment, nothing had changed, but of course it had. Those days were the past. This was pretense—a show. Still, he couldn't help reveling in the challenge of it.

As he and Reba passed, he saw that she was smiling as well. Whatever else Reba might be, she was a woman who enjoyed performing, and she could ride and shoot better than any man Max had ever known—himself excluded, of course.

They fired their last shots, expertly hitting the final target with two holes side by side dead center. They slowed their horses to a trot and met in the center of the field before taking one last lap together around the perimeter. The cast and crew cheered.

"Okay, it's a good act," Reba admitted as they dismounted and handed their horses over to a stable boy. "Exhausting, but I see the point."

"I thought it could be the finale," Max said as Bert joined them.

"I have an idea that would make it the perfect finale," Reba said, linking her hand through the crook of Bert's elbow, ignoring Max.

"Listening," Bert replied, chewing on his unlit cigar.

"I think we need to add a bit of romance to the show. After all, throughout the performance, Max and I flirt with a more serious relationship, the way he's always coming to my rescue. It seems to me the audience—especially the ladies—will want to see that play out."

Max shot Bert a warning look over the top of Reba's head. Bert ignored him.

"What'd you have in mind?" he asked.

"Perhaps instead of simply riding off together at the end of this act, we could go our separate ways, and I could dismount and be devastated at losing or, more likely, triumphant in victory. Either way, Max starts to leave, then changes his mind and rides full out toward me, scooping me up and onto his saddle, perhaps kissing me as he and I ride off together."

"I like it," Bert muttered.

"I don't," Max grumbled.

Reba glanced at him. "It's a simple kiss, Max—a stage kiss," she said. "The audience will go wild."

He knew she had a point, knew she'd hit on the one thing he'd avoided addressing in the script for the show. He also knew for Reba and him, there had never been anything close to a stage kiss.

"I'll think about it," he mumbled. "Right now, I

need to check on the chief, make sure his people got settled all right."

His friend and fellow scout, Chief Gray Wolf, had persuaded Max to add a group of Blackfoot Indians to the show earlier that year, and they'd made a real difference in bringing authenticity to the acts that involved them. Before Max had persuaded him otherwise, Bert had been satisfied with white actors smearing makeup on their skin. He and Max had argued about that—a lot. But when ticket sales went up once they could advertise "the real thing," Bert shut up. He was a simple man, and as long as the money rolled in, he was satisfied.

Max had met Wolf while working border patrol in northern Montana. The chief had attended English-speaking schools, lived for a time with a white family, and adopted the Christian name they'd given him— Wolf Sutter. That was how he'd introduced himself when he and Max met.

"Is that the name you prefer?" Max had asked.

Wolf had studied him for a long moment, then shrugged. "I prefer Mingan, meaning Gray Wolf. But Wolf Sutter is the name that gets me what I want for myself and my family, Captain."

"Very well. How about we settle on 'Wolf' for you and 'Max' for me?"

Wolf's family consisted of his siblings and their families as well as his parents, and it had taken some fast talk to convince Bert to take them all on. But once Bert realized the advantage of having Wolf and the others, he talked like it had been his idea all along. Still, not everyone in the company was pleased. Ed

Brunswick had made it clear he saw the addition of "redskins," as he insisted on calling them, as nothing but trouble.

"I get it that you two got friendly back when you were both scouts, but this is different. Folks won't take to the idea of a bunch of Injuns strutting around like they belong," Ed had argued.

"They do belong," Max had replied calmly.

He'd figured that was all he needed to say to get his message across. Ed had said no more, but he'd also refused to have anything to do with Wolf or his people.

Now as he crossed the compound, Max saw Wolf sitting cross-legged outside his tepee, surrounded by half a dozen nieces and nephews. The thing that had bonded Wolf and Max in friendship was their determination to preserve the true history of the West without sugarcoating it. Wolf could often be seen telling the children a story or teaching them some traditional custom. Max lifted a hand in greeting. Wolf finished whatever story he was telling the youngsters before sending them on their way, then got to his feet and came forward to meet Max. He was two inches taller, a detail he often liked to point out. He was barefoot and bare-chested, his ebony hair pulled straight back from his high forehead and tied with a strip of leather.

Max glanced around at the village of tepees, bustling with activity as the women tended both the children and cooking fires. "Looks like you got settled in," he said. "Any problems?"

Wolf shrugged. "The usual. A rancher and his son showed up and took exception. Bert set them straight."

Max frowned. It seemed like no matter where the show traveled, there was always some white man who objected to the idea of natives setting up their camp. More than once, Bert had had to explain why it was important to allow the Blackfoot contingent of the show to have their own living arrangements. Often the only thing that had settled the matter was Bert paying off some official.

"Cost of doing business," Bert always said afterward, but the harassment rankled Max.

"Sorry," he said now.

"Not your fault," Wolf replied. "How's the town?"

"Like most other places we've played, just better accommodations."

Wolf grinned. "I expect Reba's happy about that."

"Seems to be." He frowned, recalling the new problem Reba had handed him—the question of a kiss.

"So what's got you looking like you want to set fire to something?"

Max smiled. Wolf had always been able to see right through him. "Reba's got this new idea for ending the show. After the contest, she wants me to scoop her up on Diablo and kiss her as we ride off together."

"People are bound to like that idea," Wolf said slowly.

"Yeah. I know."

"But you don't want Reba getting any ideas about what's real and what's not."

Max nodded. Then he shook his head. "Any other man would be jumping for joy at the idea of kissing a beautiful woman every night, but this is Reba."

"And you two have a past," Wolf added.

Max groaned. "Don't remind me. That was a mistake I will regret for a long time. I never meant to hurt her, but it just wasn't working out."

"What you need is to find a new woman, somebody not with the show maybe."

Immediately, Max's mind went to Emma, and his expression must have alerted his friend.

Wolf grinned. "You've already met her, haven't you? That's why this thing with Reba is bugging you so much." He squeezed Max's shoulder. "I'll tell my mother she can stop trying to find someone for you."

"Yeah. Tell her she can focus all her attention on finding a good woman for you," Max shot back.

Both men were laughing as they went their separate ways, Wolf to help finish setting up the encampment for his people and Max to come up with a finale that would avoid him having to kiss Reba every performance. As he walked toward the converted boxcar he and Bert used as their headquarters, he found himself thinking about Emma, and just thinking about her calmed him.

∞

With Trula gone and no replacement on the way, Emma found herself spending more time than usual helping out in the dining room and at the counter. For the rest of the week, neither Max nor his manager took any meals at the hotel, and Miss Reba continued to request food sent to her room. The table in the corner remained set and ready to serve but was never occupied.

Emma could not deny the fact that she glanced up expectantly every time someone entered the dining room, nor the fact that she felt a flicker of disappointment when the new arrival was not the captain.

"You're as starstruck as any of your girls," she reprimanded herself on Sunday morning as she checked her appearance in the small mirror that hung over the washstand in her sparsely furnished bedroom. Because she had not seen Max since the morning he'd asked her to come to the showgrounds, she wondered if he even recalled the invitation. "Well, time for church," she muttered as she pinned her hat in place, collected her gloves and purse, and headed downstairs.

Outside, she joined several of the waitresses on their way to the small adobe church set on one side of the town's main plaza. As usual, the girls were tittering about the show, scheduled to open with a parade through town before its first performance later that week.

"…real Indians," Sarah was saying when Emma caught up to them. "They live in tepees and everything," she added.

"I saw one of them in Mr. Tucker's store yesterday," another girl added. "He was so tall, and he spoke English, and he was just as polite as you please and—" She broke off and nudged the girl next to her. "It's him," Emma heard her whisper.

"Good morning, ladies."

Emma had expected to see the native man Sarah had been going on about. But it was Max who tipped his hat to them and fell into step beside her.

"Beautiful day," he added.

He was dressed in black trousers, a white collarless shirt, and a buckskin coat the color of the butterscotch pudding they served in the hotel dining room. Emma swallowed and smiled.

"You're going to church?" It was an inane thing to ask, Emma thought. "I mean…"

Max grinned, and her heart beat a little faster. "Why, Miss Emma, even show people have faith."

She felt a blush stain her neck and rise to her cheeks and heard the waitresses snickering as they hurried on to the entrance.

"That was rude of me, Captain Winslow," she said. "I apologize."

He offered her his arm. "May I see you to your pew, Miss Emma?"

She rested her gloved fingertips lightly in the curve of his elbow. As they approached the entrance to the church, he removed his hat and nodded to Father O'Meara, who stood just inside the door. "Good morning, Father," he murmured.

"Welcome, my son. Several of your colleagues have arrived ahead of you." He motioned to the sanctuary where the usually half-empty pews overflowed with people from the show's cast and crew.

Max smiled and stepped aside to allow Emma to precede him down the aisle. She saw that the other Harvey Girls had held a place for her. She also saw there was no room for anyone else, certainly not a man the size and breadth of the captain. With an apologetic smile in his direction, she slipped in next to Sarah just as the organist played the prelude to the opening hymn.

Max nodded and continued down the aisle until he reached the very first pew. Emma saw him murmur a few words to Mayor Tucker already seated there before sliding in to sit next to him and then standing again as Father O'Meara took his place at the altar and invited all to join in singing the opening hymn.

Admittedly, she heard nothing of the homily or readings and barely glanced at the hymn book Sarah shared with her whenever they stood for the singing. Her focus was on Max. What made someone, who by all accounts had once thrived on the adventure and danger that was life on the frontier, decide to turn his thoughts to performing in a spectacle designed to entertain? How could that ever be enough for a man who was so physically virile?

"Miss Elliott," Sarah whispered with a glance over her shoulder at the other girls. Everyone in her pew was standing, waiting for her to lead them forward to take communion. She shook off her musings and stepped into the aisle, looking neither left nor right as she made her way to the altar and knelt. She folded her hands and bowed her head, lifting it only to receive the wafer and the sip of wine the priest offered. She crossed herself and followed the others back to their pew.

The sacrament took longer than usual given the large number of congregants to be served, but Emma was grateful for the delay. It gave her time to gather her thoughts and renew her determination to focus on her work and the tasks she faced in the coming week, among them reminding company headquarters in Kansas City of their need for a replacement for Trula Goodwin.

As if Emma had somehow conjured her, the girl strode past on her way back to her seat after receiving communion. She was dressed in a blue skirt and velvet jacket like the one Miss Reba had worn the night of her arrival. She wore a less dramatic hat than the actress had chosen, but Emma had little doubt the costume was the same. Emma found herself wondering what Miss Reba might be wearing and then realized she had not seen Max's costar among the show people gathered when she entered the church. It crossed her mind that Miss Reba might not be aware Trula had "borrowed" her clothes for the service.

That's unworthy of you, she thought. Trula had her faults, but it was uncharitable to make such assumptions about how the girl might have come by the outfit.

Organ music filled the sanctuary as Father O'Meara and two altar boys made their way up the aisle. Behind them, those in the front pews gathered their belongings and turned to greet their neighbors before joining the exit parade that signaled the end of the service. Emma saw Max laughing at something Mayor Tucker was telling him.

He did have a lovely smile.

"Miss Elliott?"

Once again, Sarah's voice reminded her she was blocking the way for the others, Harvey Girls anxious to get back to the hotel, change out of their finery, and enjoy their one day off.

"Sorry," she murmured and stepped into the aisle, nearly tripping over the captain. He grasped her shoulders. She seemed to have developed this habit of losing her balance and having him there to set her to rights again.

"Steady there," he said. And then as if it were the most normal thing in the world, he fell in next to her and continued speaking—speaking so that Emma was sure Sarah and the others heard. "I'll just go get the horses and meet you at the hotel entrance," he said. "Half hour?"

Emma nodded. Behind her, she heard her girls whispering. She drew her mouth into a thin line and kept her eyes straight ahead as she willed the line in front of her to move.

Horses! Not horse and buggy. The man expected her to ride. How did he know she could? It rankled that he would simply assume. Not that she wasn't an expert rider, but that was hardly the point.

Back at the hotel, she stopped in her office to make notes to herself on matters she had added to her list of tasks when she should have been paying attention to Father O'Meara's message. Upstairs, she was surprised to find several of the girls gathered in the hall outside her room.

"You're going riding with the captain?" Melba Connors asked, her excitement mirrored in the faces of the other girls.

"I am," she replied as she opened the door to her room and stepped inside. She left the door open, an invitation for the girls to gather in the doorway while she removed her gloves and unpinned her hat. The clothes she had chosen for her outing with Max lay on the bed. "He has invited me to tour the showgrounds with him and Mr. Gordon."

"You can't wear this," Melba said, stepping fully into the room and fingering the plain, light wool dress Emma had selected. "Unless you plan to ride sidesaddle."

"But why would she?" Nan Stone interjected. "Everyone knows Miss E is possibly the best horse-woman in Juniper." The girl had opened the small wardrobe that held Emma's clothes and pulled out a riding skirt. "Hand me that," she ordered, trading the skirt for the dress Melba held.

"I have the perfect blouse," Sarah called as she hurried down the hall to the room she had once shared with Trula.

"Ladies, I am right here and perfectly capable of choosing an outfit," Emma protested. "You are all behaving as if you need to—"

Sarah came rushing back holding a beautifully embroidered, tailored blouse. "Here," she said, handing it to Nan to pair with the skirt.

"Perfect." All half dozen girls who had gathered outside and inside her room chorused their approval.

"I hardly think we need to make such a fuss over—"

Melba blew out a huff of pure exasperation and faced her. "Miss E, you are stepping out with possibly the most gorgeous male creature God ever placed on this earth. You are fulfilling the fantasy of every girl gathered here. Please do not do that thing you do."

"What thing?" Emma probably should have been insulted, but the truth was she was mystified.

"That thing where nothing ruffles your feathers," Sarah said.

"Honestly, Miss E," Nan added, "we are all pretty

sure a gang of outlaws might one day come storming into the dining room and you would just stand there, smiling and reminding them that weapons are to be checked at the door."

"This is Captain Maxwell Winslow," Melba announced. "And for today at least, he has chosen you. Please do not pretend you aren't a little bit excited."

Emma couldn't help herself. She smiled, and then she laughed. "All right. I'll wear the riding costume."

"Good. Now for your hair," Nan said, shutting the door after all three girls had crowded into the room.

Half an hour later, Emma descended the back stairs, her long, curly hair pulled into a clip at the nape of her neck. She was dressed in her riding skirt and Sarah's borrowed blouse. Nan had offered a pair of embossed boots, but Emma had drawn the line at that. "I will wear my own footwear, thank you." All the girls had frowned when she pulled on a pair of worn brown boots.

George Keller looked up at her and grinned. "In that outfit, the captain's gonna want you to join the show, Emma."

Emma laughed nervously and hurried on to the lobby. After all, she didn't want to be late.

Max was standing with his back to her, talking to Aidan, but he turned when Aidan's eyes widened and focused on Emma. For a moment, both men stood there simply staring at her. Her usual self-confidence failed her. She had misunderstood. Her costume was all wrong. She looked ridiculous.

"You said horses," she blurted.

Max took a step toward her while Aidan returned

to the front desk, pretending not to listen. "That I did, Emmie. I meant a team. I'm not much for one-horse buggies. But if you'd like to ride…"

Emma pursed her lips. "It hardly matters to me," she said.

"Horseback might be more fun," he mused as if considering their options.

"Or I could change into something more suitable," she offered. His expression of horror was so theatrical and absurd that Emma could not help but laugh. "All right, I'll go as I am. You choose the transportation."

"Horses," he announced as he offered his arm to escort her from the hotel. "Definitely horses."

This time when he offered his arm, she linked her hand in the crook of his elbow without hesitation. She was looking forward to spending this time with him and was excited to think of the stories about the showgrounds she would have to share with the other girls later.

They walked to the livery, and while Max negotiated the exchange of wagon and team for a horse he thought suitable for her, Emma anchored her hat in place and pulled on her riding gloves.

"Ready?" Max exited the barn leading a beautiful gray mare. He cupped his hands, offering her a foot up, and once she was settled in the saddle, he handed her the reins. "Be right with you," he said and strode back to the barn. A moment later, he reappeared mounted on his famous stallion. The two horses nuzzled each other. "Diablo has a thing for the ladies," Max whispered as if the horses might overhear him.

"And does this lady have a name?" Emma asked.

"She does. It's Lady."

Emma leaned forward and stroked her mount's neck. "Well, Lady, meet Diablo, and watch your step. I hear he's a terrible flirt."

Emma couldn't help smiling at the sound of Max's laughter as they headed out of town. Suddenly, she felt a lightness and freedom she hadn't allowed herself to experience in some time. Her responsibilities had required so much of her that it was like being released from bonds to be out in the open air, riding next to the handsome Captain Maxwell Winslow.

It didn't take long to reach the compound where most of the cast and crew lived and worked and where performances of the show would happen for weeks to come. Still, Emma was unprepared for what lay before her as she and Max topped the rise that allowed them to look down on what to Emma was a settlement that seemed to have sprung up overnight.

The train she'd seen that first night now sat on a side track. She hadn't realized how many cars were involved. Besides the passenger cars, there were at least a dozen box- and flatcars, obviously empty of their freight now. Dominating the space not far from the railroad tracks was a huge arena with seating for hundreds of people covered with a canvas shelter surrounding the large, open performance ring.

"That big tent over there is the dining tent," Max said, pointing to the far end of the compound, farthest from the performance area. "Next to that are the dressing tents and the costume shop. To the other side of the arena is where we keep the horses and other livestock, the wagons and the sets we use for different acts. That tent there is the carpentry shop, and the one next to it is where we store and repair saddles and bridles and such. The native people prefer to set up their own place." He pointed to a cluster of tepees on the far side of the tracks.

"It's so much more than I imagined," Emma said.

"In the scheme of things, it's pretty small. Buffalo Bill's show carries over five hundred performers and crew members. They travel with over two dozen bison, not to mention more than a hundred horses, and they have seating for twenty thousand. They also have their own fire department." He shook his head as if even knowing the facts, he still couldn't quite believe it.

"Is that what you hope for with your show?" she asked.

He took a moment, his eyes sweeping over the expanse of tents and corrals and such below them. "Not really." He shook off whatever thought he was entertaining and smiled. "Shall we have a closer look?"

Max took the lead as the horses picked their way down the rocky trail and on through the tall grasses that brushed against Emma's riding skirt. She could smell the grainy scent of them, a scent that was soon replaced by the fragrance of onions frying and seared meat.

"Hungry?" he asked, looking back at her over his shoulder.

"Starving," she admitted.

With a loud yelp, Max spurred Diablo to a gallop. Not to be outdone, Emma let out a whoop of her own and followed him, the wind tugging at her hat and tendrils of her hair. By the time she caught up to Max, he had wrapped the reins around a post and was standing there grinning up at her.

"You can ride," he said, holding out his hands to help her dismount.

"Well, you don't have to sound so surprised," she replied, trying hard not to dwell too long on the thrill of his long fingers wrapped along her waist as he lifted her to the ground. He released her but just as quickly grabbed her hand and led her toward what he'd pointed out as the dining tent.

"Come on. I want you to meet some people."

Just outside the large tent, they passed a long cooking range where slabs of meat sizzled next to piles of onions and potatoes. Several men wearing stained aprons tended the food. They grinned when they saw Max, nodding to him but not abandoning their work.

Inside, the tent was furnished with long tables and lined with backless benches. A gray-haired woman sat alone at one table nursing a cup of coffee. She looked up and smiled. "Maxie," she said by way of greeting and then settled her gaze on Emma. "And who is this young beauty?"

"Pearl Hardin, this is Miss Emma Elliott. She's in charge of the wait staff at the hotel in town."

Pearl stood, wiped her hand on her skirt, and offered a handshake. "A Harvey Girl?"

"Yes, ma'am," Emma replied, liking her at once.

"You two ladies get acquainted," Max said. "I just want to have a word with Jason."

Pearl indicated the bench across from where she'd been sitting. "Jason's the head cook. You'll stay for lunch, I hope."

"I plan to," Emma agreed.

"There was a time when I thought I might try being a Harvey Girl," Pearl said.

"Why didn't you?"

Pearl gave her a wide grin that revealed a single gold-capped eyetooth. "I was pretty sure I wouldn't pass the Harvey Girl smile test."

Emma smothered a giggle.

"You can laugh," Pearl said. "It's okay. Truth is, perfect smile or not, I wouldn't have lasted. Watching other folks come and go, wondering what adventures waited for them at the next stop? Not for me."

Or maybe no longer me.

Emma was surprised at that thought, but it was true. She had been watching people come and go for years now and was no closer to her dream of adventure than she'd been when she joined the Harvey Company.

"What do you do with the show?" she asked.

Pearl shrugged. "This and that. Mostly, I make and repair all the costumes. I'm really taking a shine to that blouse you're wearing. Maybe something I could copy for Miss Reba and the final act."

"It's a lot of handwork," Emma said, fingering the intricate embroidery that covered the collar and cuffs.

"Do you sew, Emma?"

"I do. I find it relaxing after all the tasks of a day spent pleasing guests and managing the girls."

Pearl cocked an eyebrow. "And what's your connection with our Maxie?"

The sudden shift in topic accompanied by Emma's awareness of a flood of men and women crowding into the tent carrying plates piled high with food made her hesitate.

"The captain and I—" She caught sight of Max balancing three plates and weaving his way toward them.

"From where I sit, the captain seems to think you're pretty special. Can't recall a single time he brought a lady out to see us. Certainly not just after we got settled in." Pearl reached across the table and patted Emma's hand before standing.

"Really, we hardly know one another," Emma protested.

"Trust an old woman's instinct." She grinned up at Max. "'Bout time, Maxie. I'll see you two later. Got to have a word with Bertie." She took a plate of food from him and headed for another table.

Emma suspected Pearl had made up an excuse to leave Max and her alone. She knew matchmaking when she saw it. She'd been guilty of it a time or two herself.

Chapter 4

As Max set Emma's food in front of her, he realized she was blushing. "Don't pay any attention to Pearl's rambling," he advised. "She likes to stir the pot."

"She strikes me as someone who cares a good deal about you."

He chuckled and straddled the bench across from her. "She mothers the entire cast and crew." After cutting a bite of beef, he glanced at her untouched food. "Hey, I know it's not up to Harvey standards, but it's not bad."

Emma picked up her flatware and began cutting the slice of meat. "It's not that at all. I was just thinking how nice it is to be served, to sit quietly and have someone bring me food."

"Hard to believe you've been a Harvey Girl for eight years."

"I was first hired when I was eighteen." She shook her head as if she couldn't quite believe it.

Max studied her. He was just two years older than she was, and yet she seemed so very young.

"And you?" she asked. "I mean how long since you and Mr. Gordon formed your partnership?"

"We hooked up about six or seven years ago. He owned the show and gave me a job. In time, we found we worked well together."

"How did you come to this work in the first place?"

"I was down on my luck, and Bert hired me," he murmured and stuffed his mouth with food. She was asking about things he didn't usually talk about much. He bought time by chewing and swallowing. "How 'bout you? I mean what was life like before you joined the Harvey Company?"

"My family had a small farm and a store in Omaha. I'm the youngest of four and the only girl."

He noticed how she answered questions without embellishment. She seemed as reluctant to talk about her past as he was to discuss his present. "Older brothers who spoiled you?"

"I'm afraid so."

"Clearly, you learned to ride somewhere along the way."

"I did. My brothers were very competitive. If I wanted to be with them, I had to learn to do what they enjoyed."

He watched as she finished the food he'd brought, a helping more suited to one of his crew than a petite woman like Emma. "I think there's cake if you saved room," he said, trying not to smile.

"That would be lovely," she replied. "I'll just clear these."

When she reached for his plate, he covered her hand to stop her. "Today's your day off, remember?"

He allowed his hand to linger and noted that she did not pull away as quickly as he might have expected. Their eyes met. She looked away first, but there was an undeniable connection between them. He felt it, and he was pretty sure she did too.

He stood and picked up their tin plates. "Coffee?"

"Yes, please," she said.

A worker from the kitchen staff took the plates from him as Max made his way through the maze of tables and benches filled with performers, dressers, handlers, and others. The sides of the tent had been rolled up to allow for more fresh air to pass through, and he could hear the sounds of hammers, shouted instructions, and laughter from the men building the seating for the arena.

In the far corner of the dining tent, outsized flat trays that held the cake lined a table. Large metal urns of coffee, battered by years of use and travel, sat on a second table. Max thought of the gleaming silver-plated urns in the Harvey establishment. Still, coffee was coffee.

He filled two mugs, hooked his forefinger through the handles, and then stared at the two slices of cake he'd set aside while he went to get the coffee. How was he supposed to manage everything? Suddenly, he had a new appreciation for the work waitresses did—managing multiple dishes without dropping any. He looked around for something that might serve as a tray, saw one of the cake pans had been emptied, and loaded it with the mugs and cake, adding a creamer and spoons before making the trip back to where Emma sat. Halfway there, he stopped.

Reba stood next to the table, the sun at her back. Emma was looking up at her with a smile that seemed more polite than warm. Max hurried to join them and saw Pearl coming from the opposite direction. They arrived at the table seconds apart, in time for Max to hear Pearl say, "Why, Miss Reba, how nice you have honored us with your presence today. Have you met Miss Elliott?"

"Of course we've met. She works at the hotel," Reba said, her eyes focused on Emma. "A bit far from your usual surroundings, are you not, Miss Elliott?"

Max stepped forward and balanced the tray on the edge of the table as he unloaded it. "She's my guest, Reba, so play nice, okay?"

"You're welcome to join us," Emma added. She looked up at Max. "Perhaps Pearl and Miss Reba would also like cake and coffee?"

"Sounds good to me," Pearl said. "But we can get our own, can't we, Reba?" She started toward the cake and coffee service in the corner, but after three steps, she turned back and looked directly at Reba. "Coming?"

"I'm not hungry."

Pearl snorted. "Since when?"

Reba glared at the seamstress. "Coffee would be nice."

"Then come on," Pearl said, making it clear she was not serving the actress. "We need to talk about your costume in the opening act." Reluctantly, Reba followed.

Max sat across from Emma as she added cream to her coffee.

"I forgot the sugar," he muttered, half rising.

"This is fine," Emma assured him. "I don't add sugar." She took a bite of cake and closed her eyes. "This is heavenly," she said. "You'll have to be sure our chef has the recipe."

Max wanted to ask if Reba had said anything to upset her. He was pretty sure his costar had been rude, but that went without saying. Reba was rude to everyone she considered her inferior. More than once, he or Bert had had to remind her they'd found her on a street corner in a Nevada mining town showing off her skills with twirling a gun for pennies.

Pearl joined them after a few minutes and perched on the bench next to Max. Reba was nowhere in sight.

"She went back to her tent," Pearl explained. "Of course, first she gave me a list long as my arm of things that weren't right with her costumes. Seems she's got an idea she needs something new for that final act you two have put together. Something fancy with a low-cut neckline for when the two of you go riding off into the sunset."

"She can make do with what she's got," Max replied. "The act requires expert riding and shooting. It's not a fancy-dress ball," he added. He glanced at Emma. "On the other hand, if Reba insists, then the outfit Miss Elliott is wearing is exactly right. Reba must have something close to that, maybe not the fancy doodads on the blouse but—"

"Well, I don't have time to embroider an old blouse before we open," Pearl grumbled.

"I do," Emma said, surprising them all. "That is, I

could maybe help." She turned to Pearl. "Of course, with your guidance."

"You already have a job," Pearl reminded her. "One with a good deal of responsibility, from what I hear."

"Yes, but I have time after work with little to do, and I don't mean to brag, but I am quite good. You can ask the other girls at the hotel."

By Pearl's expression, Max knew the costumer still had doubts. "I have an idea," he said. "What if we give Emma an old blouse from a costume Reba no longer wears, and she can show us what she would do with it?"

Pearl nodded slowly. "I like that idea. It can just be between the three of us. No one else, including Reba, needs to know. That way, if things don't work out— and I'm not saying they won't," she hastened to assure Emma. "But you have your work, and embroidery takes a lot of time."

Emma raised her coffee mug in a gesture of toasting the idea. "I think that's a perfect solution." Then she grinned and, to Max's delight, released a very girlish giggle. "This is going to be such fun," she said.

Max couldn't help thinking he agreed—especially if it meant he would be seeing more of Miss Emma Elliott.

❧

After they finished their cake and coffee, Emma was pleased when Max suggested they take a tour of the grounds to give her a closer look at how the show worked.

"That would be lovely," she said. "I need some exercise after such a filling meal. Otherwise, I'm likely to fall asleep on the ride back to town."

She quickly understood how justly proud Max was of what he and Bert had created. In spite of the dusty surroundings, everything was incredibly well organized. Fred Harvey would approve. They walked through several cars of the sidetracked train, sleeping cars as well as a dining car that served as a lounge when the company was not on the move. At the very back of the passenger section of the train was a converted boxcar Max told her was the business headquarters for the show.

"It's like a traveling village," Emma said, marveling at the way every inch of space was used in the office, with furnishings and even a large safe anchored against the rocking of a train in motion.

"It's been home for some time now," Max admitted. He fingered a ledger laid out on one of three desks that filled the center of the car. He seemed momentarily lost in thought, pensive.

"And for how much longer do you see this being your home?" She couldn't shake the thought that he was unhappy and, like her, dreamed of more.

He glanced up and gave her a half smile and a shrug, then picked up a program from a stack shelved nearby. "This is the lineup for the winter season here in Juniper." He moved close enough so she could read along with him as he pointed to each act and explained it. "The idea is to entertain but also to give the audience a history lesson, so we do an act about the Pony Express and another about settlers moving West with a wagon train."

"What's this?" she asked, pointing to an act titled *American Indian Life*.

"It's a tableau that tries to get people to understand

native people are not all bloodthirsty savages." His tone was bitter, bordering on anger.

"Do you really believe that's how they are perceived?"

He glanced at her. "Don't you? These people were here long before we came, Emma, but instead of trying to find some way the two cultures might live side by side with respect, we decided they had to go."

"Sometimes progress..." Emma stammered, unnerved by his passion.

"Buffalo Bill Cody once quoted the words of Bishop George Berkeley to me. He said, 'Westward the course of *empire* takes its way.' The white man seeks to build empires, Emmie. The Indian just wants to live—at least most of them."

"But can you risk telling that tale when your audience is primarily composed of white families?"

To her surprise, he grinned. "Small steps. The tribe's chief is an old friend. He was the one who came up with the idea of showing native people in a family setting—playing with their children, cooking their food, telling their stories. We show the settlers moving West depending on them to act as guides and to help them through difficulties like finding water or crossing mountain ranges."

"And you don't show them scalping or—"

"Did you know the habit of scalping was something introduced by the Spanish?" he asked as he reached for one of several dozen books on a shelf that ran the length of the car.

Emma looked at the page he'd marked and now showed her. Still, it sounded like he was more on a mission to teach than to entertain, and that seemed to her to spell eventual doom for the show's success.

Max closed the book and dropped it on the desk, picking up the program again. "But I do understand why people come to our show, so we intersperse the history lessons with plenty of fun and excitement. Roping, trick riding, and sharpshooting are at the very core of our performances, and we're lucky to have some of the best in the business as part of our troupe. Come on. I'll show you around."

Once off the train, Max led Emma to what he called a rehearsal ring where a young cowboy was practicing stunts with a rope. He was indeed expert at his craft, and once he spotted Emma, he grinned and doubled his efforts to entertain her. When he ended by making the large loop of the rope dance across the dusty ground toward her, Emma applauded enthusiastically, and the cowboy took a bow.

"Lookin' good, Mason," Max called out as they moved on.

Over the next hour, they watched performers rehearse their riding stunts, including one woman who did all her tricks while riding sidesaddle.

But it was their tour of the encampment that Emma loved best. Chief Gray Wolf and his people welcomed her warmly, his mother insisting to Max that "This young woman needs to eat more."

Max laughed at that. "You should see what she had for lunch," he replied.

Emma blushed, and Wolf's mother frowned at Max. "You cannot say such things about a lady, Maxwell. Sometimes you and my son have the manners of bumpkins of the country."

"She means country bumpkins," Wolf explained.

"It's her new favorite insult. Come, let me show you our camp."

The chief was kind and a born leader, judging by the way many of the other actors and crew related to him. Emma felt as if she had made a new friend by the time the tour ended.

"We should be getting back to town," Max said. "Why don't you head over to the costume tent and see if Pearl has that blouse you need while I get the horses saddled?"

"All right." She started down the path but turned back at once. "Wolf, please thank your mother for her hospitality, and thank you for a wonderful visit."

Wolf grinned and ducked his head, clearly pleased. "Our pleasure, Miss Elliott. Have Max bring you back soon."

"I'd like that," Emma replied and hurried on her way. As she approached the costume tent, she heard raised voices. There was no way of knocking to make her presence known, so she simply lifted the flap and peeked inside.

Trula Goodwin was holding a yellow gown and standing over Pearl, who was seated at a sewing machine, one foot pumping the treadle furiously. "I am telling you Miss Reba needs this altered now," Trula practically shouted.

Pearl got to her feet. "And I am telling you, young lady, you don't give me orders, and neither does your boss. That gown is not part of the costumes for the show, so if it needs altering, I suggest you take it back to Rebel Reba and tell her I said when she can ask and not demand—and do it in person—then we might have reason to discuss it. Until then…" She spotted Emma waiting quietly just inside the entrance. "Ah, Miss Elliott." She stepped around Trula and picked up a small canvas-wrapped bundle. "I have everything you need right here."

Trula stood stock-still, staring from one woman to the other and then focusing on the package Pearl handed Emma. "What's that?" she demanded.

"None of your business, girl," Pearl grumbled. She turned her attention back to Emma. "Have a nice ride back to town, and remember what I told you," she added with a wink.

The woman was a hopeless matchmaker—hopeless because even if Max were attracted to Emma, their lives were far too different for anything more than a short romance to come of it. On the other hand, if she longed for adventure, why not the adventure of romance? Even one doomed to end once the show moved on to the next town?

From outside the tent, she heard horses, and she lifted the flap. "I'll get this back to you as soon as possible," she said, keeping her focus on Pearl.

"I'll be here," Pearl replied.

As the canvas fell back into place and Max stepped forward to help Emma onto her horse, Emma heard Pearl's gravelly voice bark, "You still here, girl?"

A moment later, Trula scurried from the tent and walked stiffly across the compound and up the hill to another tent, clutching the yellow dress.

"What was that about?" Max asked as they started up the trail that would take them back to town.

"I think Trula is still adjusting to her role in your

little community, Max. But I have no doubt Pearl will make sure she settles in before long."

He frowned. "She'll need to learn that in a group like ours, getting along is the key. It's not like a normal job where you work with people and then leave them at the end of your shift. We not only work together, we live together. I would think she would get that, given it's pretty much the same for you Harvey Girls."

He had a point, but Emma knew Trula had never really adapted to the communal life that came with working for Mr. Harvey. And given what Emma had observed so far of Trula's association with Miss Reba, she doubted things had changed. "She might have a chance at making a go of this with Miss Reba's help— and Pearl's."

His laughter rang out, and she couldn't help smiling and then laughing with him. She found herself wishing the show's compound was farther from town so they would have more time to get better acquainted.

"Come on," he said as they capped the rise. "I'll race you." He set off, his large stallion lengthening the distance between them.

"No fair," she shouted, but although Lady made a good attempt, it was useless trying to catch up. They arrived back in town dust-covered and breathless, and as Max stood holding her horse while she dismounted, she thought about inviting him to come sit with her on the hotel's veranda.

He took her gloved hand and pressed it between both of his. "I enjoyed today, Emmie. It's been a while since I had time to just take pleasure in an afternoon."

"It was wonderful," she agreed, reluctantly pulling

her hand free. "I had no idea what all went into putting on a show like that." When he made no move to walk back to the hotel with her, she added, "If you want to brush down the horses, I can..."

He turned and retrieved the package from her saddlebag. "I have to go back—work to do," he said as he handed her the bundle, nodding toward it. "You're sure about this?"

"I'm looking forward to it," she assured him. "Don't worry. I think you might be impressed."

"I'm already impressed," he said softly, his eyes meeting hers.

She swallowed around the sudden drought in her mouth. "Thank you again, Max. For today, I mean." She had to force herself not to ask if he might be at breakfast the following morning. Instead, she clutched the package to her chest and hurried off toward the hotel.

"See you at breakfast," he called.

Emma couldn't seem to stop smiling as she waved and ran the rest of the way to the hotel.

❧

Max worked until well after midnight, going over the books, trying to figure out where he might be able to make cuts to keep the show in business until they could go back on the road in spring. He had no doubt they would have full houses the first several performances here in Juniper, but after that? He doubted many families would come more than once, maybe twice if they changed up the acts. Most folks lived a good distance from town, and attending the show meant more than just buying a ticket. Those families had to travel and perhaps camp overnight. There was food to be bought and souvenirs for the children. Bert had set up three sideshows and insisted on charging separately for them. Max had not been in favor of that. After all, when someone came to see them perform, didn't that person deserve to see everything? But when Bert had shown him the take from the sideshows, Max had to admit they needed the money. "Just keep it reasonable," he'd told Bert.

His partner had agreed. Max knew that from time to time, Bert even made sure some families got to see the sideshows at no cost. He was a good man, but he was also a businessman who reminded Max on a regular basis that the lives of several dozen performers and crew members depended on them staying in business. In exchange for Max allowing Bert to manage the business end of things, his friend did not argue when Max decided to change the show's content, even though Bert made no secret of his opinion that what folks came to see was high drama. By the same token, when Max asked to see the ledgers, Bert did not take offense.

Max knew his friend would never cheat him, and that was not his point in reviewing the books. The point was to remind himself that a show built around his memories of what the true West had once been might not be one most people called entertainment. The show did all right in areas where their version was the only one people were likely to see, but more than once after a performance he'd stood near the exit, dressed in the rougher clothing of a roustabout, with a hat pulled low to hide his face and heard comments like "It was a nice show, I suppose. Nothing like Buffalo Bill Cody's, of course. And why didn't they do the Battle of the Little Bighorn? Every show seems to be doing that one."

Max pushed the ledger aside and removed the wire-rimmed glasses he'd taken to wearing whenever he worked on the books. With two fingers, he pinched the bridge of his nose and closed his eyes. He just hoped the finale he'd created with Reba would give people enough of a thrill that they would forget about the big battle scene they all seemed to want.

Reba.

He knew she had a point—the crowds would be delighted with the romantic ending she'd proposed. The problem was he knew Reba had a lot more than pleasing her audience in mind when she came up with the idea of them kissing and riding off together on Diablo. It wasn't that she was in love with him. No, what Reba sought was security, someone to take care of her. That business about needing an assistant had been nothing more than her way of setting herself above the rest of the cast. True, she could neither read nor write more than her name, but she was certainly capable of dressing herself and packing and unpacking as the show moved from place to place. But it had been easier to give her what she wanted than to argue the point and live with the constant threats of her moving on to another show.

On the other hand, he'd realized that Reba's assistant was one place they could find some savings.

As a former Harvey Girl, Trula Goodwin was clearly capable of finding work. Max would even do what he could to help her. After all, she hadn't worked for Reba for more than a few days. He'd agree to give her two weeks' pay so she'd have something while she sought other employment. Of course, the problem wouldn't be the Goodwin girl. The problem would be Reba. Well, he'd give Reba the choice to either pay the girl herself or let her go.

Max let out a long breath and pushed himself to his feet. He glanced at the clock and decided he'd sleep on the cot in the office, but before that he needed to stretch his legs and clear his head.

Outside, all was quiet. A campfire glowed from the midst of the tepees. The huge performance space sat empty, the wooden seating unoccupied. A lantern inside the dining tent reminded Max he hadn't eaten anything since the lunch he'd shared with Emma. Once inside the large tent, he grabbed an apple from the bowl of fruit left out and bit into it as he walked back outside. The night was clear with a sliver of a moon and thousands of stars dotting the New Mexico sky.

How many nights had Max spent sleeping under just such a sky surrounded by open prairie or next to a raging river—alone? On any one of those nights, had he ever imagined his life would have come to this?

He chewed the apple, savoring the sweetness of it. So much had changed, but the one thing he understood was that somehow, he'd always found his way. And even though he knew he couldn't hold back progress, just maybe sharing what he knew to be the true history of the frontier was exactly what he'd been meant to do. First, he'd had to live it. Now, he had to share it. He tossed away the core of the apple and stared out at the mountains silhouetted against a charcoal sky.

The world was changing—*had* changed. He needed to face that. Putting on a show of what things had once been was no longer going to be enough. Max needed to find his place in this new world. And he was surprised when his next thought was of Emma Elliott. He wondered if overseeing a bunch of Harvey Girls was enough for her. Somehow, even though he barely knew her, he had a sense that, like him, she wanted more.

Chapter 5

EVERY NIGHT AFTER HER BUSY DAY ENDED, EMMA worked on the blouse, her mind racing with some new idea for colors or stitches. Twice, she carefully ripped out what she had begun and started again. In the dining room, she found herself examining the clothing worn by female travelers and guests of the hotel. That skirt would be so much more striking with a band of velvet at its hem, or that jacket would stand out more if it fastened with black braided loops instead of just buttons.

The other Harvey Girls had taken an interest in the project as well, stopping by at night to see how things were coming along and giving their opinions on the shape of a line or the blend of colors.

"Miss Reba is to wear this?" Sarah asked, her eyes wide with this new bit of information.

"Maybe. If so, it would be for the finale," Emma said, "and please do not let her or Trula know I am working on her costume. It's entirely possible Pearl Hardin won't consider my work up to snuff and will go with something else."

Melba let out a derisive huff. "Trula Goodwin thinks she's too far above us to even so much as say a decent hello, much less stop to chat."

"Even so, it's to be a surprise," Emma insisted. "Now get to bed. Tomorrow is going to be another busy day."

"They're all busy days since the show came to town," Nan replied, covering a yawn. "Good night, Miss E."

"The parade is just days away," Sarah reminded them, "and the first performance."

"Oh, how I wish we could all go," Melba sighed.

"The show will be here for weeks," Emma said. "I'm sure Mr. Campbell will make certain we'll all have the opportunity to see a performance, maybe more than one. Now scoot."

She closed her door behind them, enjoying the sound of their excited chatter as they went to their rooms. They were truly nice girls, and sometimes she felt such a maternal love for them.

Maternal?

She wasn't *that* much older than they were—at most eight years older than the youngest. She stabbed her needle into the pincushion and set the blouse aside. Was this to be her life? Shepherding young women until they found husbands or moved on while her life remained the same?

She'd had two serious relationships in her life. The most recent had been with Aidan. Her first romance had been with a boy she'd known in Nebraska who had abandoned their plans to marry one day in order to join Theodore Roosevelt's Rough Riders and fight in the Caribbean. She'd been so young then and so brokenhearted that she'd been certain any chance she might have for marriage and family was over. On the other hand, if they had married, she might never have pursued the adventure she'd found in joining the Harvey Girls, but at least she would have known...

What? Security? From what? Loneliness?

No, loneliness wasn't an issue. She had the girls and her good friends. Grace Hopkins and Lily Daniels had come to Juniper with her, and until each found her true love, they had all shared a room just down the hall from where Emma was now. They had also shared laughter and tears and dreams for the future. Grace and her husband, Nick, lived close enough that Grace and her children were in town at least every couple of weeks, and she and Emma always found time for a quick visit. Lily split her time between Washington, DC, and Santa Fe where her husband, Cody, served as territorial representative and was rumored to one day become the territory's first governor should statehood ever be achieved. Emma chuckled at the idea of Lily as the first lady. Of the three friends, Lily had always been the one who tested rules and followed the more dangerous but thrilling path.

Emma had always wished she could be more free-spirited like Lily. But here she was—head waitress and housemother to a crew of girls who reminded her of the good times of her younger days as a Harvey Girl. She studied her face in the washstand mirror, running her fingers over her skin. The outing with Max was the first she'd taken in weeks. Even when the dining room and counter were closed, she still spent hours in her office filling out the multiple reports required by her superiors at headquarters. And in the evenings, she felt compelled to be available should any of the girls need to talk or take ill or try to slip in past curfew.

More than once, she had lectured Trula or another girl on the dangers of allowing any young man to expect her to break the rules for him. No wonder Trula rolled her eyes and pursed her lips. Even to Emma's ears, her words had sounded preachy. But she had a duty to these young women who were far from home and family, didn't she?

And what of your duty to yourself—your happiness?

She shook off the thought, moving to the window that looked out over the town—the railway station across the street, the darkened shops, the church on the far side of the plaza. The church where Max had walked with her, giving her all his attention while the younger and far more attractive Harvey Girls trailed along behind.

She had to wonder if his kindness and attention had been born of respect rather than attraction. Stiffening, she wondered if she had indulged her girlish fantasies that the handsome captain and showman found her attractive when the truth was it was far more likely he viewed her the same way he thought of Pearl. She'd allowed herself to become caught up in the romance of a new handsome man coming to town, breaking the boredom of what had over the years become routine.

Well, Emma Elliott was no longer seventeen and ready to marry the first boy she'd ever kissed. She was a grown woman with serious responsibilities. She would finish the blouse and deliver it as soon as possible, even if it took all night. After that, when it came to Max, there would be no cause for anything other than the polite interaction of a Harvey Girl with her customer.

Unless, of course, she was wrong, and he didn't think of her as he did Pearl at all. Unless he also felt a connection.

∽∞∾

When Max took the last stool at the counter the following morning, planning to grab a quick breakfast before meeting with Frank Tucker and other business owners to thank them personally for all the town had done to make the troupe welcome, he glanced around, hoping to see Emma. Seemed like her smile might be a good way to start the day, especially one that promised to be as busy as this one did. Although Aidan Campbell had pressed him to have his breakfast in the dining room where he was less likely to be recognized and disturbed, Max saw no reason for special treatment. After all, it was part of his job to be recognized, to build interest and excitement for the show. If he got a good meal on top, he counted that a bonus.

Harvey Girl Melba was working the counter. He'd taken to addressing the girls that way since he did not know their last names and could not seem to break them of referring to him as Captain Winslow. Melba smiled and nodded as she turned away to prepare his orange juice.

"Is Miss Elliott around?" he asked when she brought him the glass filled with juice served on a bed of shaved ice. It was unusual for Emma not to be within sight or at least earshot, making sure everything was up to the Harvey standards.

Melba frowned. "No one has seen her yet this morning, and we got so busy, we figured she'd be down any time now." She glanced toward the kitchen as if expecting her supervisor to come through the door any moment. "I hope she's not made herself sick. She's been working late every night on that costume and…"

Just then, Emma entered the lobby from the dining room. She was balancing a brown paper package under her chin as she tied the sash of her apron. There were shadows under her eyes, and her hair was not nearly as perfectly bound as usual. She looked like a girl who'd been caught showing up late for school, and that made Max smile. He left his place at the counter and approached her.

"Good morning, Emma."

"Yes…I…that is…" She lifted her chin, and the package fell to the floor. He bent to retrieve it at the same time she did.

"Are you unwell?" he asked.

She straightened. "I am perfectly fine." When he tried to hand her the package, she refused. "That's for Pearl—the costume. I hope it meets her standards. Please let her know I enjoyed working on it."

Max studied her. Something was different. She was not the woman he'd shared the previous Sunday afternoon with. She seemed…grumpy was the only word he could find. "I'm sure Pearl will be grateful to have had the help."

"If you want to look at it to make sure it's up to *your* standards…" Her voice cracked, and he realized she was nervous.

He smiled. "Not sure I know the first thing about costumes and such, Emma."

"Well, I won't keep you. Enjoy your breakfast, Captain." And with that, she walked quickly back through the dining room doors, closing them behind her.

Max glanced at the counter and caught Melba's eye. The waitress had clearly overhead the exchange, but she just shrugged and went to serve another customer.

Max finished his breakfast, his mind chasing reasons for the sudden change in Emma's reaction to him. Maybe Reba had said something? Although he didn't think Emma was likely to be taken in by anything Reba might say. And then he had a thought. He hadn't offered to pay her for the work on the costume. Was that it? Surely, she knew he wouldn't expect her to do all this work for free. He wiped his mouth and set the napkin on his plate, left a tip for Melba, and headed for the dining room.

"Uh, Captain?" Melba was clearing away his dishes. "If you're going to see Miss E, this way's closer."

"Just forgot to tell her something," he said.

Melba smiled. "She'll likely be in her office." She indicated the waitresses' exit to the kitchen.

"Thanks."

He followed Melba's instructions, nodded to the cook and kitchen staff, and knocked on the partially closed door of the office.

"Yes?"

She was seated behind a small desk, a sheaf of papers

scattered in front of her and a pencil tucked behind her ear. She peered up at him and then stood. "Captain Winslow," she said, a little breathless with surprise.

He half expected her to salute, so stiff was her posture. Not waiting for an invitation, he closed the door and pulled out the single chair across from her. "I've come to apologize, Emma."

"I'm sure I have no idea…"

Max felt his temper rise. There was no call for games. He waved the package between them. "I came to let you know I have every intention of paying you for the work you've done and for any work you might do in the future."

She stared at him for a moment, then sank slowly back into her chair. "I do not expect to be paid. It was a test. We agreed."

"I agreed to no such thing. Bert and I pay people a fair wage, and I will do the same with you. I assume you kept track of the time spent?"

"No," she murmured, studying her hands.

He let out a sigh. "Then I'll ask Pearl for a fair remuneration and get that to you."

"Really, that's entirely unnecessary. I enjoyed doing it."

Max ran a hand through his hair. He did not understand this woman, and he considered himself a pretty good judge of the female of the species. "If it wasn't that you thought I'd taken advantage, then what?"

She glanced up and then back down. "I don't know what—"

"All that business in the lobby, Captain this and that, treating me like we'd never met before."

He saw her hands tense. "I was simply being polite—and professional."

"I thought we were friends, at least becoming friends, Emma."

She stood. "I apologize if I have offended you, Captain, but the truth is we are both exceedingly busy people, and eventually you will be gone and—"

"I didn't come in here for an apology. I came to apologize to you. For the life of me, I can't figure you out." He stood. "The thing is, Emma, I'm pretty stubborn when it comes to stuff like that, especially when it comes to somebody like you—somebody I think is well worth knowing. So get ready. I'm not planning to give up." He put on his hat and reached for the door. "What do you say we take a walk later tonight once you're off duty?"

Her lips hardened into a thin line that told him she was about to refuse, so he added, "I mean, by then I'll have delivered this package to Pearl and can let you know what she had to say about your handiwork."

That did the trick.

"Very well, Captain. And if there's anything I can do to correct any problems—"

"There won't be any problems, Emma, unless you decide to keep on calling me Captain," he added with a wink as he left.

∞

His natural charm was impossible to resist, Emma thought as he closed the door with a soft click. She heard him walk away, heard him laugh at some exchange with George. She sat at her desk and tried to concentrate on the schedule she'd been working on before he came through the door. All six feet plus with his broad shoulders that seemed to make the room suddenly too small.

He was incredibly good-looking even when he wasn't smiling. And he could captivate anyone he set his sights on. But Emma had been fooled before, not only by the boy back in Omaha but by her very own father, a man she had adored and one she thought had adored her in return. Of course, that was before he left the family one day without a word and was never heard from again.

"Enough!" she hissed as she slammed the scheduling journal shut and stood. Things had been going along so well. She had her work and solid friendships, and she was well liked and respected within the community. She held to the hope that one day she might meet someone who would share her interests in music and nature and become—if not a romantic partner—a sort of companion.

And then Captain Max Winslow had walked into the dining room, and from that moment, it was as if she found breathing difficult whenever he was nearby. Still, hadn't she held her own during the afternoon they'd spent together at the showgrounds?

That's because you were interested in something other than him. You met Pearl, and the opportunity to do some creative work presented itself and...

A knock at her office door had her pressing her palms across into the wood of the desk before taking her seat again. "Come in," she called as she pulled the scheduling journal closer. When she looked up, the bellboy was standing just inside the door. As always, he looked nervous.

"Yes, Tommy, what is it?"

He handed her an envelope she recognized as hotel stationery. "The captain asked me to deliver this," he mumbled as he folded his hands behind his back and waited.

"Thank you, Tommy. That will be all."

The boy shifted from one foot to the other and made no move to leave. "He said I should wait for an answer, miss."

Emma found herself at odds with wanting to roll her eyes at the man's schoolboy tactic while at the same time wanting to smile. She slid her thumb under the seal of the envelope and removed the single sheet of paper.

Forgot to ask—are you fond of ice cream?

Max

It was a ridiculous question, but it made her lips twitch. She considered a response and decided to give it in writing. Scribbling her reply on a piece of paper, she folded it and stuck it into the envelope Tommy had delivered. "Thank you, Tommy. Please see that the captain receives this."

Tommy stared at the envelope she held out to him. "Should I wait for an answer?" His voice cracked, and there was a bit of panic in the way he looked at her. She imagined he might see himself being a kind of carrier pigeon between Max and her, and the image made her laugh, which made Tommy relax slightly.

"No need to wait, Tommy. I'm sure you have other responsibilities that need your attention. Thank you."

The boy straightened his shoulders and fled her office before she could change her mind.

Ice cream?

She smothered a giggle—a girlish giggle—and then Aidan entered her office without knocking.

"You have a problem," he said. "Trula Goodwin."

Emma was at once all business. "Trula is hardly my concern, Aidan," she said. "She no longer works for the Harvey Company."

"But she is a guest—of sorts."

"Then don't you mean *you* have a problem?"

Aidan sat across from her and leaned closer. "She is creating difficulties on a number of levels, Emma."

"What sort of difficulties?"

"She treats the housekeepers as if they are her personal servants. Two of them are ready to quit. And George told me if I don't keep her out of his kitchen with her special demands in the name of Miss Reba, he'll leave as well."

"Maybe since she claims to be acting on behalf of Miss Reba, that's the person you need to speak with."

Aidan rolled his eyes, and Emma couldn't help but pity the man.

"Come on, Aidan. Turn on the charm and she's bound to come around and bring Trula along as well."

"I have my doubts. If you would just speak with Trula, I'm sure—"

Emma stood. "Trula is not at the root of the problem, Aidan. We both know that."

Aidan got to his feet and turned toward the door, then stopped and smiled at her. "How about you speak to the captain? Ask him to talk to Miss Reba?"

"Again, that would be your job, Aidan, not mine."

He studied her for a long moment, his eyes narrowing. "You've changed, Emma. You used to be so willing to do whatever was needed to make sure everything here at the hotel ran smoothly."

Emma straightened. "And I continue to be dedicated to my work. Are you dissatisfied with the job I'm doing managing the wait staff and the dining room and counter?"

"Of course not. It's just you used to be willing to go beyond that. I thought we were partners in this."

"We are. I manage the wait staff, George handles the kitchen staff, Tilly Hobson takes care of running housekeeping, and you manage the running of the rest. Isn't that what you once told me?"

She was deliberately recalling a night during their brief courtship when she had made several suggestions for ways they might improve services. She had thought he would be interested, but instead he had reminded her of her place in the organization and brushed off her suggestions as untenable.

Now Aidan started to say something, thought better of it, and opened the office door. But he hesitated before leaving. Once again, he glanced at her, his brow furrowed in a frown. "Like I said, Emma, you've changed."

For one brief moment, she wondered if he was

giving her a warning. After all, he had the power to express concerns about her job performance to the home office in Kansas City. She considered calling out to him, saying she would speak to Max about Reba. But she didn't.

Why should she?

Maybe because she was in her late twenties, and without this job, she really wasn't sure how she would fend for herself. Her brothers had all married and were scattered across the country. They had sold the farm, and her mother kept the shop in Omaha open— barely. This job had allowed Emma to send money to her mother regularly.

Hearing the distant blast of a train whistle that signaled the arrival of a swarm of hungry travelers, she hurried off to the dining room to be sure everything was ready to receive them. They would have only half an hour to eat and get back on the train. In addition, there would also be the regulars—townspeople and guests staying at the hotel. Her chest swelled a little when she saw that everything and everyone were ready. Her crew of girls stood at their posts, their uniforms spotless and their smiles already in place as Emma opened the double doors and welcomed their first guests.

She let out a breath of relief when she saw that neither Max nor Bert Gordon were among those streaming into the dining room. The business partners rarely showed up for lunch. On the other hand, just as the last of the travelers from the train found a seat, Miss Reba swept into the room, and there was an audible gasp as diners recognized her. She glanced around as if she were taking her curtain call, smiling at everyone, and even allowing her gaze to linger on one or two of the younger men before taking a seat alone at the table reserved for her, Max, and Bert.

Emma's table.

A moment later, Trula entered the room and took the chair across from her employer.

Emma greeted them with a forced smile. "Ladies, welcome," she said. "May I take your beverage order?"

Trula pointed to their cups that she'd already set in the Harvey code and looked up at Emma with a smirk. Coffee for Reba and tea for her.

"The chef has prepared his signature flank steak today," Emma said as she presented menus to both women. "We have a lovely selection of side dishes for you to choose from. I'll give you time to decide," she added and stepped away, signaling Nan, the beverage girl, who hurried forward to serve the coffee and tea.

Emma was aware of the other girls glancing at Trula, their smiles wavering. She signaled the staff to join her just inside the kitchen. "Trula works for Miss Reba now," she reminded them. "As such, she is as much a guest as anyone else dining with us today."

"And she's gonna play that to the hilt," Melba said.

"But, ladies, we do not have to play along with her. Give those diners seated at your stations your undivided attention. I'll take care of serving Miss Reba—and her guest."

The girls nodded and stepped aside as George entered the dining room holding a tray of steaming sliced beef high above his head. As always, the diners from the train buzzed with expectation. The waitresses surrounded George, filling trays with plates of meat for their guests and then serving the sides they'd chosen, always with a smile.

Emma took two plates of beef to Reba and Trula.

"I'll have the boiled potatoes and green beans," Reba said, handing her menu to Emma.

Emma nodded. "And for you, miss?"

Trula ignored her and leaned forward. "Have you ever tasted the chef's stewed peaches, Miss Reba? They are divine, simply divine."

"I didn't see that listed on the menu." Reba glanced up at Emma, her penciled eyebrows lifted in question.

"Oh, I'm sure George will make some special for you," Trula gushed before Emma could reply. "You'll see to that, won't you, dear?"

Since assuming the position as head waitress and housemother, Emma had always been Miss Elliott or, in more casual circumstances, Miss E. Even those waitresses she'd worked with before the promotion never called her by her given name and certainly would never dare refer to her as "dear." Emma felt her smile stiffen as she turned her attention back to Miss Reba. "I'll be happy to convey your request to the chef," she said before looking at Trula. "And for you, miss?"

The girl tapped her forefinger on her chin as she studied the selection listed on the menu. "The peaches, of course, and perhaps the creamed corn... no, the lima beans...although I do love—"

It was Reba who lost patience. "Oh, for heaven's sake, girl, make a choice. My meat is getting cold."

Trula's cheeks turned a splotchy red. "Creamed corn," she muttered.

Emma took the menus and returned to the kitchen to place the order. It was understood that any reasonable request made by a guest was to be taken seriously and honored if possible. But George was not in the mood to accommodate this one.

"That girl is behind this," he said, his eyes boring into Emma's, waiting for confirmation.

"Still, the order is for Miss Reba, and—"

George held up his palm, signaling silence. "I have had my fill of Trula Goodwin strutting around here like she owns the place. No more," he snapped and turned away to attend to the bread pudding he was preparing for dessert.

"George, I know Trula is out of line. Aidan and I were discussing the matter just before we opened the dining room. He's going to speak to the captain."

"And what good will that do?"

"The captain will speak to Miss Reba."

George's shoulders slumped. "I'll do it for *you*, Emma. I don't want to leave you in a bad place."

"Thank you. I'll serve them their other sides and come back for the peaches." She prepared single servings of creamed corn, green beans, and boiled potatoes, loaded them onto a tray, and returned to the dining room.

"Good news," she said brightly as she served their vegetables, keeping her focus exclusively on Reba. "The chef is preparing peaches especially for you."

"Excellent," Miss Reba said as she attacked her food. She might be the star of a national traveling company, but she ate like a field hand.

"This corn is cold," Trula snapped.

Before Emma could respond, Reba reached across the table and scooped up a forkful of the corn and tasted it. "It's piping hot," she said, frowning. "Delicious, in fact." She glanced up at Emma with a radiant smile. "I don't suppose I might have a side of that as well?"

"Of course," Emma replied and hurried off to the kitchen.

When she returned with the corn and two servings of peaches, Reba was pulling apart a roll and slathering it with butter. Trula was gazing out the window, a sour expression on her face. She made no attempt to acknowledge the delivery of the peaches.

"When you are ready, the chef has prepared a lovely bread pudding with caramel sauce for dessert," Emma said, refilling their coffee and tea. "Will there be anything else?"

"Just the bread pudding," Reba said, still chewing the roll and dismissing Emma with her focus solely on her food. Emma noticed Trula's order of peaches and the rest of her food remained untouched, and as she moved away, she heard Reba say, "If you're not going to eat those peaches, pass them over. And let's discuss where you got the idea I would approve of you parading around town in my gowns."

It occurred to Emma that Aidan's concern about Trula might be short-lived. Clearly, Miss Reba did not suffer fools—or young women who stepped beyond the bounds of their employment. With a genuine smile, she returned to the kitchen to prepare the orders of bread pudding.

"What are you so happy about?" George grumbled.

Certain Reba's comment to Trula would lighten George's foul mood, she told him what she had overheard. His full-bellied laughter caused the rest of his staff to glance up from their work, and Emma was glad she'd broken her rule to never repeat conversation overheard in the course of her day. When she returned to Reba's table, she removed the dishes from the main meal and replaced them with crystal bowls of bread pudding, the caramel sauce steaming as it pooled around the dessert.

"Lovely," Reba announced, clapping her hands with delight. When Trula said nothing, only probed the pudding with the tines of her fork, Reba once again lost patience. "For heaven's sake, girl. You overstepped. It's hardly the end of the world. Stop pouting. You're spoiling my lunch."

As she returned to her post near the kitchen, it occurred to Emma that perhaps Trula and Reba were two of a kind, focused first on what each of them individually needed and wanted. Given Miss Reba's starring role in the show, she had the upper hand in this, and Trula had best watch her step.

The remainder of the day passed in a blur of passengers and other guests coming and going as well as making sure the uniforms in need of laundering were bagged and loaded on the afternoon train and fresh ones had been delivered. By the time the last guest had left that evening, Emma was looking forward to having a hot bath and curling up in bed with the penny novel she'd fallen asleep reading several nights before. She closed the door to her office and crossed to the back stairs that led up to her room. George was standing in the open doorway that led outside, talking to someone. He turned when he heard the click of her leather heels on the tile floor.

"Here she is now," he announced and stepped aside. "You folks enjoy your evening," he added before heading back through the kitchen and out into the dining room.

Max was standing in the yard, grinning at her. "Ready?" he asked.

Chapter
6

SEEING EMMA HESITATE IN THE KITCHEN, MAX suspected she had forgotten all about meeting him. "You don't do much for a guy's confidence, Emmie," he said with a shake of his head.

"I'm sorry. It's been a busy day, and as you can see, I haven't even had time to change out of my uniform. Perhaps another time?"

"Perhaps. Or we could just sit in a couple of those rocking chairs out front and take in the night air. Guaranteed to help you sleep better." He saw her glance toward the stairway. "Half hour," he bargained before pulling out his ace. "I want to tell you what Pearl said when she saw your handiwork."

"Very well. Half an hour." She stepped into the yard and headed around the side of the hotel, taking a seat in a rocking chair and smoothing her skirt. "Well?"

Max played dumb. He took his time removing his hat, setting it on the small table between his chair and hers. "Well, what?"

"What did Pearl say?"

It was dark, but he would have been willing to bet her question came through gritted teeth.

"She loved it," he said. "In fact, I've never heard her go on about anything the way she was carrying on about the work you did. She must have shown it to pretty much every woman in the company. They were all chattering about such small, even stitches and something about the way you used color and such. Meant nothing to me. I just thought it looked fine."

"She liked it then," Emma murmured, and she sounded pleased, a little excited even.

"She told me to tell you if you ever decide to give up working for the Harveys, you might want to think about heading east and opening a shop. Something about how those high society ladies would beat a path to your door."

"I'm just glad I could be of help." She set the rocking chair in motion.

Max wished he could see her more clearly. He leaned back in his chair. After a moment passed without either of them saying anything, he cleared his throat. "Do you ever think about that, Emmie? I mean doing something other than working for the Harvey outfit?"

"Do you?" she countered. "That is, do you think about something other than traveling across the country putting on shows?"

"Asked you first," he said with a chuckle.

She took her time answering him. "Nothing is forever." Her voice was soft, even a little wistful.

"So dream a little, Emmie. If you could do anything at all, what would it be?" He assumed the answer would be the usual—settle down, marry, raise a family.

"I joined the Harvey Company because I wanted to travel," she admitted. She laughed, but there was an edge of bitterness to it. "That hasn't exactly worked out."

"Where would you go if you traveled?"

"I saw an article once with photographs of something the article called 'a national park.' I really didn't know anything like that existed, and the photographs were so…unusual. Geysers and mud pots and steaming rocks." She stilled the rocking chair and sat forward, her hands gripping the chair arms. "Did you ever see that part of the country, Max?"

"I have. It's like nothing you can imagine, Emmie. It's all so grand and wild." Instinctively, Max covered her hand with his. "I hope one day you get to go there." He felt her relax slightly, her hand soft beneath his. He decided not to let go.

She let out a breath. "I've never shared that dream with anyone else, Max, not even my dearest friends. I imagine they would be quite surprised at this side of me. They see me as someone who is content with the life I have, and I guess I liked the way they relied on me, the way the girls now rely on me. Does that make any sense at all?"

"It does, at least to me. I think we have that in common—that sense of responsibility for others, putting that ahead of what we might need ourselves. For me, it's also the show and the way people think they know me when they don't."

They started the chairs rocking again, their hands still touching. He laced his fingers with hers, and she did not pull away. A couple of businessmen came up the walk and entered the hotel. From down the street came the faint plinking of the piano in one of the saloons. Otherwise, all was quiet except for the rhythmic squeak of their rocking chairs.

"Emmie?"

"Hmm?" Her voice was sleepy and relaxed.

"If it means anything, I think you could probably do pretty much anything you set your mind to."

She was so quiet, he thought maybe she had dozed off. But then she giggled. "I couldn't star in a Wild West show," she said.

He smiled and tightened his hold on her hand. "Would you want to?"

"Not really, but it does all seem like a grand adventure." She stifled a yawn. "Excuse me. I assure you it's not your company."

"Shall we call it a night?" he asked but made no move to rise and hoped maybe she would stay as well.

She slid her hand free of his and pushed herself to her feet. "I have an early start tomorrow," she said. "Thank you, Max. I'm so glad Pearl was pleased with my work. Let her know I'm happy to help with special projects or even alterations if she's in need and I have the time."

Max felt disappointed that she had focused on Pearl and the sewing project rather than the personal conversation they had shared. *Give it time.* He stood and faced her. "I'll be sure to pass along your offer to Pearl. In the meantime, do you think we might do this again?"

"This?"

"Spend time together."

She looked down at the floor. "Max, please don't feel you need to—"

"To what? Spend time with you? Try to get to know you?" He moved a step closer and hooked his forefinger under her chin. "Look at me, Emmie. The more I learn about you, the more I like you. I like talking to you. Truth is I was looking forward to tonight all day long. It made me smile just thinking about it. *You* make me smile." He trailed his thumb over her lower lip. "And if you don't walk away right now, I'm liable to think pretty seriously about kissing you good night."

She lifted her eyes to meet his. Something in the way she lingered told him she was coming to a decision, one she did not take lightly. "Still here," she finally murmured.

Max lowered his mouth to hers, kissing her gently, knowing it would not do to give in to his baser instincts to take her fully in his arms and deepen the kiss. "Good night, Emmie," he said before kissing her a second time, unable to resist one more taste of her soft, full lips. He was surprised by his restraint, surprised to realize that whatever he was feeling for Emma Elliott, it was a lifetime away from the purely carnal need he'd acted on with other women. With two light kisses, he felt something that had always been missing in his life. He felt a kind of contentment, as if maybe the world was going in the right direction after all.

He stepped away to allow her to pass.

"Good night," she said softly and crossed the veranda to the front entrance of the hotel.

"See you tomorrow?" he called after her as he leaned against a post and watched her go.

She paused before walking on. "That depends. Are you planning on taking any meals with us?"

"You know what I'm asking. After. Can I see you after?"

She did not turn to face him, and her voice was so soft, he almost missed her reply.

"Seems to me there was some suggestion of ice cream, so yes."

Max shoved his hands in his pockets and headed for the livery where he'd left Diablo. He couldn't seem to stop grinning like a schoolboy.

❦

On her way to her room, Emma felt a lightness she hadn't known in months. The weight of her responsibilities often left her feeling tired and out of sorts by the end of the day, but not tonight. She touched her fingers to her lips. He'd kissed her, not once but twice. She wanted to tell someone. She wished Grace and Lily were waiting for her at the top of the stairs, anxious to hear all about her evening with the handsome showman.

But it had been three years since the days when she, Grace, and Lily were Harvey Girls together. They had each found adventure of their own and followed it. The reminder of passing time brought Emma's high spirits back to earth. She sighed and climbed the stairs, doing a quick check of the rooms along the hall to tally which girls were still out. It was not a perfect plan, but when she'd told the girls she would make this nightly visit and anyone who was still out would need to knock at her door when they returned to be marked off the list, they'd groaned but so far had followed the plan. Of course, Emma was not so naïve that she didn't understand a girl—like Trula, for example—might check in at the stroke of curfew and slip out again later, but for the most part, the system worked.

On this night, every girl was accounted for, most of them already in their nightgowns. She bid them good night and returned to her room at the top of the stairs. When she opened the door, she saw a small envelope on the floor and recognized Grace's blue stationery. She slid her thumbnail under the sealed flap and removed the contents.

Planning to be in town tomorrow. Let's meet for tea and catch up. It's been ages. Meet you at Miss Lorna's Tearoom after the three o'clock pulls out.

Grace

Emma smiled. Despite the fact that it had been years since Grace had worked as a Harvey Girl, she still gauged time by the coming and going of the trains. Emma clutched the message to her chest and laughed. It was almost as if Grace had known. How many times had it been just that way for the three friends? She wished Lily lived closer and they could all be together, but she would not be greedy. A shared cup of tea with Grace was exactly what she'd been hoping for.

Outside her door, a floorboard squeaked. Emma

glanced at her watch. Quarter past curfew. She opened her bedroom door and stepped into the hall. Melba was on her way down the stairs, fully dressed. Emma cleared her throat and waited.

Chin lowered to her chest, Melba retraced her steps, squeezed past Emma, and headed down the hall to the room she shared with Nan.

"Good night, Melba," Emma called out, not bothering to lower her voice, wanting to sound a warning to all the girls.

"Good night, Miss E," Melba muttered as she entered her room and shut the door.

And just like that, all the youthful joy Emma had felt following Max's kisses and finding Grace's invitation melted away. She may as well face facts—her time for romance and adventure had probably passed. Nothing could possibly come of a liaison with Max. He would move on, and she would stay. Her choice was to enjoy whatever time they might have with the knowledge it was not permanent or cut it off before she suffered the misery that was sure to follow.

She undressed and pulled her nightgown over her head. Tomorrow, she would have tea with Grace. Grace would listen and sympathize with her dilemma and perhaps offer advice.

⤬⤬⤬

Miss Lorna's Tearoom was a new addition to the growing string of businesses that stretched along two sides of Juniper's plaza, a sign of the times. More and more people were settling in the area; more and more tourists came from the East to experience the wonders of the mountains and desert, marveling at the strange foliage and rock formations that rose like buildings across the land.

As soon as Emma made sure the dining room and counter were cleared of the effects of serving a steady stream of guests and that the dining room was set for the supper clientele, she left her apron in her office, pinned on her hat, and hurried away. Grace was waiting, having already chosen a table by the lace-curtained windows and ordered a pot of tea and plate of finger foods for them to share.

The two of them hugged and sat across from each other at the small round table. Two other tables in the tearoom were occupied, but Emma focused only on her friend. Grace always looked so young, so fresh. How did she do it? "Where are the children?" Emma asked, spreading her napkin over the black skirt of her uniform.

"I left them home with Nick. Let him answer their endless questions and keep up with their constant need to move from one activity to the next every few minutes." She laughed. "Besides, when he heard you and I planned to get together, he offered."

"Have you heard from Lily recently?" Emma was fairly bursting to talk to Grace about Max but understood there was a protocol to be honored.

Grace rolled her eyes. "You know Lily. One day she'll simply show up, full of excuses and apologies for not being in touch, and you and I will hang on her every word as she regales us with the adventures of her life in Washington." She poured tea for Emma and herself, then selected two small sandwiches from the tiered plate between them, setting them on a smaller hand-painted plate. "Are you not eating anything?"

Emma realized Grace was waiting for her to choose sandwiches and hurried to do so. They ate and drank in comfortable silence, but then Grace frowned.

"Okay, what's going on?"

"Nothing out of the ordinary," Emma lied.

Grace cocked an eyebrow. "Really? Then why do you look as if you have the weight of the world on those shoulders? It's Aidan, isn't it? Is he still upset that you broke things off with him? Because it's been months, and he needs to move on and let you do the—"

"I've met someone."

Grace's scowl softened into an expression of surprise that spread to delight. She leaned closer and lowered her voice. "Really? Tell me everything."

As they shared the sandwiches and sweets and lingered over cups of tea, Emma told her friend about the day Max first walked into the dining room, the afternoon they'd spent at the showgrounds, and finally the kisses they'd shared just the evening before.

"My stars," Grace murmured, her eyes cast down as she sipped her tea. "I mean, Emma, don't you think perhaps… That is, he is a showman after all, an actor and, well, we all know that sort of person can be…" She glanced up and then set her cup down as she took hold of Emma's hand. "Not that he is that sort of person. He might well be a perfect gentleman. After all, as you said, he served our country and was a decorated hero."

"You think I'm being a fool," Emma said softly, half believing it herself. Why on earth would a man like that be interested in her?

"I think you're being uncharacteristically spontaneous, Emma. Of the three of us, you were always the cautious one. Now you tell me you've known this man barely a week and already allowed him to kiss you, not once but twice?"

"I did not allow..." she protested. But she had. Her high spirits at the promise of a visit with her friend plummeted. "They were hardly passionate kisses," she grumbled. In fact, now that she really thought about them, they had been little more than chaste pecks, albeit on her lips rather than her cheek or forehead. "I'm sure they meant nothing to him."

"But they meant a good deal to you," Grace said. "I just don't want you to be hurt, Em."

Emma smiled. "I know. Let's talk of other things. Did I tell you Trula Goodwin is now working for the show's female star?"

"Really?"

Grace set down her teacup, eager for details and clearly relieved at the change in topic. So Emma told her all about Rebel Reba's grand arrival at the station that first night, Trula appearing in church wearing one of the actress's gowns, and the uncomfortable lunch she had served the actress and her assistant. "Wait until Trula learns I did the embroidery on her boss's costume," she said with a rueful laugh. "I doubt that's a piece of clothing she'd look forward to borrowing."

"You always had such a gift for needlework," Grace said. "I remember all the nights the three of us talked well into the night, and you'd always have some sewing project in your hands. You made my wedding dress," she recalled.

"Well, based on Lily's design," Emma said, remembering that day vividly. They had all been so young, and none of them had thought that Grace—fresh off the farm and innocent as a newborn—would be the first of them to find her true love.

"Emma?" Grace was watching her closely. "Maybe it's time you thought of leaving the Harvey Company. Maybe open a little shop of your own if you want to stay here in Juniper, or maybe move on to Santa Fe. You always seemed the perfect candidate to take on the duties of head waitress, but none of us ever thought it would be forever."

"That's true. What we thought was that one day— like you and Lily—I would find my true love, and the fairy tale would be complete for the three of us. Sadly, 'twas not to be."

Grace pursed her lips. "Emma Elliott, stop this right now. You act as if you are past your prime and destined to live out your days alone. That is simply unacceptable. So if you have feelings for this show-man, then who am I to dissuade you? I just want you to be careful." Then she brightened. "I have an idea. Bring him out to the ranch for Sunday dinner next week—no, make it two weeks. Nick must be away on ranch business next week, and I want both of us to have a look at this man. You trust Nick's opinion, don't you?"

Emma nodded and smiled. "I trust both of you. It's a good idea. I'll ask him tonight."

Grace lifted her eyebrows. "Tonight? Two nights straight? This man moves fast, Emma. Just watch your step."

"Enough about me," Emma said. "Tell me what's happening with you. Every detail."

They lingered so long over their tea and Grace's stories of her wonderful family that Emma had to rush away in order to be at the hotel in time to be sure everything was ready for the arrival of the late afternoon train.

"Even if the captain can't come that Sunday," Grace called as Emma hurried up the street, "promise you'll come spend the afternoon with us."

"Promise," Emma replied and blew her friend a kiss before they went their separate ways.

⸺∞⸺

Max's desk chair creaked as he leaned back and stretched his arms over his head. The meeting with Bert and the show's advance man, Ed Brunswick, had gone on longer than usual. Without warning, Ed had reported that the town council refused to issue a parade permit without certain advance assurances. That probably explained why the town's leaders had been so reserved when Max had met with them earlier in the week.

"They want a cut of ticket sales," Ed reported.

"We're barely meeting expenses as it is," Bert reminded him.

Ed shrugged. "No cut, no permit."

"I have to go into town tonight," Max said. "Let

me have a word with Frank Tucker. As mayor, maybe he can have some influence."

"I can handle it, boss," Ed protested. "I'm on good terms with the mayor. Just tell me what you want me to do."

Max's mind clicked to alert. "You know him?"

"Met him at the council meeting. Didn't have time for more than just a friendly chat, but you know me—I can talk anybody into anything."

Lately, Max had begun to wonder if Ed was the right man for the job of traveling ahead of the show, making arrangements for permits and such. More often than not, it seemed as if demands from the town fathers had increased. "I'll handle it this time," Max said and stood, signaling the end of the meeting. Bert and Ed moved toward the door. Max waited for Ed to start down the short wooden stairway that led from the railway car to the ground and said, "Bert, you got a minute?"

His partner waved Ed on his way and turned to face Max. "You don't have to say it, Max. We're thinking the same thing."

"Ed's stealing from us?"

Bert nodded and picked up a ledger from his desk. "I didn't catch it at first, but he's getting more brazen. Look at these numbers." He opened the ledger and pointed to a column that showed their costs for printing posters and securing permits and leasing land for setting up the show. The numbers had steadily increased over the last few months.

Max ran his fingers through his hair. "I was check-ing the books the other night and missed that. I wasn't comparing current expenses to past months." This was the part of the job he hated most—having to confront an employee and probably let him go. But the evidence could not be denied and at least required giving Ed the chance to explain himself.

"I've saved all the receipts he turned in," Bert said. "Comparing this last season to the season before, there's a big difference and not in our favor."

"I gave him this job," Max said, more to himself than to Bert. He was recalling the man he'd once served with, then lost track of, then had stumbled across one night when the show was on tour. Ed had been out of work with no prospects and winter coming on. As Bert had done for him, Max had offered Ed a job with the crew that set up and dismantled the show at each stop. He had proven himself a hard worker and popular with the other members of the cast and crew. He'd had a natural gift of gab, and that made Max consider him for the advance man's position. At first, Ed had handled the job as if he'd been born to do it. Now it looked like all that had changed.

"I'm going to town," Max said. "I'll talk to the mayor and get his side of the meeting with the council."

Bert nodded. "Clock's ticking, boss. That parade is day after tomorrow. We can't do it without the permit."

Max took his hat from the rack by the door. His gun belt hung there as well. There'd been a time when strapping on that belt and shoving a loaded, ebony-handled six-shooter in the holster had been as natural as putting on his hat. But the world was supposedly more civilized these days—no need for men to always be armed. He had tried to remind himself that was progress, but the truth was it only reminded him of how things had changed.

"I'll see you for breakfast," he said as he started down the short flight of wooden steps.

"Gonna see that Harvey gal, are you?" Bert teased.

"None of your business," Max grumbled, but he smiled as he unhitched Diablo's reins and mounted the steed that seemed as anxious as Max was to be off to some new adventure.

❧

Max was waiting outside the kitchen entrance as he had been the night before. On this night, he sat alone on the wooden bench in the yard. Emma watched him for a moment from the kitchen window. He looked pensive, and it occurred to her that he might have had a rough day, that he was as exhausted as she was, and that making time to see her could easily have been postponed. He could have sent word that something had detained him at the showgrounds. Of course, he had a room in the hotel, so he would have ended up here anyway.

Oh, she wanted so much to believe he was out there waiting for her because there was nowhere else he'd rather be. But when it came to trusting the male of the species, she had such doubts. Her father's abandonment had scarred her badly and devastated her mother. It occurred to her that her attraction to the boy who'd run off to fight with Roosevelt had been nothing more than a failed attempt to prove to herself that a man would want her.

And then there had been Aidan. The two of them had started stepping out once Grace and Lily had both married and Emma was promoted to head waitress and housemother, a managerial position on a par with his. Not long after, she had come to realize that it was her promotion, not ardor, that had spurred him to pursue something more personal. He saw them as two lonely souls with great responsibilities and the need for companionship. But Emma wanted more than just companionship. She longed to be courted because she was desirable and interesting and not because she was merely "suitable." She wanted what she'd seen Grace and Lily find—passion that would not desert her, no matter what.

"You gonna just leave the poor fella sittin' there, Emma?" She hadn't realized George was still in the kitchen.

"He's a guest of the hotel," she reminded the chef primly. "He can come inside any time he likes."

"And as a guest, he would come through the lobby. He's in the kitchen yard, and he's waitin' for you. That makes the question what are *you* waitin' for?" He arched his bushy eyebrows, then turned away and busied himself checking the dough he'd set to rise for the next morning's baking.

Emma removed her apron and took a shawl from the hook behind her office door, wrapping it around her shoulders. This time of year, the days were pleasantly warm, but once the sun set, it could get quite chilly. She touched her fingers to her hair and nodded to George who nodded in return as she opened the back door. "Good evening, Max," she said.

Max stood and snatched off his hat. He smiled as he ran his hand through his thick dark hair. "Evenin', Emmie. Care to take a walk?"

He did not offer the formality of his crooked arm for her to take but rather stretched his hand out to her, and it seemed only polite to take hold. His hand was warm and swallowed hers in a way that made her feel protected.

"I found this trail back of the hotel here," he said, leading the way.

"I know the one," she replied, her voice so unsteady that she hoped he would assume it was the exertion of the climb and not the fact that she was trembling with pleasure. "It goes up to the cemetery, and there's a lovely view of the town and sunset from up there."

It was a short climb to the low adobe wall that surrounded the cemetery. "I'll bet there are some interesting stories in here," Max said.

"Yes…sad stories."

"You knew some of these people?"

Emma nodded as she released Max's hand and bent to brush away debris from the grave of Jake Collier. "Like this one."

"Who was he?" Max asked.

"A friend—a wonderful, funny, and caring man. He worked in the hotel kitchen and was in love with my dear friend, Lily. He got mixed up with some bad men. They threatened to harm Lily, and Jake tried to stop them…and paid for his courage with his life."

"And Lily?"

"Jake always understood the feelings didn't run both ways, but he knew Lily cared for him, and when he died, she was inconsolable. Later, she married Cody Daniels, who became the territorial representative in Washington, so now she lives out there most of the time."

"Most of the time?"

"She and Cody come back to Santa Fe a couple of times a year. Hopefully, she'll make one of those visits while you…the show is camped here. She would love seeing a performance."

"Let me know, and I'll have tickets waiting. I'd enjoy meeting your friends."

She continued clearing debris from Jake's grave while Max walked along, looking at the markers. "Speaking of my friends," she said, "I had tea this afternoon with another former Harvey Girl who married and stayed in the area. Grace Hopkins. She, Lily, and I arrived here in Juniper together and were roommates. She's invited you and me for the afternoon Sunday after next if you'd like to go. Her husband, Nick, is a rancher and I think the two of you might have a lot in common."

Max grinned. "Why, Miss Emma, are you asking me out?"

Emma felt the heat rise in her cheeks. "I'm relaying an invitation from my friend," she said. "If you're busy, she'll understand." She shrugged as if it hardly mattered, even though it mattered a good deal to her.

"Tell your friend I accept with pleasure. But I'm going to need directions, and since you've been invited as well, maybe we could go together…I mean, since you know the way." He held up his hands. "But I understand it's not a date."

Emma couldn't help but laugh. "Stop teasing me."

"Can't help it. I like the way my teasing makes your eyes sparkle. Of course, I'm never sure if that's irritation or just surprise, but it's nice."

While Emma reset the bouquet George and his staff had left on Jake's grave, Max stopped before a massive headstone with the surname *PERKINS* emblazoned across it in deeply etched capital letters. "This guy must have been important."

"I suppose he was to some people. He was president of the bank. Unfortunately, he was also obsessed with Grace, and to that end, he almost got her killed in the fire that killed him. After that, Grace was arrested on a charge of murdering him, which was, of course, nonsense."

"I take it she was found innocent?"

"Not for lack of his wife trying to see her hanged," Emma grumbled. She gathered the sticks and other debris she'd cleared and carried the pile to the edge of the cemetery where she scattered it on the barren ground. When she turned around, Max was standing close by, watching her.

"I didn't mean to upset you, Emma. Shall we leave this sad place and go watch the last of the sunset?"

Emma brushed the dirt from her hands and pointed. "The best view is from that outcropping of boulders up there," she said, linking her fingers with his. "Come on or we'll miss it."

She was glad to leave the cemetery. Too many memories of times she'd rather forget. Times when she and Grace and Lily—and Jake—had spent their days together working and their time off enjoying hayrides and picnics and such. They had been so very carefree, and it had seemed as if whatever the world had to offer lay ahead of them.

She led the way as they climbed the narrow rocky path until they reached the cluster of boulders, smoothed and polished by centuries of weather. She directed Max's attention to the spectacular view. "There," she said, her voice softened by the awe of seeing the red-orange orb suspended above the mountains.

Max climbed onto the largest flat boulder and then pulled her up to stand beside him. When her shawl slipped, he caught it and tenderly arranged it over her shoulders before turning her so that her back was to him and they were both facing the setting sun. "That's about the prettiest sunset I've ever seen," he said.

And his saying that made Emma realize how silly it was to think a sunset in Juniper might be unique for this man who had traveled the land and must have witnessed countless sunsets and sunrises in his years as a frontier scout and army officer. "You're kind to say that," she murmured. "I'm sure you've seen others equally as special."

He stepped closer and rested his hands lightly on her shoulders. "Not so, fair lady. I didn't see those with you."

Oh, how she wanted to believe him, but caution was her way. Working for the Harveys, she'd had more than her fair share of men making flattering statements. Part of her early training had been in ways to rebuff such advances without upsetting the man, usually a customer. Drawing on her training, she stepped away from Max's touch, turned, and looked up at him. He reached for her, and she stepped back, her foot slipping on the loose shale rock at the edge of the boulder. She scrambled for traction before falling to her knees. She looked down into the abyss below, her heart hammering just as Max's hands closed around her upper arms and dragged her back to safety.

Her breath came in short gasps as he held her upright and examined her face closely. "Are you hurt?" he asked, not releasing her.

"I slipped," she said, trying to smile, but suddenly the reality of how bad the fall might have been hit her. They'd scaled the rock on the side closest to the path but stood watching the sun go down closer to the edge that was a sheer drop into the arroyo far below.

"You're shaking," he said and pulled her fully into his arms. As he held her, he moved closer to the safer side of the flat rock.

"I'm...I'll be..."

"Shh," he whispered, his breath warm on her forehead. He was cradling the back of her head with one hand while his other hand spanned her back, pressing her to his chest. "Take a moment," he instructed.

She looked up at him. "Thank you," she said softly.

Their eyes locked. A question was asked and answered in silence. He cupped her chin and lowered his mouth to hers, and this time, there was nothing guarded about the kiss he gave—or her reaction to it.

Her fingers closed around the lapel of his jacket as she urged him closer. When he stroked her lips with his tongue, she opened to him and thrilled to the deep sigh that elicited from him. He tightened his hold on her, and she in turn pressed herself more fully into the solidness of his chest. She felt the outline of his long legs against the fabric of her skirt.

Then he was kissing her throat and her eyelids and earlobes. His fingers were undoing her hair and combing through the tangles. She heard the hairpins ping against the granite they stood on. Their breaths came in lung-filling gasps before they dove back in for another kiss. His stubble, which would be clean-shaven by morning, scratched her cheeks, marking her with the scent of the sandalwood soap he used.

And all too soon, it was over.

Once again, he cradled her head to his chest. She heard the steady beat of his heart and felt the rise and fall of his rapid breathing. When she opened her eyes, the sun had fully set, and only shadows surrounded them, the mountains outlined against a clear night sky. Once their breathing had steadied, he stepped back enough so he was still holding her but also looking at her. He touched her cheek, and she leaned into that touch, savoring the warmth of his fingers on her skin.

"I have something I need to handle with the show," he said. "And there's the parade and opening day after tomorrow. I may not be able to get away for the next few days," he added.

"It's all right," she said, moving away so she could readjust her shawl.

"No, it's not," he replied. "It's not all right, Emmie, because I find I want to see you every day, every night. To not see you for a couple of days?" He shook his head.

She wanted to remind him that each of them had work to do and that he was only here for a matter of weeks. In time, they would have to face facts. He would move on with the show, and she would stay to attend to her duties. But not tonight.

"Aidan has said the girls and I can watch the parade from the hotel balcony," she said, knowing it was not what he wanted to hear. "We'll wave and cheer, I promise." She kept her tone light and playful.

He traced her features with his forefinger. "You're very beautiful, Emmie," he said softly. "I don't think you see that, but I do."

No one had ever called her beautiful. Appealing, even attractive, yes. But never beautiful. She didn't know how to respond, so she simply said, "We should get back." She pulled her shawl tighter.

Max leapt down from the rock and held out his arms to her to help her down. Those long fingers she had admired that first morning spanned her waist and stayed there even after she was safe on the path. "I meant what I said, Emmie."

She smiled. "And coming from what my girls are sure is the best-looking man they've ever seen, I'll take that as words to treasure." She started down the path. He walked beside her or a little ahead when the path narrowed, but they were halfway back to the hotel yard before he spoke.

"Why do you do that? Brush aside compliments the way you do?"

They had reached the yard behind the hotel. She let out a long breath and turned to face him. "I have my reasons, Max. Maybe one day I'll explain, but not tonight. Tonight I want to remember a lovely walk, a shared sunset, and…"

"A kiss?"

She nodded. "Good night, Max." She stood on tiptoe to kiss his cheek before hurrying away.

As she let herself into her room, it occurred to her that he still owed her ice cream. She thought of having Tommy deliver a note reminding him of the promise. It would set a more lighthearted tone to an evening that had become far too serious. But as she passed the window on the landing of the back stairs, she realized he was still standing where she'd left him. He was looking up at the back of the hotel. In her room, she lit the lamp and walked to the window. When he saw her, he smiled, swept off his hat, and bowed before walking away, whistling.

Chapter 7

AFTER LEAVING EMMA, MAX DECIDED TO TAKE A WALK through town to clear his head. This business with Ed had rattled him. He'd trusted Ed, had given him a real opportunity. But there was evidence that Ed had gotten greedy. Seeing a light on in the back of the mercantile Mayor Frank Tucker owned, Max decided to pay the man a visit instead of leaving a note as he'd first intended.

Tucker greeted him cordially but was clearly surprised to see him.

"Sorry. I know it's after hours," Max said as he followed the older man inside the back entrance to the shop. "I saw the light and…"

"How can I help you?" Frank asked.

Max liked a man who cut right to the heart of things. "It's about this parade permit. I think there might have been a misunderstanding."

"Not on this end. The fellas on the council just want to be sure we have the fee in hand before we give you the go-ahead."

"And remind me of the amount of the fee."

Tucker named the price the council and Bert had originally agreed on.

"No surcharge on top?" he asked.

The mayor looked confused. "Surcharge? No. Why would we…" He slowly shook his head. "That young man is cheating you, isn't he?"

"Looks that way," Max said as he pulled cash from his pocket and peeled off the payment for the permit. "Does this make us square?"

"Yes, sir. I'll have the permit delivered first thing tomorrow."

The two men shook hands, and Max walked to the door. "Mayor Tucker, from here on out, as long as my company is in town, you and the council deal directly with me or Bert Gordon, okay?"

"Good plan." He walked Max out to the street where they shook hands again. "Good having you folks in town," he said. "Good for business."

Max headed for the livery to get Diablo and return to the compound. He planned to confront Ed Brunswick before any more time had elapsed. Knowing Ed's temper, it wasn't likely to be easy. On the other hand, if he let Ed go, they probably could afford to keep Reba's assistant. So one less problem.

∞

On the morning of the parade, clouds blotted out the sun, but to Max's relief, that did nothing to lessen the throngs of people already gathering along the boardwalks of the main street. As usual, Reba was late, but he had no doubt she would make her entrance at the last minute. Bert, on the other hand, was a worrier.

"Everybody else is in place," he grumbled as he checked his pocket watch for the third time in as many minutes.

"She'll be here," Max assured him. He was far more interested in whether Emma and the rest of her staff would gather on the balcony as she had said they might. But the only action he saw was the girl Reba had hired running toward him.

"Captain!" She reached him and gulped air, trying to regain her breath and speak.

"What's happened?"

"Miss Reba's costume...the jacket's whole back seam...ripped...stem to stern."

Bert joined them. "Tell her to wear something else and get over here now," he barked.

"All her costumes are at the showgrounds in her dressing tent."

Max could see the girl—Trula, he recalled—was genuinely upset and suspected she'd suffered the full brunt of Reba's rage at this unexpected disaster. Pearl Hardin had stayed behind at the showgrounds to make sure all costumes for the afternoon's show were properly repaired, pressed, and waiting in the dressing tents. A movement on the hotel balcony caught his eye. "Come with me," he said, taking hold of Trula's elbow and guiding her back to the hotel.

"What about the parade?" Bert shouted.

"Stall," Max answered. When he was near enough to the hotel entrance, he yelled up to the balcony. "Miss Elliott, could you join us in Miss Reba's room, please? And bring your needle and thread." He did not wait to see if she would comply but strode through the lobby and up the stairway. When he reached Reba's room, he banged on the door. "Reebs, cover yourself. I'm coming in."

He stepped inside, leaving the door open. The room was a mess of discarded clothing on the bed, on the chaise, on the floor. Reba stood in the midst of it, dressed in her underwear—pantaloons, chemise, and a corset that was only half laced. "I simply can't go on," she said with a dramatic sigh as she threw herself onto the bed.

"Sure you can." Max picked up a gown. "Wear this."

"Nothing fits," she screamed at him. She burst into tears and collapsed onto a stack of pillows.

Both Bert and Max had noticed Reba's recent weight gain. The woman had always had a healthy appetite. In the past, she'd worked that off riding and rehearsing for hours on end. But once Max ended their romantic relationship, Reba had claimed a variety of ailments. She rehearsed only when she deemed it necessary to practice a new act.

Still, he could see now that Reba's distress over the torn costume was genuine. He stepped carefully over a pile of discarded clothing on the floor and pulled a chair closer to the bed. "Come on, Reebs. We're going to fix this. The show must go on, right? Now where's this jacket?"

Trula picked up an item from the pile of clothing near the open door just as Emma came down the hall. She was clutching a small fabric-covered box that Max hoped was her sewing kit.

"Look, Miss Elliott has come to our rescue." He stood and, with a wave of one hand, indicated Trula should hand the jacket to Emma.

Reba raised herself to a half sitting position. "I do not need a waitress, Max. I need a seamstress."

Emma set her sewing box on a side table and held the jacket up to examine it.

"Can you fix it?" Max asked.

"I can mend it well enough to hold through the parade." Without saying more, she moved farther into the room, pushing aside the nest of clothing on the chaise as she turned the jacket inside out, spread it flat, and opened her sewing box.

"Reebs, get laced up and put on your skirt," Max instructed. "We need to get this parade started." He picked up a white blouse with a frilly lace collar and cuffs and showed it to Emma. "If the jacket can't be fixed, maybe she can wear this. Do your best," he said and started for the door. "And thank you," he added before stepping into the hall and shutting the door behind him.

❧

Emma nodded, her focus on the ripped garment. Fortunately, there was ample room in the seam to let it out. Up close, the alteration would be evident, but not from a distance.

"It won't work, so don't waste your time," Reba said as she held onto the bedpost while Trula laced her corset.

"There's a nice wide seam I can let out," Emma

replied around straight pins she'd lined up between her lips to pin the new seam. "Let's try this." Once she'd set the pins, she held the jacket as she might a coat for a hotel guest.

With a skeptical frown, Reba slipped her arms through the sleeves and stepped in front of the full-length pedestal mirror near the window. She preened and turned as she buttoned the jacket. "It's a little better," she agreed. "Not perfect, but it will do for the parade."

Emma heard Trula release an audible sigh of relief. From outside came the sounds of the show's band playing song after song and the show's narrator urging those waiting for the parade to sing along.

"Very well," she said. "I'll stitch it up while Trula helps you finish dressing." Reba removed the jacket and tossed it to her. Emma perched on the end of the chaise, threaded a needle, and began sewing.

"Well, hurry up," Reba urged, and Emma was unsure of whether that was directed at her or Trula, who was scurrying about retrieving the hairbrush and combs that had clearly been victims of Reba's tantrum.

Once dressed, Reba swept from the room without a word of thanks to either of them. Trula gathered some supplies—the hairbrush and extra hairpins, plus a clothes brush—and hurried after her. Neither of them so much as glanced at Emma.

She poked the needle and pins into the padded satin lining of her sewing box and closed it. She was tempted to restore the room to order by hanging up the discarded garments but decided she'd done enough. Max would be grateful, even if his costar was not. Closing the door, she climbed the back stairs to her room. After leaving the sewing box on her dresser, she returned to the balcony to enjoy the parade.

By the time she got there, the crowds lining the street were cheering a contingent of costumed riders that had stopped just past the hotel to put their horses through a routine of tricks. Behind them came a wagon carrying actors portraying a frontier family, followed by Chief Gray Wolf in full costume riding a large chestnut stallion. Several members of his family walked behind, including women dressed in the most beautifully beaded dresses Emma had ever seen. How she would love to have a closer look at that handiwork!

Across the street, she saw Trula clinging to the arm of a stocky young cowboy. So this was the young man the former waitress had slipped out repeatedly to meet. Emma took a closer look and noticed that although Trula was talking to him, he was looking elsewhere, not paying her much attention at all.

Oh, Trula, Emma thought, *you deserve a man who does not take you for granted, as this cowboy seems prone to do.*

Her instinct was to have a talk with Trula as she might with any one of the young women in her charge. But Trula was no longer one of those young women, and Emma doubted she would appreciate advice, even if it was well-meant.

Suddenly, a cheer went up, and Emma turned her attention back to the parade—and Reba. The show's female star sat sidesaddle on her white horse and waved a white lace handkerchief to the crowd as she passed. The girls on the balcony all buzzed about her hat, her beauty, and her stylish burgundy riding outfit.

Not one of them pointed out the temporary stitches Emma knew were holding the back seam of the jacket together, stitches she hoped would last the duration of the parade.

As Reba's horse passed the hotel, the crowd gave a shout and turned their attention back to the railway station where the parade had originated. Max came around the corner. He wore a coordinated costume of black trousers, a cream-colored shirt with a bolo tie, and a fringed deerskin coat, this one the color of vanilla. He wore his black hat and silver-studded black boots and sat in a saddle also decorated in silver. Diablo was equally as impressive, tossing his shiny mane while high-stepping down the street.

When they reached the hotel, Max reined in the horse and put the animal through its paces—rearing to its hind legs, counting by striking the ground with a front hoof on Max's command, and finally kneeling on front legs in a bow. That was when Max's eyes caught Emma's. He removed his hat and smiled.

Around her, the girls all let out an audible sigh. "Oh, Miss E," Sarah said. "He looked right at you. That smile was just for you."

"Really, girls, I think—"

"She's right," Melba interrupted. "That man likes you, Miss E, as in he *really* likes you."

Emma could feel her cheeks starting to color. In the street below, the parade was winding up and the crowd was beginning to scatter. Emma clapped her hands to gain the attention of her staff. "All right, time to get back to work. The noon train will be arriving within half an hour."

"He likes you," Nan murmured as the girls turned to go.

"Shoo," Emma said, but she could not deny she was basking in the warmth of Max's smile. No doubt he was letting her know how much he appreciated her help in repairing Reba's costume. No doubt knowing his costar as he must, he was aware there had been no gratitude from her. And just maybe he was letting her know he was still thinking about that sunset—and that kiss.

Because Emma seemed incapable of thinking of anything else.

❧

Behind his showman's smile, Max's mind raced with the unpleasant discussions he would need to have later with not only Ed Brunswick but Reba as well. Frank Tucker had confirmed the members of the town council were more than willing to accept the usual percentage of box office receipts. The problem had been Ed telling them the figure was ten percent more—an extra ten percent the front man no doubt planned to pocket.

Bert had suggested it would be best to get through the opening performance before letting Ed go. Further, Max knew they could not afford a new wardrobe for Reba. The incident before the parade had raised the question of whether he needed to have a talk with his costar. He hated the thought of that. Reba was performing as well as she ever had, and the woman did love her ice cream.

Ice cream. He'd promised Emma ice cream. He'd planned to take her to the small ice cream parlor across from the tearoom, but with her schedule and his and the fact that the shop closed early and did not open on Sundays, that seemed unlikely. As the parade wound its way down to the church where it disbanded, Max caught a glimpse of George Keller and had an idea. The hotel served ice cream, and with George's help, maybe Max could pull off the kind of quiet shared moment he'd been planning.

"Bert!" he called out to his partner who was barking out instructions to the crew. "Got an errand. See you back at the showgrounds."

"Don't be late," Bert demanded as he turned to face Reba. "That goes for everyone else," he shouted and stalked off, chewing on his cigar.

❧

Due to the parade and the arrival of the noon train, the hotel's dining room was thronged with customers, and the counter was doing a lively business as well. Aidan even seated a party at the table reserved for the stars and manager of the show. "The three of them have gone back to the showgrounds to prepare for this afternoon's opening performance," Aidan explained when Emma questioned the decision. "We need every table we can find plus every stool at the counter, and we need to turn things around as quickly as possible. There are more people waiting in the lobby."

Emma gathered the waitresses for a quick meeting. "Maintain your usual calm and charm, but keep an eye on your tables and try to get the guests served and on their way as quickly as possible. Nan, I'll serve all beverages today. Your help is needed with filling orders and getting side dishes out to the tables." She drew in a long breath and let it out with a smile. "Ready, ladies?"

"Ready," they chimed and hurried back to their posts.

The travelers from the train would not be a problem. They were well aware the stop was only for thirty minutes and they risked missing their train if they lingered. But those who had come in from watching the parade were a different matter altogether. Those with tickets for the performance had a couple of hours to dawdle. It was going to be a hectic lunch hour for both the waitresses and the kitchen staff.

So Emma was mystified when after serving coffee and tea to numerous guests, she was on her way through the kitchen to refill a coffeepot when George greeted her with a broad smile and a wink. George rarely smiled, and he never winked, she was quite sure of that. And under the circumstances, she would have expected more of a frown and grumble. But there was no time to even exchange a word with the chef, so she smiled back at him and hurried on.

Throughout the long lunch hour—extended to make sure they accommodated every person—Emma moved around the dining room, keeping an eye out for how the cups had been set by the waitress assigned to serve each new batch of guests. For several people taking lunch with them, this was their first time in the dining room, and they marveled at the way she seemed to know without asking what they had ordered to drink.

"It's just the Harvey way," she told them. And in the rare case someone caught onto the system—usually a child—she put her finger to her lips, swearing them to secrecy.

Gradually, the crowd thinned until there were only a few tables occupied and the counter was empty of customers. Emma gave each waitress a genuine smile and her thanks. "You've done excellent work today," she told them. "Thank you."

With obvious weariness, the waitresses trooped up the back stairs. They would have a couple of hours to rest before they'd be back for the supper crowd.

"I just want to take a nice hot bath," Emma heard Melba say.

"Get in line," Nan replied, and with a whoop, the girls were off to see who might lay first claim to the claw-footed tub in the common washroom.

Emma watched them go, picturing how she, Lily, and Grace had once vied to be first in line. Lily usually won and always took the longest time. Emma smiled at the memory as she headed back to her office.

"You going to see the show, Emma?" George asked. He was standing at a double sink scrubbing a large pot that had held soup.

Emma laughed at the ridiculousness of that idea. "Well, certainly not today." She perched on the wooden stool next to the sink. "That was the busiest day I can remember, and we still have supper to serve to travelers from two more trains."

George snorted. "I thought Aidan was going to

drive me crazy the way he kept popping back here to check up on everything, like me and my boys don't know how to do our jobs."

The *boys* were George's crew, and they ranged in age from fifteen to nearly fifty. They cooked and cleaned, unloaded and stored supplies, and in general made sure Emma and her waitresses had exactly what they needed at a moment's notice. Emma understood while the Harvey Girls might be the face of the company, it was those who served behind the scenes who made it all work.

"Aidan has ambitions," she reminded him. "And we can never tell when someone from headquarters might decide to come to Juniper. In fact, since Captain Winslow and Mr. Ford Harvey are apparently friends, I expect Aidan has been looking over his shoulder for days expecting one of the Harveys to show up."

To her surprise, George grinned. "Speaking of the captain, he stopped by after the parade. Wanted to talk about a little surprise he's planning for you."

"I can't imagine why."

"Why he'd talk to me or why he'd want to surprise you?"

"Both, I guess." Emma stood and examined a small spot of coffee on her apron. "This needs laundering," she muttered as she untied the sash and removed the garment, wadding it in a ball and placing it in a bin set by the door.

"He likes you, Em. Anybody with eyes can see that. Truth is we're all pretty pleased about it."

"We?" Emma understood her girls were going to talk, but George? And who else?

George set the pot aside and dried his hands on a flour sack turned dish towel. "Come on, Emma. We're a family here, and families talk to one another and wish the best for one another. The way you're always taking care of everybody else, seems like it's past time for you."

She knew better than to argue with George, so she changed the subject. "What's the surprise?"

Again the loopy grin, this time with another wink. "Ah, that's for the captain to reveal. Just thinking you might want to be looking your best once that last train leaves." He walked away and out into the yard.

"George!"

"Got to check the smokehouse, Em. See you for the supper shift." He waved and kept walking.

Men.

❧

As Max had expected, every seat was filled for the opening performance. People cheered each act, rising to their feet a couple of times in their enthusiasm. Everything had gone off like clockwork, and the time had flown by. He could hardly believe he and Reba were taking their places for the finale.

"Nice costume, Reebs," he said with a nod toward the blouse she wore...the blouse Emma had embroidered.

"Oh, this?" She tossed her head. "I'd forgotten all about it until Pearl found it. Funny, I had put it aside because it always seemed too large, but it fits perfectly."

Max figured Pearl had decided not to say anything about Emma embellishing the garment. He heard the band's fanfare as the show's announcer called for the audience to welcome the stars of the show.

Side by side, he and Reba rode into the ring. The targets were in place, and the audience looked on with hushed expectation. Per the script, Max tipped his hat to Reba and started slowly circling the ring. Reba acknowledged his greeting with a nod before heading in the opposite direction. When they were positioned across from each other halfway around the ring, they removed their six-shooters from their holsters and checked them for ammunition. Then as the announcer counted down from five to one, they locked eyes across the expanse dividing them.

"One!"

Almost before the word was out, Max and Reba urged their horses to a canter, circling and crossing as they wove their way around the circle. They took turns firing at the nearest targets—blue for Max and red for Reba—and the crowd applauded every shot that found its mark. On the second round, they spurred their mounts to greater speed and again hit every target dead center.

As they made the third pass, they paused opposite each other, and Max could practically feel those in attendance holding their breaths. Then with a whoop, Reba took off, her horse galloping full out around and around the ring. Max followed suit, riding in the opposite direction. All eyes were on them, and he suspected few people noticed the crew setting up identical targets side by side at the far end of the ring.

On their fourth circle when they reached the point where they had passed each other, they pulled up and dismounted.

Standing side by side, they reloaded and took aim. At the announcer's signal, they fired in turn, each at a separate target. The audience quickly grasped the contest and chose sides, some cheering every shot Reba took and others wildly applauding Max's efforts.

He glanced at Reba. She met his eyes and frowned. He grinned. This was the Reba he liked best—the girl who was a damn good shot and proud of it.

The announcer continued to build suspense by calling for a pause as he walked to the target sheets and compared them. "A draw," he shouted.

Beside him, Max heard Reba snort. "Not likely," she muttered.

"You doubt Arnie?"

"It's your show, Max," she reminded him. "Arnie knows where his bread is buttered."

The truth was that regardless of how this first round turned out, it would be called a draw, necessitating the posting of two fresh target sheets and Arnie's dramatic explanation that in order to break the tie, the shooters would fire six shots each. "Five shots to hit every ring of the target in a straight line that leads to the bull's-eye and then that final shot." He returned to his position on a platform at the side of the ring. "Ready! Set! Fire!"

In a blaze of noise that included not only the firing of their guns but also the shouts of the crowd, they fired. Five shots apiece delivered in a matter of seconds. A pause as everyone stared at the targets and saw each featured a line of bullet holes pointing straight toward the center.

Once again, the arena was silent.

"One target left," Arnie announced. "Ladies first."

Reba took aim, adding to the drama by allowing her hand to visibly shake before drawing in a dramatic breath, steadying herself, and firing. When the bullet found its mark, a cheer erupted from the stands. *The captain can't do better than that*, Max figured they were thinking.

He shook his head as if defeated. He reloaded his gun and tucked it in his side holster, then turned his back to the targets, pretending surrender. The audience booed and grumbled. He mounted Diablo, his head low, his back still turned to the targets. The protests rang out until Max silenced them by removing a small mirror from his coat pocket, positioning it above one shoulder with his six-shooter over the other, and firing. Six shots in rapid succession—five that formed a perfect circle around the bull's-eye and the sixth right through the center.

The audience was on its feet. Max half suspected the cheering could be heard ricocheting off the surroundings hills. Reba pretended to stalk off in defeat, leaving her horse behind as she walked toward an exit. But as they had agreed, Max went after her and scooped her up and onto the saddle in front of him as together they rode past the cheering crowd.

"Kiss," Reba reminded him, even as she was smiling and waving at those they passed.

"We don't need that. Listen to them."

He maneuvered Diablo to the center of the show ring and coaxed the horse into a bow, and as he doffed his hat and waved it high over his head, Reba tightened her arms around his neck and kissed him full on the lips.

Once again, the audience roared their approval.

They had barely cleared the exit when Max swiped his hand across his mouth and dismounted. He reached up to lift Reba down, but she ignored him, sliding from the saddle and facing him toe-to-toe. "It worked, Max. Do not tell me it didn't."

"I'll give you that, Reba, but before we do that again, we're going to get some training in stage kissing." Without thinking, he once again rubbed his lips with the back of his hand. "Understood?"

Reba glared up at him. The slap she delivered came out of nowhere, and by the time Max recovered from his surprise, she was stalking back to her dressing tent. Fortunately, the exit they used was on the opposite side of the show ring from where the audience exited the bleachers, so no harm done there. But Bert had seen, as had Pearl, and both lifted their eyebrows as if to question whether Max was truly up to the task of corralling his costar.

Max handed Diablo off to one of the stable boys. "Brush him down and get him settled, then bring me one of the spare mounts. As soon as I get changed, I'm heading into town." He strode toward his dressing tent, ignoring Bert and Pearl.

But Bert was not so easily put off. He followed Max inside and sat on a trunk while Max removed his jacket and shirt, splashed water on his face, and studied his reflection, trying to decide if he needed a shave before going to see Emma.

"It worked," Bert muttered around the stub of his cigar.

Max did not have to ask what "it" was. "She ambushed me. We agreed to a stage kiss, a chaste—"

"Nobody ever said nothing about chaste, Max."

He pulled on a freshly laundered shirt, tucked it in, and snapped his suspenders in place. "We don't need the damn kiss."

Bert chewed his cigar while Max combed his hair and put on a vest and his hat.

"We don't need it maybe," Bert said. "But you know it'll sell tickets. The truth is the more folks who believe there's something perking between you and Reba, the more they'll want to be in that front row seat."

Max knew Bert had a point. He felt the anger he'd carried into the tent relax. He touched his cheek where Reba had slapped him. "Woman delivers a solid punch," he muttered. Then he grinned. "Bert, I'm on my way to town. We had a good start here, and I'm in the mood to celebrate. We'll figure this out tomorrow."

Instead of seeming relieved as Max might have expected, Bert frowned. "Stepping out with that Harvey Girl does nothing for the show, Max. In fact, it's bound to upset folks wanting to think it's you and Reba."

"Stepping out with that Harvey Girl does something for me, Bert, and right now that's all I care about."

He lifted the tent flap.

Bert followed him as Max headed for the corral.

"On the other hand," he continued, "if folks get to thinking there might be a love triangle—two beautiful women vying for your attention…"

"Drop it, Bert. We're not using Emma to sell tickets," he replied as he saddled the horse the stable boy had brought.

Bert stroked his jaw and looked off toward the horizon. "When you gonna talk to Ed?" he asked, a reminder of yet another problem Max didn't want to think about.

He let out a long breath and started back toward the office. "Get him over here and we'll do it now."

"Can't. He took off for town before the show even finished."

"He'll be at the saloon next to the railway station. The Sagebrush," Max said as he mounted up. "I've seen him heading there a couple of times. I'll take care of it."

"You want me to come along?"

"I said I'll handle it," Max replied and saw relief cross his partner's face. He spurred his mount to a gallop, setting his sights on town—and Emma.

Chapter 8

HAVING PRACTICALLY COUNTED THE TICKS OF THE large clock in the lobby, marking time until the supper shift ended, Emma changed out of her uniform, released her hair from the bonds of its chignon, and fastened it with a barrette at the nape of her neck. George had mentioned a surprise, but she wasn't sure what she should do. Wait in her room? Wait outside the kitchen door where he had come before? Of course, the surprise might be tomorrow or next week for all she knew.

In the end, she settled on a compromise. She would sit in one of the rocking chairs on the hotel veranda. It was not at all unusual for her to do that before retiring for the night. No one would think it odd. Yes, that was the right choice. She carried along a basket of knitting. She could form stitches even in the dark if necessary, although there was always light coming from the lobby windows.

Knit one, purl one, repeat.

As she worked, she kept an eye out for Diablo. The stallion would be the clearest sign of Max's arrival. As the minutes clicked away, she counted out the pattern, nodding politely to guests returning to the hotel for the night while she waited. She was about to pack up her yarn and needles when from behind her, she heard the unmistakable sound of dishes rattling on a metal tray.

She turned and saw Max struggling to keep two glass ice cream dishes plus spoons and napkins at an even keel.

"This is harder than it looks," he grumbled.

Emma set her knitting aside and relieved him of the tray. "What on earth?"

"I promised you ice cream."

"That you did," she said, setting the tray on a small side table.

"I can't take full credit. I had help. George is responsible for the whipped cream and the cherries. He insisted. Truth is, he was so set on getting it all perfect, I figured you'd be long gone by the time I got here."

"How did you know where to find me?"

Max chuckled. "Folks tend to keep an eye on you, Emmie. One of the waitresses came through the kitchen while George was fussing with the sundaes, and I reckon she just assumed this was all for you. She reminded George vanilla is your favorite and then told me you were out here." He handed her a cloth napkin and spoon, waited for her to drape the napkin over her lap, and then presented the stemmed glass bowl brimming with the sundae.

"Thank you. It looks delicious."

"It's not for admiring, Emmie. Take a bite before the whole thing melts." As if to demonstrate, he filled his spoon with a heaping bite of his chocolate ice cream and savored it. "Mm-mm."

Emma took a much smaller bite and relished the cold sweetness that filled her mouth. "Oh, that's so good," she murmured and quickly took another bite.

"If you think that's good, try this," he said, offering her a bite of his.

The gesture seemed far too intimate to be proper, and yet it was hard to resist his enthusiasm. She opened her mouth, and he slid the spoon between her parted lips. The chocolate was rich, almost decadent. She closed her eyes. Slowly, Max withdrew the spoon. When she opened her eyes, he was watching her, the spoon still suspended between them.

"Do you really prefer vanilla?" he asked, his voice husky.

"I prefer variety," she replied and, to prove her point, took a bite of her ice cream.

"You could share."

This was getting out of hand. She was not immune to the game he was playing, but really, they were seated in a public place where they might easily be observed by anyone. Instead of filling her spoon and feeding him, she handed him her dish. "Help yourself."

He set his dish on the tray and accepted hers, filling his spoon not once but twice before she objected.

"I didn't say take it all," she protested with a laugh. When she reached for her dish, he turned away, protecting it. "Very well," she announced. "Two can play this game." She picked up his dessert. Caught up in the silliness of their contest, she ate three small bites of his chocolate sundae in quick succession, then closed her eyes as the cold went straight to her head, giving her a sudden headache.

Max set the dish he was holding aside and took hers from her, then clasped her hand. "Are you okay?"

She nodded and smiled as she shook off the headache. "One forgets ice cream is to be savored, not gobbled like a last meal." She leaned back in her chair as did he. She noticed he did not let go of her hand. They set the rockers in motion.

After a moment, he said, "You gonna eat that last cherry?"

She laughed. "It's all yours." She watched him pop the fruit in his mouth. "How did the first show go?"

"I think we were a hit, as they say in this business. Folks were definitely on their feet cheering."

"Someone mentioned they could hear the roar of the crowd all the way in town."

Max chuckled. "I kind of doubt that, but it's nice to think about. You should have seen Reba in that blouse you fixed up for her."

"You didn't tell her I did the work, did you?"

"No, but why shouldn't I?"

"I just think Pearl should have the credit."

She heard him let out a long breath. He sounded exhausted, and it occurred to her that if she thought her day had been long and hard, his had begun well before dawn and included not just the parade and the show but also the emergency of Reba's costume. And that was just what she knew. Yet he'd made time to come to meet her.

She stood and set the dishes and her napkin on the tray. "Thank you, Max, for this lovely treat."

"You're leaving me here alone?"

She couldn't help laughing. "Tomorrow is another day. I have four trainloads of people to serve, and you have two performances to deliver. I think we could both use some rest."

"Are we still going to meet your friends a week from Sunday?"

"Are you sure you have time?"

"Show's up and running, and we don't perform on Sundays, so the answer is I'm looking forward to it."

"Me too," she admitted.

"I'll rent a buggy if that suits."

"That would be fine." The playfulness they'd shared while eating their ice cream had disappeared. Emma wondered if there would ever come a time when they could be completely at ease in each other's company.

Max took a step toward the back of the hotel.

"There's no need to see me to the door," Emma protested.

The lamplight from the lobby caught Max's smile. "Now what kind of gentleman allows a lady to walk home alone?"

"It's no more than a few steps," she reminded him.

"You'd be surprised what can happen in just a few steps," he replied.

They walked along the path that led around the side of the hotel and on to the kitchen entrance. Emma balanced the tray with their dishes while Max reached for the door.

"Well, here I am, safe and sound," she said, wishing there were more time. "Good night. Thank you for the ice cream."

"Emmie?"

She looked back at him with a questioning smile. Gently, he relieved her of the tray, setting it just inside the door, then took hold of her shoulders and turned her so their faces were only inches apart. He was wearing his hat, and his face was in shadow, and yet she knew what he wanted—what she wanted.

As if driven by outside forces, she placed her hand on the back of his neck and raised herself to her toes. "Yes," she whispered, although he had not asked, at least not in words.

She felt the warmth of his breath and then the fullness of his lips meeting hers. She felt as if she could stand in that place all night.

Suddenly distant shouts and a single gunshot shattered the moment. Max looked toward the saloon down the street. "Go inside," he said as he held the door open and nudged her through. "Lock the door," he called as he took off running toward the commotion.

"Wait," she shouted, but he was already gone. Max wasn't armed. These days, few men in town for the evening were, but they had heard the unmistakable sound of gunfire, and Max was running headlong toward it. She needed to get help right away.

She raced through the kitchen to the lobby. Aidan looked up from his position behind the front desk, and once he saw her face, he hurried forward.

"Emma? What's wrong?"

"The saloon…gunfire…Max…" Her heart was beating too fast for her to form proper sentences. "He needs help."

"Stay here," Aidan instructed as he headed for the front entrance.

Emma went behind the desk and retrieved the pistol she knew Aidan kept there on the off chance there might be trouble in the hotel or on the grounds. "Take this," she said as she followed him outside. "I'll go rouse the sheriff."

"He's probably already there or on his way," Aidan said, staring at the gun she held. "Put that back, Emma."

"No. Max is unarmed and…"

"And whatever was going on is over," he said, jerking his head in the direction of the saloon where the only sounds now were angry voices. "Just wait here, and I'll go make sure the captain gets back to his room unharmed."

Behind him, Emma saw two men coming their way. One was Max, and he was practically carrying the other man. Ignoring Aidan's commands for her to stay put, she dashed into the street.

"Max, bring him inside," she called, pointing the way to the hotel.

As Max moved into the light spilling from the open hotel door, she saw that the other man was Chief Gray Wolf, and he was bleeding badly.

"Aidan, send Tommy to fetch the doctor," she shouted as she led Max and Wolf inside.

"I'm afraid we can't have…that is…this man is not…" Aidan stood frozen by the door, staring at Wolf.

"This man is injured, Campbell," Max growled. "And either you send for help or I'll find other accommodations for myself and my friends."

Emma could practically see the wheels turning in

Aidan's mind as he calculated what upsetting Ford Harvey's friend might do to his ambitions. And yet if the other guests saw Wolf being helped to a hotel guest room, they would surely disapprove.

"Tommy!" Aidan banged three times on the brass call bell that sat on the front desk. The boy emerged from a back room, rubbing sleep from his eyes. "Get Doc over here," Aidan ordered. "Now!"

Tommy took off.

"Thank you," Max said. "Now if you would help me get him upstairs to my room."

"I'll bring fresh towels and some first aid supplies," Emma said as she rushed off to the kitchen. By the time she collected everything and ran up the back stairs, she saw Max and Aidan had managed to get Wolf settled on Max's bed. She also saw that Reba and Bert had left their rooms and crowded inside Max's. She squeezed in and shut the door.

"We can't do the show without the chief," Bert was saying more to himself than anyone else. "This is a disaster."

Reba stared down at Wolf. "What was he doing in there in the first place?"

"I don't know, Reebs. Maybe he had the audacity to think he had as much right as any other man to be there," Max snapped. He glanced at Aidan. "Let's get him settled and have the doctor examine him. Plenty of time for questions after that." He took the stack of towels from Emma and placed them on the bureau. "Where's that doctor?" he muttered, and Emma saw his fists clench as he turned back to the bed and began removing his friend's boots.

Footsteps in the hall announced the arrival of Dr. Waters. Ignoring everyone but the patient on the bed, he set down his black bag and leaned in for a closer look at Wolf. "Emma," he said without looking at her, "get me a pan of water, and let's get some of these cuts cleaned up so I know what I'm dealing with." He reached inside his bag and brought out a bottle of smelling salts, and by the time Emma returned from the washroom with the pan of water, Wolf was moaning softly, and his eyes were half-open.

That was when the sheriff showed up.

Max's room was overflowing with people—Reba weeping after Max's caustic comment, Bert wringing his hands, the doctor trying to bring Wolf around, Emma running errands, and now the sheriff. Max stepped between the lawman and Wolf. "This isn't the time," he said.

"I'll be the one who decides that," Sheriff Bolton said quietly. He stepped around Max and looked down at Wolf. "What's the verdict, Doc?"

"He'll live. Might wish he didn't once he starts feeling the pain." He moved aside and nodded to Emma, who began gently washing away the crusted blood caked on Wolf's face. "Couple of broken ribs at the least, judging by the way he reacts when I touch his torso and the way he can't seem to draw a proper breath," Doc continued. "That knife cut on his arm is superficial, and the puncture wound on his chest could have done the job if it had been a couple of inches lower."

Bert squeezed in next to Max. "How long will he

be laid up for? I mean, we've got two shows tomorrow and…"

Doc shrugged. "A month…six weeks."

Wolf turned his gaze toward Max. "Sorry," he mouthed through lips that were bruised and swollen.

"There was a gunshot," Emma said.

"That was me getting their attention," the sheriff replied. He pushed his way closer to the bed. "You up to telling me what happened, Chief?"

Wolf's voice was raw, and he grimaced with pain. "Followed one of my nephews into town." He glanced at Max. "Chogan—Black Bird."

"Where's your nephew now?" Sheriff Bolton asked.

"Pro'ly hiding out…somewhere 'tween town… showgrounds." Wolf licked his lips and swallowed with difficulty before adding, "Won't want 'splain to his mother."

The sheriff glanced out the window for a moment. "Did you get jumped?"

Wolf grimaced. "Yeah. Once somebody realized… who I—"

"Was it Ed?" Bert interrupted.

"No need…" Wolf replied, but Max had his answer when his friend refused to meet his gaze.

Before coming to see Emma, he'd confronted Ed outside the saloon. The show's advance man hadn't denied anything. In fact, Max hadn't even had to lay out the reasons he was letting Ed go.

"You gonna turn me over to the sheriff?" he'd demanded. "Because if that's your plan…"

"Don't threaten me, Ed. Just pack your gear and be gone by morning." He'd reached in his pocket and peeled off several bills. "Here. This should hold you until you can find something."

"I don't need your money, Max." He'd struck a match and lit his cigar. "Are we done here?"

"Just be gone by morning," Max had repeated.

Ed had laughed. "Since I don't work for you no more, that's not your call, Max." And with his usual swagger, he pushed open the double half doors of the saloon and called for a beer.

Knowing Ed was angry and inclined to want revenge, Max was pretty sure he'd had a part in the attack on Wolf. "Was Black Bird at the saloon?"

Wolf nodded. "Hiding in back. Find him, Max. Tell his mother…go easy."

Unlikely, Max thought. Wolf's older sister was a grizzly when it came to protecting her kids. Black Bird, her sixteen-year-old son, was an angry young warrior who saw no reason why he should not have the same rights and privileges as any white boy. Her daughter, Koko, was an innocent, but she was also a beauty who looked older than fourteen. More than once, Max had had to warn a new crew member that the girl was off-limits. He recalled Ed Brunswick had been one to receive that warning.

"I'll find him," he told Wolf. "You get some rest." He pulled on his hat and headed for the door. Aidan was blocking his way.

"Captain Winslow, of course we want to do everything we can for you and your company." He glanced toward the bed. "However, in this case—"

"However, a Blackfoot Indian being housed and cared for in your hotel goes beyond that?"

He saw the flush rise above Aidan's stiff collar. "The other guests…" Aidan's eyes pleaded for understanding.

"Your guests believe I am the one occupying this room. No need to give them reason to think otherwise. As soon as Doc here says Wolf can be moved, he'll be out of your hair, okay? In the meantime, keep the door closed and cancel housekeeping. No one in or out except me, Bert, the doctor, and Miss Elliott."

"What about me?" Reba demanded.

Max turned to stare at her. "Since when are you so close to Wolf or his people, Reba? Seems to me you were the one trying to persuade Bert there was no need for *his kind* in the cast."

"Well, I can't see why *she* has any more business here than I do." She jerked her head in Emma's direction.

"Miss Elliott is a trusted employee of the hotel and can see to Wolf's needs while he's here." He paused and stroked his chin. "On the other hand, Reebs, if you want to sit by the bedside—keep a vigil, so to speak—I suppose as long as you show up for performances, that might indeed be a comfort for Wolf. You could bathe him and apply new dressings to his wounds, maybe help him down the hall to the washroom when necessary."

"You made your point, Max," Reba said as she swept past him, shouldered Aidan aside, and planted herself near the window.

Meanwhile, Aidan turned his attention back to Max. "The housekeeping staff will wonder about the sudden change."

Max smiled. "Hey, Aidan, you can handle this.

Give them that weary smile of yours and mutter something like 'Show folks,' and that'll take care of it." He glanced back at the sheriff. "I'll find the boy," he said.

Sheriff Bolton nodded. "No need to bring him to town. I'll stop by the showgrounds tomorrow to get his side of this thing."

Max left the room and stood for a moment in the corridor. There were only three rooms on this offshoot of the main corridor. Those rooms were occupied by Reba, Bert, and him, and they were close to the service stairway. It was a perfect setup. As he moved into the hallway that led to the main stairs down to the lobby, he saw that every door was closed. He hurried down the stairway and out to the street. Apparently, the saloon had returned to its normal business—cowboys going in and out, the twang of a badly tuned piano, the clink of a bottle of whiskey filling a glass, the laughter of one of the bar girls. Otherwise, the town was quiet.

Max first checked along the boardwalk and behind the saloon before turning back and walking to the church. It was a likely place for a kid who was scared and figured he couldn't go home to hide. Removing his hat, Max stepped inside, standing at the back of the sanctuary as he studied the shadowed rows of pews dimly illuminated by banks of votive candles representing the prayers and hopes and sorrows of those who worshipped there—and probably more than one who didn't.

"Chogan?" He kept his voice calm and low as he started down the side aisle. The sixth sense he'd acquired from years of tracking and pathfinding for settlers and the army told him the boy was somewhere nearby. Nothing moved beyond the flicker of the candles. He paused and took one of the rough, thin sticks provided as tinder for lighting the candles. "Wolf's gonna be fine," he continued as he touched the end of the wooden stick to a flame and then to the wick of an unlit candle. "Pretty banged up, but you know your uncle."

Behind him, he heard someone sniff, and when he turned, Chogan was seated on the edge of a pew, his head in his hands. "Ma's gonna kill me," he muttered miserably.

"Unlikely, but I wouldn't want to have to be the one telling her Wolf got beat up."

The boy gripped the back of the pew in front of him. "I can't be the one to tell her."

"Sure you can." Max tossed his hat onto the seat and slid in next to Wolf's nephew. "First, you'll need to explain what made you go into town in the first place. Then you'll explain how you came to understand that was a mistake, and if it hadn't been for your uncle…" He studied the boy. "What on earth are you wearing?"

Now that he was closer, he saw that the young brave was dressed in a pair of plaid trousers held up with suspenders, a purple shirt, and a newsboy's cap pulled tight to hide his shoulder-length hair.

"I borrowed a couple of things from the costume shop."

"Were you trying to get yourself beat up?"

"This peddler came around our camp the other day. I saw the way he kept looking at my sister. Nothing happened, but I figured maybe if I—"

"In that getup?" Max was having trouble keeping his laughter under control.

Chogan looked down at his clothes, and then his shoulders started to shake. At first, Max thought the boy was crying, but then he realized the shaking came from trying to hold in laughter that—like his—threatened to explode in the peaceful quiet of the church. He wrapped his arm around Chogan's thin shoulders. "Come on. Let's get you home."

"She's gonna kill me," the kid muttered.

"I'll go with you, but if you ever pull a stunt like this again, she won't have to. I'll do the job myself."

They started across the open land behind the church, walking in silence as they climbed the hill that led to the mesa overlooking the showgrounds. Once there, they stopped for a minute to enjoy the expanse of a starlit sky.

"Max? Why can't it be like everybody says it was in the old days? When our people roamed the land without anybody telling them where to go?"

Max knew those times had already passed by the time Chogan was old enough to appreciate the history of his people. "We can't go back. All we can do is try our best to shape what's before us now."

As they started down the rocky path, Chogan lagged behind. Max knew the kid didn't believe him. Truth was those words rang hollow to Max as well.

❧❧

Emma had never in her life seen anyone as badly beaten as Wolf was. His left eye was swollen shut, and his lips were purple with bruises. Every time he moved, he groaned with pain. Doc had treated the knife wounds and bandaged his chest, saying it was all he could do for the ribs he was certain were broken. Once Max left, Doc handed her a vial of pain medication with instructions on how to administer a dose every few hours.

"Other than that and redressing his wounds and watching for any sign of infection," he said as he packed up his stethoscope and put on his coat, "only time will work. He needs rest. I'll be back in the morning. We'll get him on his feet in a day or so, but until then, he needs to stay pretty still."

"I'll set a schedule with my girls to stay with him," Emma volunteered. "We can certainly manage for a few days on short staff."

"Don't see why that should fall on you," Doc said, glancing at Bert and Reba. "Seems to me his friends might take over."

The expression on Reba's face was one of abject horror. "I know nothing about caring for the sick. Besides, he's a man and I—"

"That dog don't hunt with me, missy," Doc interrupted. "Miss Elliott here is also of the female persuasion, in case you haven't noticed." He turned to Bert. "What's your excuse?"

"I'll take my shift, but I've got a bunch of other folks depending on me," Bert replied.

"Maybe one or two of them could help out. Why don't you and Miss Elliott work that out together?" He collected his black bag and hat and headed for the door. "Main thing is to keep him calm at least until morning and try to get some fluids in him."

Emma nodded. "Thank you, Doctor."

Once the door closed, leaving her with Reba and Bert, she was unsure of what to say or do. She pulled a straight-backed rocking chair closer to the side of the bed and sat facing Wolf, her back to the others.

Bert cleared his throat. "Well, if you've got this, Emma, maybe Reba and me could get some rest ourselves."

"Yes, that would be best," Emma agreed. Anything to have them leave.

"I'll send Trula to relieve you," Reba said as she hurried to the door.

Bert frowned and hesitated, his hand on the door-knob. "I don't know, Reba. Trula's young—a girl, really—and if anyone found out we'd left her alone with a man…"

Reba chewed her lower lip. "I just can't," she whispered.

Emma stood. "Please. I'll be fine through the night. Perhaps tomorrow, Bert, you could send one of the crew or maybe Pearl?"

"Pearl! Dandy idea. I'll take care of that." He opened the door, and Reba scurried through. "Thank you, Miss Emma," Bert said. "Doc was right. This isn't your problem, and I'm gonna make sure after tonight we do what's needed for the chief."

"Good night, Bert."

He hesitated as if he'd expected more but then nodded and stepped into the hall, closing the door behind him.

Emma looked down at Wolf, who was sleeping or perhaps passed out. She rinsed a washcloth in cold water and wiped the sweat from his forehead, then refolded it and pressed it to his lips. He moaned, then relaxed. After a while, Emma realized he was sleeping soundly, the first dose of pain medication having taken hold.

With a sigh, Emma walked to the window, passing a wardrobe where she caught a glimpse of the deerskin jacket Max had worn the first day they met. This was his room. It felt odd being here. Not that she hadn't been in the guest rooms of the hotel before, but never had a room seemed so personal to her. She felt his presence, certain that the scent of the sandalwood soap he used permeated the air around her. The writing table near the window was covered with notes and papers, lists and maps and such. She had thought of him as a showman, someone whose smile made female hearts flutter. Here was the evidence of a more serious side of the man—a man who held the futures of others in his hands.

She moved the lamp closer and studied the papers. Lines of numbers and dates. She quickly realized these represented the shows they'd done on their way to Juniper. The total was impressive until she looked at the second ledger sheet and saw the expenses, which were greater. Having grown up helping her mother manage the shop, she understood clearly what the discrepancy meant. The show was in trouble, at least financially speaking. She wondered how Max managed to maintain his optimism in the face of such a hard reality. She tried to make sense of the accounts, but she was so exhausted that sometimes the numbers seemed to run together. She leaned back and closed her eyes to rest them.

Outside, the town clock over the railway station

sounded midnight. Realizing she had dozed off, Emma stood and rubbed sleep from her eyes on her way to check on her patient. Behind her, she heard the click of the door handle and turned to see Aidan enter the room. He glanced first at the bed and then at her. "How is he?"

"The pain medicine has had its effect," she replied. "I'll stay with him through the night."

Aidan tapped his fingers to his chin, a gesture she knew meant he faced a decision he'd rather not make. "That man cannot stay in the hotel, Emma." He kept his voice low and quiet.

"That man has a name—two, in fact. Wolf Sutter is probably the more comfortable one for you."

"Don't fight me on this, Emma. You know as well as I do tha—"

"What I know is that Mr. Sutter was stabbed and badly beaten earlier tonight. He needs to rest at least until morning. If you have any thought of moving him out tonight, I'll have to—"

"What, Emma? You'll have to what?"

"None of the other guests know he's here," she reasoned, "but if you insist on moving him, he's bound to cry out. The man is in pain with possibly broken ribs. Think, Aidan. If you move him, even using the service stairs, there's bound to be a commotion. Do you really think no one will take note?"

Aidan stared out the window. "Well, we can hardly move him in broad daylight."

"So why move him at all?"

"The other guests are bound to see Doc coming and going."

She knew he had a point. "What if Doc only uses the kitchen entrance and the back stairs and only comes when most guests are downstairs having a meal?"

Aidan glanced at her. "I suppose, if he used the back stairs…"

Emma nodded, encouraging him to work the idea through until it was the solution he wanted. "Dr. Waters indicated Mr. Sutter could get up in a couple of days," she said. "And once he's able to move around, it will be far easier to take him back to the camp."

Aidan focused on the man in the bed. "You can keep him quiet until then?"

Emma was ready to agree when Aidan's expression told her he'd come up with another problem. "We can't use the girls to sit with him. Too much chance they might talk and someone overhear."

"Mr. Gordon is going to have people from the show come. Between them and me, I think we can manage for a few days."

"You can't work all day and tend the patient all night, Emma."

"Let's get through tonight first and make decisions once Max returns."

"I don't like it, Emma."

"Oh, for heaven's sake, Aidan. Mr. Sutter is a good man and hardly in a position to cause me any harm even if he weren't."

Aidan turned to the window and said so softly Emma first thought she'd misunderstood, "I'm not worried about the patient."

"The captain? You think the captain…?"

"He's got eyes for you, Emma. Anyone can see it. And if anyone should see you coming from his room—I'm thinking of you."

Emma's temper found escape in sarcasm. "I suppose I could always come and go by climbing through the window," she mused.

"I'm serious, Emma. You have a reputation to uphold, if not for yourself then for this establishment and as an example to your staff."

And there it was, as clearly as anything Aidan had ever said to her before. It was the business he worried about—not her. Slowly, she turned to face him.

"Make whatever arrangements you need to make with the captain," she said as Wolf began thrashing about and moaning with pain. "But in the meantime, Mr. Sutter needs care, and I intend to stay right here and provide that." She walked past Aidan to the bureau where she'd placed the pain medication and the bowl of ice she'd had Tommy bring her. She measured and mixed a dose of the powder in water, then wrapped a piece of ice in a towel and approached the bed. "The cold soothes his swelling, and Doc says he needs fluids," she explained when Aidan moved to the opposite side and stared at the towel wrapped around the ice.

"Do you need help? Shall I lift his head and shoulders?"

"Yes. Thank you."

It occurred to Emma they always worked well together when they were equal partners. It was only when Aidan insisted she simply accept his way as the only way that they crossed swords.

After Emma had managed to get Wolf to swallow most of the medicine, Aidan gently laid him back against the pillows and straightened. "Have you eaten anything, Emma?"

"I'm fine." She pressed the ice to Wolf's swollen lips.

Aidan smiled as he shook his head. "You'd never admit it if you weren't." He walked to the door. "I'll have George prepare a tray and send it up to you."

"Thank you," she said softly, suddenly aware of how very tired she was. "Coffee," she added as he stepped into the hall.

"Coffee," he repeated and closed the door with a soft click.

Chapter 9

JUST AFTER DAWN THE FOLLOWING MORNING, THERE was a knock at the door. Emma hesitated, knowing neither Max nor Aidan would knock.

Tap. Tap. Tap.

"Emma? It's Pearl Hardin."

"Come in," Emma said, opening the door and ushering the older woman inside.

Pearl was carrying two large baskets filled with fabric. "Mending," she explained when Emma took hold of one basket by its bentwood handle. "Figured it would help pass the time." She removed her coat and hat and looped both onto hooks near the door, then went directly to the bed. "How's our patient?"

"I think the medicine is helping. He had one bad stretch a couple of hours ago before it was time for his next dose. I've tried to make him as comfortable as possible."

Pearl brushed Wolf's hair away from his forehead—a mother's touch, Emma thought. "Well, he's sleeping now. Why don't you show me how to prepare the medication properly, and then I want you to get out of here. There's time for you to have at least an hour of rest before you start your day."

"I'm so very glad you're here," Emma admitted.

Pearl grinned. "Of course, I'm not Max," she teased.

"I'm sure he has things to do," Emma replied as she busied herself writing out the times Wolf should receive the pain powder.

"He said if I can handle the days, he can take the nights. Seemed right worried we were involving you in something that might upset that guy who acts like he's in charge around here."

"As long as our guests are served properly, Mr. Campbell has no cause for concern." Emma explained how to measure out the powder and water and how to get Wolf to swallow it even when he resisted.

Pearl nodded. "Got it. Now you get out of here. Max and me have got this covered."

"If you're sure…"

"I'm sure." The costumer herded Emma toward the door.

"Thanks for coming, Pearl. If you need anything, just sound the buzzer here." She pointed to a button near the door. "Tommy will come right up. He knows what's happened, and he can be trusted."

"Understood. Now git!" Gently, Pearl pushed Emma into the hall and shut the door.

Emma stood in the deserted corridor a moment before climbing the service stairs to the top floor and her room. From behind closed doors along the narrow hall, she could hear the others starting to awaken and stir. A door at the far end of the hall opened, and

Sarah, still dressed in her nightclothes, headed for the common washroom. The waitress was completely unaware of Emma standing at the top of the stairs. Before any of the others could pop out and see her in her sleep-deprived state, Emma stepped into her room and quietly closed the door.

There was no time for a nap, so she stripped down to her undergarments and poured fresh water from a large pitcher into the washbasin that was one of the advantages to having a room to herself. The water was tepid but refreshing as she splashed handfuls over her face. It would be a long, exhausting day, but she'd faced those in the past, and tonight she would retire early and not worry about Melba or any of the other girls slipping out.

She considered her reflection in the small oval mirror. *Not likely*, she thought, for it was well known that Emma Elliott was dedicated to her job and everything it entailed. She released her hair and began brushing it. Staring at the woman in the mirror—the woman who, with her hair undone, looked nothing like the oh-so-proper head waitress and housemother—she wondered what her life might have become if she'd never joined the Harvey Company. She thought of her mother, a woman who had never talked about her husband's abandonment. She thought of all the long hours her mother had put into keeping the family fed and clothed. It occurred to her that the paths she and her mother had taken had not been so different—both lived to serve others with little thought of what might address their own needs, never mind their hopes and dreams.

Maybe it's time...

She found she had no way to finish that statement. Time to what? Move on? Settle down? Not likely. She'd spurned the best chance she'd had for marriage when she'd broken things off with Aidan.

But Max...

She shook off the thought, rejecting it as the foolish daydreams of a girl who still believed in such impossibilities. His was the life of a nomad—always had been. He'd never really spoken of settling down, just about his drive to make sure the West he'd always known and loved was not forgotten.

Outside her room, she heard doors open and shut, and she hurried to pin up her hair and step into a fresh uniform. By the time she opened her door, most of her staff were already scampering down the stairs. They froze and looked back at her with shocked expressions. Not once had any of them managed to make it to their posts before Emma was already down.

"Yes, I overslept," she said. "And yes, ladies, despite rumors to the contrary, I am human. Shall we get to work?"

⧜⧜⧜

Max looked up as Bert stormed into the office. "The sheriff arrested two locals for attacking the chief—a powerful local rancher and his son," his partner announced. "This is bad news, Max. Really bad news."

It wasn't necessary for Bert to explain. The show depended on locals to buy tickets and fill the seats. Any hint of scandal that involved any of the company—especially a nonwhite member, even if he was completely innocent of wrongdoing—would spell disaster for the company's future.

"This is not something we need, Max," Bert added, his always-present cigar bobbing up and down between clenched teeth.

"Okay, calm down."

"Calm down? Folks in town are talking about coming after the chief. They figure he's holed up here. Rosie at the saloon told me she heard a couple of cowboys plotting a raid—a real live raid."

Max leaned back in the ancient swivel chair, which groaned in protest. "We'll have to cancel performances for the rest of the week while we figure out how to handle this. Let the cast and crew know. Assure them they'll still be paid, then get somebody to town to post the cancelled notices there."

"That's just going to rile folks more, Max. A lot of people have already bought tickets."

"Refund their money and give them a free ticket for a future performance. We're going to be here for a while, so that should work. Talk to Mayor Tucker. Maybe he'd be willing to let you handle refunds and exchanges at his store. That would make it convenient for everybody and show we're working hard to clear this up."

Bert stared at him. "You're bleeding money we don't have, Max."

"I'm open to other ideas."

Bert grunted. "And what about the chief?"

"I'll handle that end of things."

Bert drummed his stubby fingers on the desk. "You know Ed Brunswick is behind this, don't you?"

"Figured as much."

"He's staying around. Rosie said he took a room at the boardinghouse and asked her for a job. She turned him down, but that don't stop him looking. She also said it was him who made sure others knew Wolf wasn't one of them last night. He didn't do the beating, but he might as well have."

"I'll take care of it, Bert." Max could not recall a time when he'd felt more exhausted. Physical fatigue was something he could handle—it was usually tied to a job well done. But this constant need to put out the wildfires of running a business was a different breed altogether, and he hated it.

"What are you gonna do?" Bert could sometimes be like a dog with a bone filled with marrow that was impossible to reach.

"I'm going into town to talk to the sheriff, Bert. But first, if he's up to it, I'm going to talk to Wolf and get his side of things. After that?" He shook his head as he reached for his hat and headed across the compound toward the corral. "Chogan! Get me the sorrel," he shouted. This was not a time to come riding into town on Diablo.

As he rode past the hotel, Max calmed himself by thinking of Emma. This time of day, she was usually in the dining room. He was tempted to show up for lunch. He imagined the way her eyes would widen in surprise at his unexpected appearance before she caught herself and switched to her Harvey Girl demeanor. The very image of her lifted his spirits as he dismounted outside the sheriff's office and wrapped the reins around the hitching post.

His intent was to cross the plaza to the hotel and speak to Wolf if possible, then return to meet with the sheriff. But Sheriff John Bolton stood in the open doorway of his office as if he'd been waiting for Max to arrive.

"Sheriff," Max said.

The lawman nodded and motioned Max inside. He pointed to the single chair across from his desk, then walked to a door that led to the jail cells and shut it. Max realized the two local men arrested for attacking the chief were back there.

With a weary sigh, Bolton took the chair behind the desk, stretched out his legs, and looked up at the ceiling.

"Captain, we got ourselves a real problem here," he said. "You might as well know, the truth is I never wanted you folks to set up camp here."

"Wolf Sutter didn't start this," Max reminded him.

"Got no idea who this Sutter fella might be. What I know is that redskin fanned the fires, coming into the saloon where he had no business being, dressed like a white man." He slowly shook his head and spat a stream of tobacco toward a brass spittoon.

He missed.

Max understood what they were up against in a way he hadn't fully appreciated until that moment. This was not something the lawman was interested in working out. "What do you want, Sheriff?"

Another spit, this one at least hitting the outside of the spittoon with a definite ping. Given the dried pile of tobacco juice on the floor, Max was pretty sure the man missed more than he hit his target.

Suddenly, Bolton sat forward and focused his entire attention on Max. "Way I see it, you've got two choices. One, you send those redskins back to the reservation and do your show the old-fashioned way. It's a show you're putting on, not real life."

"And the second choice?"

"You strike camp, load up your fancy train, and are gone by end of the week."

"We've got a contract."

Bolton shrugged. "That don't mean a hill of beans to me, Captain. Folks expect me to keep the peace, and right now I've got Seymour Gilmore and his son, RJ, back there in custody. The Gilmores are right popular in these parts, and I reckon me locking them up won't sit well for long. I'm sitting on a keg of powder sure to go off unless—"

Max stood and knew the move surprised Bolton, because he too was on his feet at once. "You leavin'?"

"I'm going across the plaza to talk to Mayor Tucker. You're welcome to come along. I just want to make sure everybody on the council has agreed to this *choice* you're offering."

"Don't question my authority, cowboy," Bolton growled.

Max didn't reply. He was aware that Bolton followed him as far as the boardwalk, but he refused to look back or say anything more. He just hoped Frank Tucker had not been part of coming up with this plan.

When Max entered the store, Tucker was finishing up with serving three women, wrapping their purchases and taking payment. One of the women spotted Max right away and whispered to the others. The trio gathered their packages and marched past him to the door, noses in the air as they ignored his greeting and doffed hat.

Frank Tucker's lips thinned until they practically disappeared beneath the fullness of his mustache. "Did you talk to Sheriff Bolton?"

"I did. Are you and the rest of the council in favor of his so-called choices for how to resolve this?"

Tucker turned away and busied himself stocking a shelf with pots and pans. "Juniper is a peaceful town, Max."

"It sure wasn't all that peaceful last night from Wolf Sutter's point of view."

"The man should know better. Coming into town, dressed like a white man…"

"You want him walking around in moccasins and deerskin? He dresses like a man—any man—because that's what he is." Max drew in a breath, forcing himself to calm down. "Look, his nephew had come ahead of him, looking for trouble because some ped-dler insulted the boy's sister. Wolf wasn't trying to start anything. He was trying to stop it."

Tucker paused, set a stack of stew pots on the shelf, and turned to face Max. "That may be, but the end of the story is that there was a fight, and now two good men are sittin' in jail, the rest of their family left on their own to manage one of the largest spreads around here."

Any attempt Max might be making to remain calm failed. "And Wolf Sutter is barely able to lift his head.

He was stabbed, and Doc thinks he's got broken ribs to boot. On top of that, those 'good men' did a real job on his face. He can't open one eye, and his mouth is so swollen I doubt he can eat anything more solid than applesauce. Oh, and he has a family as well—a family that depends on him the same as the families of his attackers depend on them."

"Come on, Max. You know as well as I do this goes deeper than a barroom brawl. Your man overstepped. Maybe he was in the right in that he was trying to protect his nephew, but he shoulda known better."

"So that's the answer? Either he and his people go or the whole show goes?"

"Nobody wants the latter, Max. We're not stupid. Having you set up shop here for a few months is good for business, and what's good for business is good for those who live and work in and around Juniper, including the Gilmores. So how about a third choice?"

"I'm listening."

"You and your friend agree that the fight last night was not an attack, just an old-fashioned barroom brawl. No charges and no arrests."

"And that'll end this?"

"Not quite. In the meantime, you have the chief and his people take jobs behind the scenes. In a month, this whole business will be forgotten, and you can start to quietly bring them back in the show."

"Any way you look at it, Wolf was the victim in this, and you're making him pay the price."

Tucker shrugged. "Best of a bad situation. Of course, you can do as the sheriff wants—pack up and leave altogether. But if you do that, the council will hold you to the terms of the contract—the payments for the land use and such."

Max knew when he'd lost. He didn't like it, but there was no more to be gained by beating this particular dead horse. "Give me some time to discuss the options with my partner," he said.

"We can work this out." The mayor put a hand on Max's shoulder as he walked him to the door. "You've already gone the extra mile. Your partner already sent word you plan to refund money and give away free tickets. Folks won't forget that, and it'll make this whole unfortunate business go away a good deal faster."

"I'll be in touch," Max said and headed for the saloon to see what he could find out about Gilmore and his son.

Both in the dining room and at the counter, the conversation fairly buzzed with whispers about the fight at the saloon and whether show people were the proper influence for the impressionable young people of Juniper. Just a day earlier, Emma recalled, many of those same customers had been raving about the show and how everyone associated with the production was just like normal folks. Now they were sympathizing with the Gilmores, murmuring about how unfair it was for outsiders to accuse upstanding citizens.

The day seemed to go on forever, and all the while she was thinking of the man upstairs who had done nothing to deserve his injuries. All he'd wanted was to prevent his nephew from doing something he might regret. Twice she had managed to slip away and make sure Pearl had something to eat. Doc Waters had come and gone. According to Pearl, he'd increased the dosage of pain medication, stating that the more Wolf slept, the less likely he was to thrash about and possibly injure himself further. Once while serving customers, Emma had glanced out the dining room window and seen Max crossing the plaza. He'd looked weary—and worried.

In the times they had shared, he had talked about the show only as a vehicle for educating people about what the West had been in an earlier, more primitive time. It occurred to her that he'd never expressed any pleasure—much less joy—at being in the show. And now she recalled that when she'd seen him in parade, his smile had captured none of the thrill of a crowd's roar of approval and admiration. More and more, she was certain that Max Winslow was not happy in his work.

Like me.

It was the last thing she would have guessed they had in common. Of course, she could be wrong. But in her experience, recognizing something of yourself in another person was possible. How often had she surprised one of the new waitresses by suggesting the young woman might be homesick? It was because she had missed her home and mother so much once the realities of being a Harvey Girl had set in. Not that she would ever have admitted it. Of course, she'd had Lily and later Grace to lift her spirits. She wondered who Max had. Who did he talk to? Bert, of course, but that was more likely business. Perhaps Wolf. So many people depended on him, and now his friend had been attacked. She vividly recalled how she had felt when Grace had been falsely accused and later when Lily had been attacked. Her heart went out to Max.

Emma served her last table of customers—traveling businessmen from the train. Just as she was clearing their plates, Reba made her entrance, just minutes before the dining room was due to close for the afternoon. Emma drew in a breath and approached the actress.

"Good afternoon, Miss Reba." On the posters, she was Rebel Reba, but at the moment she looked more distressed than rebellious. "May I ask the chef to prepare something for you?"

"I'm parched," the actress replied. "How anyone can stand this dry climate is beyond me." She flung herself into a chair at the round table and stared out the window.

"Perhaps a nice tall glass of lemonade?"

"A pitcher would be better." Reba looked directly at Emma for the first time since entering the dining room and beckoned for her to come closer. "Have you heard any more about…the incident?" she whispered.

Emma hesitated. "Pearl is staying with the patient," she replied. "I'm sure if you wanted to visit—"

Reba brushed off her words with a wave of her hand. "Not the chief. What are people saying about what's going to happen now—to the show? To *me*?"

"I really haven't heard anything definite," Emma said. "Perhaps the captain will have some news."

Reba sighed deeply and returned to looking out the window.

"I'll get your lemonade," Emma murmured as she hurried off to the kitchen.

George and his staff were finishing with the washing up before starting preparations for the next meal. Emma took lemons from the supply on a sideboard and began slicing them in half. To her surprise, George sidled closer.

"This ruckus at the Sagebrush last night is no good, Emma," he muttered, glancing over his shoulder to be sure the other kitchen workers weren't overhearing. "Locking up locals for roughing up the chief will come to no good, not for business and definitely not for the captain."

"Are you saying Max—the captain—might be in danger?"

George shrugged. "Folks don't like when those people don't know their place and try to mix in."

"The chief wasn't trying to mix in, as you say. He was trying to stop his nephew from getting into trouble."

Again the shrug. "It don't matter what his intent might have been, Emma. What matters is what others think."

"Well, it seems to me if *others* were so concerned, they might have tried asking questions instead of lashing out at an innocent man."

George stared at her for a long moment. "What I'm trying to tell you, Emma, is don't go getting mixed up in this business. I heard you spent the night up there. You need to think on what that might do to your reputation should word get out. Can't imagine Fred Harvey would cotton to any hint of scandal."

Emma's temper was close to the boiling point, and only the fact that she and George had worked together and been friends for years kept her from letting it explode. She forced herself to take a deep breath and measure her words as she concentrated on preparing the lemonade. "I'm grateful for your concern, George," she finally managed as she spooned sugar into the lemon juice to create the syrup. "Miss Reba is waiting for her lemonade. Could you fill this pitcher with ice while I mix the syrup with water?"

To her relief, George did as she asked. When he brought her the pitcher, she added the syrup and stirred it, then filled the pitcher with water. George handed her a small tray and a glass and napkin. "Does Her Highness want anything to eat?" he asked in a normal tone, a signal he had said what he wanted to say to her and was now ready for them to get back to business.

"I doubt she could resist some of your coconut cookies."

George chuckled. "That woman never saw a sweet she could resist," he said as he placed four cookies on a doily-lined saucer and added it to the tray. "Now, you'd best scoot or she'll be complaining about the service."

Reba was scowling and drumming her fingers on the table when Emma crossed the now-deserted dining room, but the cookies did their magic. "Ooh," the actress squealed, her scowl transformed into a delighted smile. "Cookies."

After filling the glass with lemonade and setting the pitcher and cookies on the table, Emma stepped back. "Will that be all, Miss Reba?"

Reba brushed cookie crumbs from her bosom. "Sit

with me. I hate eating alone. Get a glass and have some lemonade."

Technically speaking, she was no longer on duty, so Emma took a glass from a nearby table set for the supper service and sat. To her surprise, Reba lifted the pitcher and filled the extra glass. Raising hers in a toast, she took a long swallow, then set the glass down and leaned forward.

"Let's talk about Max," she said.

Rarely did anything a customer said fluster Emma, but this time she was taken aback. "I don't... The captain is..."

"Falling for you—hard and fast. The question is, what are your intentions?"

Emma almost laughed. It was a question her father might have asked a beau calling on her if he'd been around to know such things were part of her life. "My intentions?"

Reba's shoulders dropped, and she sighed heavily. "Do not play coy with me, Emma. You and I both know he is taken with you."

Emma stiffened. "I'm not sure my association with the captain is any concern of yours."

"Oh, but it is," Reba replied. "You see, I love that man, and although he does not return my feelings, that does not stop me from looking out for him. He's so wrapped up in the show and keeping it afloat and taking care of all of us who work for him that he's prone to leap before he looks. So one more time, what are your intentions?"

"I have none. He has none. We live different lives. Mine is here, and his is..."

Reba rolled her eyes. "You cannot tell me you wouldn't give up all this if the right guy came along." She swept her hand in the air, taking in the room. "Is Max that guy?"

Taking a sip of her lemonade to stall, Emma's mind raced with possible replies. Reba ignored her hesitation and lowered her voice even though they were the only occupants of the room.

"This business with the chief is not going to turn out well," she said. "The chances are we're going to have to move on—not for the first time, and as usual, not through any fault of our own."

"But they arrested the men who attacked Wolf and—"

"And that is the problem. Two white men in jail for something most folks around here would consider fair play? From what Trula tells me, there are some who think Max and the rest of us should be run out of town. Wake up, Emma."

Emma thought about the whispers she'd overheard while serving lunch. "I don't see what this has to do with my relationship with the captain."

"Max—his name is Max. Do you call him 'the captain' when he's kissing you?" Reba sat back, drained her lemonade, and refilled her glass. "Now, talk to me."

Emma studied the actress for a long moment. "I do have feelings for the...for Max, but—"

Reba held up both hands to stop her saying more. "Next question...if he asked, would you leave your job here and go on the road with us?"

"Of course not. I have a reputation to uphold."

"Let me put that another way. If he asked you to marry him, would you?"

This time, Emma could not restrain a laugh. "You're being ridiculous. Max and I barely know each other. Granted I would hope we could become better acquainted, but the idea there will ever be more is absurd."

"What are you—thirty?"

"Twenty-six," Emma replied, offended.

Reba shrugged. "Either way the clock is ticking—for both of you. This is no time to follow traditions. I'm not sure how you decided to become a Harvey Girl, Emma, but I'd be willing to bet at least in part it was the promise of adventure? A more exciting life?"

Realizing she had badly misjudged Reba, Emma leaned forward. "There are rules, Reba, and times to break them. This is not such a time."

"So you're giving up? He packs us up and leaves, and you wave your little lace hankie from the hotel balcony?" She pushed herself away from the table and stood. "Then you're a bigger fool than I thought." She plucked the last cookie from the plate and bit off half of it. "Life is short, Emma, and trust me, you will not have that face and figure for much longer." She popped the rest of the cookie into her mouth and licked sugar from her fingers. "Can I ask you to let me know if you hear anything from the locals that might put Max—or the rest of us—in danger?"

Emma nodded and watched as Reba left the dining room.

Surely things were not as dire as the actress had predicted. Surely there was no real danger now that Wolf's attackers had been arrested.

She leaned back and looked out the window

toward the plaza, filled with people going about their shopping and other business. Perhaps in the West of olden days, there might have been trouble, but this was 1903. Surely by now they were past any sort of vigilante justice. She focused on the large colorful poster tacked to the side of the mercantile and saw that it had been vandalized—someone had thrown red paint on it. Was that a warning of trouble to come—trouble for Wolf and his family? Trouble for Max?

Emma shivered. She had no doubt that anyone attempting to harm the chief or his people would have to deal with Max first. And not Max the showman, but Max the veteran of prairie wars and frontier life—the man who was known for his expertise with a gun. And the man who, she suspected, would do anything for a friend.

❧

Max left the saloon no wiser than he'd been when he walked in. Rosie, the owner, wasn't there, and everyone else was tight-lipped. As Bert had reported, the two men the sheriff was holding at the jail were popular locals. The only piece of information he'd gathered was that the son, RJ, had been stepping out with Trula Goodwin.

As he passed through the hotel lobby, he nodded to the few guests gathered there. It was important to act normal, as if everything was fine. It was also important to be seen, to make people reconsider any preconceived notions they might have about the character of traveling show people. He considered handing out passes for a performance of the show but decided that might be too much. Upstairs, a maid ran a carpet sweeper over the hallway rug. *Normal.*

Pearl looked up when he opened the door to his room and stepped inside. His gaze went immediately to Wolf, who was half sitting up against a pile of pillows. Wolf gave him a crooked smile. "Nice place you got here, boss." His words were slurred, but his grin was genuine.

"Was Doc here?"

Pearl stood. "All business as usual, I see. Hello, Max. So nice to see you, Max," she said in a singsong voice.

"Not in the mood, Pearl. What's Doc say?"

"He says we can move him tonight. He's been up twice today, getting a little steadier on his feet."

"I'm right here," Wolf reminded them, his voice soft but stronger than before. Clearly, the medicine and sleep had helped.

Max turned to his friend. "You almost weren't," he snapped, the frustrations of the day erupting. Seeing the look of surprise Wolf gave him, Max stepped closer to the bed and clasped his friend's hand. "Sorry."

"Have you eaten anything today?" Pearl asked.

Max shrugged. "Look, I need to talk to Bert. But let's keep this simple. When you get back to the show-grounds, tell him to bring a wagon after midnight and come up the back stairs. We'll move Wolf and then figure out what comes next."

Pearl nodded and began packing up her sewing, preparing to leave. "How about I ask Emma to make sure you have a decent supper?"

Emma.

The chances were sooner rather than later he would

have to leave town, and whatever they might have had together would be behind them. Selfishly and despite everything going on with the show, he wanted every moment he could find to spend with her. In other circumstances and another place, they might have had more time, but this was now. "Ask her to bring up the tray herself," he said.

"Will do," Pearl replied as she opened the door a crack, checked the hall to be sure no one was around, and left.

"You saw the sheriff?" Wolf asked.

"Him and the mayor. I also had a talk with some men at the saloon."

"And?"

Max shrugged. "Nothing of value from the saloon unless you've had dealings with a rancher named Gilmore and his son?"

"Never heard of them. What'd the mayor say?"

Max laid out the three options. "I hate giving in to them, Wolf—on any level."

Wolf shifted and grimaced. "Well, truth is I'm not gonna be much use. Doc says weeks. Seems to me like the mayor's making the best offer. At least we can stay put for a while and…"

Max was pacing the small confines of the room. "It's still letting them win. And who's to say Ed Brunswick and those men the sheriff locked up won't try to provoke something else once they learn they didn't get what they wanted, which is forcing you to leave?"

"Then you'll deal with that," Wolf said. He drew in a breath, and Max saw the effort he was making to be reasonable. "Ed was drunk. Way I see it, if we follow the mayor's plan, it gives us a small chance to maybe change some minds. There's always going to be some who will want us gone, but I'd like to think most people here are—"

"Impartial? Fair?" Max clenched his fists.

"Max, think of Chogan. If we pack up, he's gonna see that as running. If we stay…"

Max knew Wolf was right, but he didn't have to like it. "You're a better man than I am, Chief."

Wolf laughed and then grimaced, placing a protective hand on his bandaged ribs. "Practice, my friend. Lots of practice."

Max looked at the slip of paper Pearl had given him with the times and directions for mixing Wolf's pain medicine. The dose wasn't due for a half hour yet, but Max could not stand seeing his friend in pain. "Close enough," he muttered as he mixed the powder in water.

Not long after Wolf had swallowed the medicine, he drifted off, and Max took a seat at the writing table, going over the cast list as he reconfigured each act. He was determined not to allow white actors to portray native people wherever he could help it, even if that meant changing the storyline to eliminate scenes that included Wolf and his people.

He'd worked his way through the entire first act of the show when he heard a soft tap at the door.

"Max?"

Emma.

He hurried to open the door for her and relieve her of the tray she carried. Behind him, Wolf slept soundly, the medicine doing its job. Max set the tray on top of the papers that covered the writing table. "Thank you," he said.

"How is he?" Emma was standing near the bed.

"Good enough that Doc says we can move him later tonight." He lifted the cover from the food. "This looks delicious."

Emma smiled and, after straightening Wolf's covers, came to stand next to the table. She was still dressed in her uniform.

"Join me," Max invited. "Tell me how your day was."

She hesitated, then perched on the edge of the extra chair across from his. "There was a lot of talk about the attack—and the arrests."

It seemed as if there was more she wanted to say. "Things like this tend to upset people, Emma."

"What are you going to do? I mean, Reba says—"

"You talked to Reba?"

Emma looked down at her hands folded in her lap. "Yes. She says the show might have to move on to another place. That seems so unfair, Max. I mean, Wolf is the victim in this after all, and to punish the entire company—"

Behind them, Wolf snorted and groaned.

Emma lowered her voice. "It just isn't right."

Max smiled as he scooped up a fork filled with a mix of beans, chilies, and beef. "In my experience, life isn't always fair, Emma."

"Well, it should be," she muttered and stood. "What time will you move him?"

"Bert's bringing a wagon after midnight. I'll make sure the kitchen door is unlocked. We'll come and go by the service stairs, and hopefully no one will be the wiser."

"I'll come back once I've made sure all the waitresses are in for the night. You'll need help."

Max was torn. He wanted nothing so much as to have her nearby, and yet moving Wolf might not go off as easily as he'd indicated. If someone saw the wagon or was watching Max or Bert to see what they would do, there could be trouble. Most folks would be asleep and unaware, but there was always the possibility someone might see.

"Too dangerous," he said.

"I thought you said—"

"I lied—sort of. Truth is things might go off without a hitch, but there's no guarantee." He watched her wrestle with an objection and decide not to make it. "However, it seems to me you and I have plans to visit your friends at their ranch on Sunday. I mean, unless you think your friends might have changed their minds about hosting me?"

"They are not at all like that," Emma protested.

Max grinned. "I didn't think so. Just checking to be sure that was still a date."

"Speaking of that," she said, her voice cracking, "Reba seems to think—"

"I wouldn't put too much stock in what Reba thinks," he interrupted. "She and I have—had—a past. Unfortunately, I'm not sure she sees it as over."

"Actually, she wanted to know my intentions concerning you."

Max nearly choked on his food and reached for his water glass, gulping down a good third before speaking. "Intentions?"

Emma nodded. "She seems to think…it's ridiculous, of course, and you may want to set her straight."

"She seems to think what?"

Emma interlaced her fingers and looked down at her lap. "Never mind. It was just talk."

"Just tell me, Emma."

She met his gaze. "She says you have feelings for me." It was a question wrapped in a challenge. She was daring him to either deny or concur.

He took his time wiping his mouth with the cloth napkin and laying it aside, then leaned closer. "And if I do?"

She glanced up at him from under hooded eyes. "I don't know," she whispered. "It's too soon, but Reba says—"

Max covered her fidgeting hands with his. "Stop telling me what Reba says. I want to know what you say, Emma."

"I say one or both of us is likely to end up regretting it, but if you want to see where this all goes while you're still here, that would be all right as long as we both understand that a future for us is...unlikely."

He cupped her cheeks, forcing her to look at him. "Yes, Emmie. Let's see where it goes."

As he leaned in to kiss her, Wolf let out a yelp of pain and woke. "Water!" he cried hoarsely.

In an instant, Emma was on her feet and across the room, filling a glass and then gently supporting Wolf's head as she helped him drink.

Lucky man, Max thought, envying his friend the touch of Emma's hand, her concerned face close as she urged him to drink.

Chapter 10

EMMA WATCHED THE CLOCK. IT WAS PAST MIDNIGHT. Her waitresses had been in bed for hours now. The town was shut down tight. And still she'd heard no wagon coming to the kitchen entrance. Had something gone wrong?

Despite her promise to stay in her room and let Max handle things, Emma simply could not sit still a minute longer. She wrapped her shawl around her shoulders and slipped down the service stairs to the second floor. Just as she was about to approach Max's room, she heard the jingle of a harness and felt a breeze working its way up the stairs. Turning back, she peered down the stairs from the landing.

George was down there talking to a man. The man was apologizing for being so late, and she remembered George telling her he'd found a source for the best chilies in the area.

"The guy's bringing them over tonight," he'd said.

Emma was happy for George—the man loved coming up with new chili dishes. But the delivery was late, and somewhere out there, Bert was probably coming with a wagon to move Wolf. George knew none of this, of course.

"Emma?" Max crept down the steps to the landing. "What's going on?"

"Shh," she warned, then motioned for him to follow her to the stairway that led to the third floor. She shut the door that closed off the staff area from that of hotel guests, then explained what was happening in the kitchen.

"But Bert's on his way, and Wolf's ready to go."

She placed her finger against his lips. "I'll take care of George and the delivery man. You go through the lobby to the street and watch for Bert, then wait for my signal."

"Emmie, I don't like getting you mixed up in this."

"Too late and not really your decision. Now go."

He grinned. "Yes, ma'am." He gave her a quick kiss and left.

Emma stood frozen for a moment, her fingers touching her lips where he'd just kissed her—again.

But then she heard George's voice and shook herself. There was work to be done. She pulled her shawl closer and hurried down the back stairs, slowing as she approached the kitchen.

"George?" She forced a yawn and hoped she looked as if she'd just wakened. "What on earth?"

"Emma, meet Sam. He's the chili man." There was no denying the excitement in her friend's tone. She offered Sam a handshake.

"Pleased to meet you, but so late…"

"Sorry about that, miss. One of my horses came up lame."

Behind the chili man, Emma saw Max waving his arms at something she couldn't see but assumed was Bert. "Well, no harm done. George has his chilies, and I cannot wait to taste them." She stifled another fake yawn. The town clock cooperated by striking the half hour. "Oh my, I didn't realize it was so late. You should probably start home, Sam, and George, that morning counter crowd will be here before you know it. Good night, gentlemen."

She made a show of reclimbing the stairs but paused as soon as she knew she was out of sight but not out of earshot. To her relief, she heard the wagon pull away. George returned to the kitchen. She heard water running, a glass being filled, and George's sigh of exhaustion.

Please go to your room.

Finally, she heard the door to his room just off the kitchen click shut. She crept down the stairs and waited for the lamp to be put out before tiptoeing past the cook's room and easing open the back door. Stepping into the yard, she glanced up at the hotel windows—all dark. Behind her, she heard footsteps. Her heart in her throat, she turned to see who might be coming out of the shadows.

Max walked toward her with a tall young man and Pearl.

"Where's Bert?" she whispered.

"Stayed with the wagon. Emma, this is Wolf's nephew, Chogan, and of course you know Pearl."

"Enough chatter," Pearl grumbled as she strode toward the hotel.

Emma, Max, and Chogan followed her through the

kitchen and up the stairs. Emma could hear George's heavy snoring even through the closed door.

When they reached the room, Wolf was standing by the window. "What happened?" he asked.

"I'll tell you on the way," Max said. "Right now, we need to move." He wrapped Wolf's arm around his shoulder and instructed Chogan to take the same position on the chief's other side. The three of them started down the stairs with Pearl leading the way, carrying a bag that contained medicine and extra bandages as she guided them with hand signals. When Emma followed, Max looked back at her and frowned. "Emmie, go to bed. If there's trouble, I don't want—"

"I'm coming, Max," she said. "You might need someone to cause a distraction."

He muttered something that sounded like "You're the distraction," but she couldn't be sure.

By the time they reached the wagon, Wolf was in a lot of pain, but Emma saw that Pearl was prepared for that. The wagon bed had been lined with straw and covered with blankets. As soon as they got Wolf settled, Pearl crawled in next to him while Chogan climbed up to ride with Bert. With a signal from Max, Bert snapped the reins, and the wagon rolled slowly into the blackness of the night.

"He'll be all right," Emma murmured.

Max wrapped his arm around her shoulder. "Yeah, he will. Thank you, Emma."

"I really didn't do that much."

Max turned her so they were facing each other, and although the night was moonless and starless, they closed the distance between them, their lips meeting as if they knew the way. She felt his hand cup the nape of her neck, drawing her closer. It wasn't that she'd never been kissed or felt a man's passion. It was that kissing Max felt different. It felt like this was where she belonged.

∞

The following morning, Max was on his way to tell the mayor that he would agree to temporarily removing any native people from the cast when he saw Trula Goodwin sitting on a park bench in the plaza.

"Miss Goodwin, you're out early," he said.

She twitched nervously and avoided looking at him. "I…my…friend is due to be released from the jail this morning."

"I see. RJ Gilmore is your friend?"

She nodded and twisted a hankie into a wad. "He didn't mean to hurt the chief," she blubbered, her chin quivering, her voice pleading with Max to believe her. "People say it was Chief Gray Wolf who struck RJ's pa and RJ was just defending him."

"Is that what you've heard? Maybe. Maybe things got out of hand, but I expect since you know the chief, you also know he's a peaceful man so unlikely to have started this business." He sat beside her, maintaining a proper distance between them. "Trula, the chief was badly injured while, by all accounts, your friend and his father were unhurt. That tells me the chief didn't fight back."

"RJ says those people don't belong in town. He says it's one thing for them to be part of the show, but that gives them ideas about putting themselves above their station."

"And what do you say, Trula? You know the chief. Your friend doesn't."

"I…" Tears rolled down her cheeks, and she swatted at them with the hankie. "He's… I know the chief is a kind and good man, but I love RJ," she admitted as if that explained everything. Then she looked directly at Max, and her eyes grew wide with anxiety. "Are you gonna fire me?"

"Not for choosing to stay loyal to a friend. Besides, you work for Miss Reba, and how do you think she'd react if I overstepped and fired you without consulting her?"

"Then she's gonna fire me," Trula mumbled miserably. "The chief is her friend, and she doesn't like it that I'm seeing RJ. She already warned me he wasn't right for me, but she doesn't know him the way I do."

This was going in a direction that was decidedly uncomfortable for Max. When it came to affairs of the heart, he was hardly an expert. For that matter, neither was Reba. He stood.

"Look, Trula, just do your job and remember that anything you may think you know about the chief is not for sharing with your beau. Do we understand one another?"

She squinted up at him, bobbing her head up and down repeatedly. "Yes, sir," she mumbled, then looked beyond him. She was on her feet in an instant and running across the plaza. "RJ!" she shouted.

Max turned and saw the sheriff shaking hands with

the older Gilmore while a younger man stood by and
ignored Trula calling out to him. Apparently, the
two men responsible for Wolf's beating were being
released. All three men were looking at Max, so he
raised two fingers to his hat and walked across the
plaza to the mayor's store.

This wasn't over. The sheriff releasing Wolf's
attackers without knowing whether Max would
accept terms told him that as clearly as any spoken
words could. This was a warning, and Max was
relieved to know Wolf had been safely moved back
to the showgrounds during the night. Remembering
how Emma had taken charge of the entire procedure
made him smile.

⸙

On Sunday, Max called for Emma just after church.
He seemed to be in good spirits given everything
Emma knew he was dealing with.

"Ready?" His smile was genuine. As he helped her
into the buggy, Emma realized he was truly looking
forward to their visit with Grace and Nick.

"As I recall, you aren't much for buggies," she
teased.

Is that a blush crawling up the captain's neck?

"I told you—I want to make a good impression on
your friends," he said as he took up the reins. "And
on you," he added.

"You needn't worry. Grace and Nick are going to
like you."

"Because you like me?"

She laughed. "Now you're just fishing for a compliment."

He took hold of her hand as they left the town behind.

"How's Wolf doing?" she asked.

"His mother and sister have taken over his care. They're feeding him some kind of herb concoction and making a poultice from the roots of desert plants to rub on his wounds. He'll be fine."

"And has there been any more trouble? I mean, since Mr. Gilmore and his son were released from jail?"

"Not so far."

His answer told her he still expected trouble. "You're worried." It wasn't a question.

He shrugged. "Usually, it's a couple of locals who want a fight."

"Isn't that what happened?"

"In Wolf's case, I'd just had to let the show's advance man, Ed Brunswick, go earlier that day. He was there when Wolf was attacked. It's no coincidence. Ed has a big mouth, and I expect he pointed Wolf out to the others."

"Is that what Wolf thinks?"

"Wolf won't say. Over the years, he's learned the hard way to let things like this go."

"That hardly seems fair. He was the victim in this attack."

Max slowly shook his head and stared straight ahead, his brow furrowed. "I'm not sure Wolf and I did his people any favors by bringing them into the show. At least on the reservation they'd be relatively free from this kind of thing."

"How did you meet?" Emma hoped her question

might move him away from troubling thoughts back
to something more positive, and it worked.

He chuckled. "I'd just been assigned to work
border patrol in Montana. A fella by the name of Tyler
Newton was the man in charge. He paired me up with
Wolf to go out on patrols. Thing is, at first Wolf and
I couldn't stand each other."

"But clearly, you both got past that."

"If you spend enough days and nights with nobody
else to talk to, you start to make adjustments."

"And now you're the best of friends."

"We are," he murmured. "Newton—the guy who
was our captain back then—now manages the regiment stationed at Yellowstone."

"The national park?" Emma couldn't hide the
excitement in her voice.

"Yeah. Newton has been after me to come work
for him. Seems they're having a lot of trouble with
poachers and gangs using the park as a hideout."

Emma had never thought of the park as a place that
might be dangerous and was about to say so when
Max suddenly looked over at her, a big grin on his
handsome face.

"Maybe that's the answer," he said. "Wolf is as
good a tracker as any man I've ever known. What if
he and his people went there and settled?"

Ever practical, Emma saw potential problems with
that idea. "I can understand recommending Wolf, but
would the commanding officer be interested in taking
on Wolf's family as well? I mean it might be one thing
if Wolf were married with a child of his own, but
parents and siblings and their children?"

"It's worth looking into, don't you think?"

She saw the hope in his eyes, the hope that he might have come up with a way to protect his friend from further harm. "Definitely worth it," she agreed before turning her attention to the road ahead. "We're almost there," she added and adjusted her hat and checked her hair to be sure she looked all right.

"Hey," Max said softly, "you look just fine. I'm the one who should be nervous."

"Oh, Max, they are going to love you."

Because I do.

The thought seemed to spring from nowhere, and yet nothing had ever rung truer. She tucked her hand in the crook of his arm and scooted a little closer as she pointed out the lane that would lead them to Grace's home.

∞

Max felt at home the minute he and Emma climbed down from the buggy. Nick had been waiting by the barn, ready to help unhitch the horse and lead it to the corral, while Grace fussed at Emma for bringing one of the hotel's cakes.

"Not at all necessary," she scolded, but she peeked under the towel covering the basket and squealed with delight. "It's George's famous applesauce cake—my favorite!" She turned her attention to Max. "And you must be the famous Captain Winslow," she said, extending a hand in greeting.

"Guilty," he replied. "Thank you both for inviting me."

Grace laughed. "By the time our two ruffians get through with you, you might regret that."

Just then, two small children came running from the house as if the place might be on fire. "Emma!" the boy shouted as he collided with Emma, who had bent down to greet both children. Max watched as she gave the boy a slobbery kiss on his cheek, one he protested and wiped away with his fist. "Ah, Emma," he complained.

"What? I can't kiss my best cowboy?"

"Ma says you've got a new best cowboy." He gave Max a shy look and frowned. "Is this him?"

"James Arthur Hopkins, manners!" Grace spoke the kid's full name with a warning tone that the boy took to heart.

"I mean, pleased to meet ya, mister."

Max followed Emma's lead and knelt to be more on eye level with the boy. He extended his hand. "The pleasure is mine, James Arthur."

"It's just Jimmy," the kid said with a roll of his eyes.

"And I'm Max." He leaned in a little closer. "Who's that?" He jerked his head toward a toddler clinging to Emma's skirt.

"That's my sister," Jimmy whispered. "She's just two—a baby. I'm going on four."

Max nodded. "I see. Does your sister have a name?"

Jimmy snorted. "Everybody has a name. That's Daisy, like the flower."

Max stood and started to hum "Daisy Bell," popularly known as "Bicycle Built for Two."

"My song!" Daisy released her grip on Grace's skirt and placed her hands on her hips. "That's Daisy's song."

Max stood. "Really? How does it go?"

"It goes like dis," Daisy said. "Daisy! Daisy," she sang in a high-pitched squeak. "Did you my dancer coo."

Max tried hard not to laugh. He picked Daisy up and began waltzing around with her, humming the song.

"Mama, we're dancing," she crowed.

But Max was not looking at Daisy or her mother. Instead, he saw Emma watching him, and in that look he saw such affection. When he realized that fondness was directed not at the child in his arms but at him, his heart seemed to skip a beat.

❧

If for one moment Emma had questioned her feelings for Max, that moment disappeared as she watched him dancing with Daisy. She imagined him as a father, a husband—*her* husband. So caught up was she in her fantasies that she barely realized that Max had set Daisy down and Grace was urging them all to come inside out of the sun.

"Emma?" Nick was waiting for her to precede him up the path from the corral to the house. She saw that Grace had engaged Max in conversation, so she fell into step with Nick.

"Grace and the children are looking well," she said.

"So are you," Nick replied with a grin. "Grace thinks the captain might be responsible for that."

"Ever since she married you, Grace has become an incurable matchmaker. First for Lily, and now nothing will do but that she finds someone for me."

"And has she?"

"I'm not sure Grace believes Max is the right one. She may be right."

"You have doubts?"

How to explain to Nick—or Grace—the barriers to taking her feelings for Max too seriously? "We enjoy each other's company," she said as they climbed the porch steps. "Let's leave it at that for now."

Nick chuckled. "Sounds like it's not me or Grace you need to convince."

Inside the rustic house, the lace curtains were drawn to filter out the strong midday sun. Grace had set the table for four with her best linens and dishes.

"I fed the children already," she said. "It's nap time for them, and that will give us grown-ups time to catch up."

Nick herded the two children up the steps to the loft. "And I don't want to hear any giggling or talking," he said with mock sternness.

"But—" Daisy protested.

"Or no dessert later," Nick added, and that threat sent the children scrambling.

"Why don't you and Max sit on the porch while Emma and I get the meal ready?" Grace suggested.

Emma was well aware Grace had planned this day in detail, from having the children take their naps to the meal to making sure Nick and Max had time to get better acquainted.

"Well," Grace said, lowering her voice as the screen door closed behind the men, "your Max is certainly a good-looking charmer."

"He's hardly *my* Max," Emma protested.

"Pshaw!" Grace snorted. "This is not a time for false modesty, Emma. The man can hardly take his eyes off you. The question is what will you do about that?"

"Really, Grace, we've only just met. I mean, he's been in town only a few weeks now."

"But if he is the one? I know I warned you to take things slow, but when I see the two of you together... Look, the one thing I know for certain is that you do not want to spend the rest of your life guiding a new crop of Harvey Girls each year because last year's girls have left to marry or find adventures of their own. As Lily pointed out, this is *your* time, Emma."

So that was what lay behind Grace's sudden change of heart when it came to Max—Lily. "When did you and Lily discuss my future?"

"I wrote her just after we met for tea, and she wrote back at once. We're both concerned about you, Emma—about your happiness."

"I'm not unhappy," Emma protested.

Grace paused, the spoon she was using to stir the stew held in midair. "Will you listen to yourself? 'Not unhappy'? That's not the same as being happy, Emma."

An uncomfortable silence settled between them. Emma sliced a loaf of bread while Grace filled a tureen with stew and set it on the table, then went to the door. "Gentlemen, I hope you're hungry," she said, and Emma heard the scrape of the porch chairs and the squeak of the door as the two men came inside.

"That stew smells mighty good, Grace," Max said. He and Nick waited for the women to be seated before taking their places at either end of the table.

Nick stretched out his hands to Grace and Emma, and Max followed suit as Nick offered a prayer of thanksgiving for the meal and the friendship.

"Amen," Max murmured, giving Emma's hand a slight squeeze before releasing it. He turned his attention to Grace. "Nick tells me your brother is in the army and serving as part of the regiment overseeing the national park," he said.

"Yellowstone?" Emma asked. "I didn't know that, Grace."

"He just received his assignment," Grace replied. "Nick and I are hoping to find some time to visit him with the children. You should come with us, Emma. I know it's been a dream of yours to see the wonders of the park."

"Max knows the officer in charge," Emma said.

"That so?" Nick questioned Max about the connection as they ate, and to Emma's relief, the conversation remained focused on the park and Grace's brother and Max's service as a scout in the years before he became a partner in the Wild West show.

"Do you miss it, Max?" Grace asked.

"I do," he admitted. "I've tried to replicate the lifestyle in the show, but the truth is that's all make-believe."

Emma could not help being surprised at Max's frankness. He'd certainly hinted at his disappointment in the life he'd chosen, but this was an outright admission. Grace had always had that effect on people. Certainly, Emma and Lily had shared their hopes and disappointments with her.

"Well, judging by my brother's letter, the national

park is still wilderness and open country," Grace said, then her eyes widened. "You should come with us. It might give you some new ideas for your show."

Max chuckled. "I'm afraid my schedule won't allow for side trips, but Emma, you should definitely go."

"I'm not sure my schedule will allow the amount of time I would need," she replied.

"When's the last time you took a day off?" Nick asked.

"I can answer that one," Grace replied. "Try never." She gave Emma a grin. "Our Emma is devoted to her work."

"Maybe we can change that," Max said, and while Emma knew Grace was teasing her, it certainly looked like Max was serious.

"I would remind all of you that I have taken today off," she protested as she helped Grace clear their plates.

"Doesn't count," Grace said. "It's Sunday."

Nick stood and patted his stomach. "That was a wonderful meal, Gracie." He kissed her forehead, then turned to Max. "Would you like to take a ride and see some of the ranch?"

The way Nick glanced at Grace, Emma knew this was part of her plan. Nick's job was to spend as much time as possible learning what he could about Max.

"I'd like that," Max replied. "As long as we don't miss that apple cake." He winked at Grace, and she laughed.

"Go on, the two of you. By the time you come back, Emma and I will have everything cleared away, the children will be up from their nap, and we can all enjoy dessert."

Emma helped Grace wash and dry the dishes. She

was grateful that Grace seemed to have gathered she'd rather not discuss her relationship with Max. Their conversation focused on Emma's role as head waitress and housemother, and Grace's children who could be heard whispering and giggling in the loft.

"All right, sleepyheads," Grace called, pretending she hadn't noticed they were already awake. "Who wants cake?"

Daisy and Jimmy hurried down the loft steps, their hair mussed from their naps.

"Where's Pa?" Jimmy asked.

"He and Captain Winslow went for a ride. They should be back shortly. Until then, how about we sit on the porch, and you can tell Auntie Emma what you've been up to since her last visit."

"I can read," Daisy announced.

"Cannot," Jimmy muttered as they went out to the porch.

"Can so," Daisy insisted and grabbed a thick book from the small table next to the swing. "Come on, Auntie Emma, and I'll show you." She placed the book on the swing and climbed up to sit, indicating with a nod that she expected Emma to join her.

"That's quite a thick book," Emma said.

"I know. There's hardly any pictures, so it's real hard." She opened the cover and pointed to an inscription. "This says it's a book Pa's boss gave him last Christmas. It says, 'Merry Christmas, Nick,' right there."

"So it does," Emma said.

"Here comes Pa now," Jimmy announced and jumped off the porch to run to the corral and wait for Nick and Max to dismount and unsaddle the horses.

The thing that struck Emma was that both men were laughing, and it was the easy, comfortable laughter of friends. Her heart swelled with pleasure as she realized Max had passed whatever test Grace had charged Nick with administering.

"Well, seems your captain has made a favorable impression," Grace said.

"I knew he would win over Nick and the children. But you…"

"Have been won over as well," Grace assured her. "It's clear the two of you are a wonderful match, Emma."

Just then, Nick hoisted Jimmy onto his shoulders, and Daisy dropped the book and scrambled down from the swing to run to her father. "Me too," she shouted. "I want a ride."

And as if it were the most natural thing in the world for him, Max caught her and swung her high on his shoulders so that she and her brother were even. Then he exchanged a look with Nick, and the two men started running for the porch, the children bobbing up and down and shrieking with glee.

For a moment, Emma felt as if she couldn't catch her breath. It was a side of Max she had never seen, a tenderness and obvious love of children that had her entertaining preposterous fantasies of Max with children of his own—of Max and *her* with children of their own.

❧

On the ride back to town, Max could not get past the thought that this day had changed him—had changed everything about what he thought his future held. He and Nick had a lot in common—their love of the land and their concern at how things were changing. And watching Nick and Grace with their children, laughing and exchanging looks that spoke of their deep love for each other, triggered something inside Max. He'd always thought one day he would find a wife, have kids, settle down. But he kept postponing that, telling himself the vagabond life he led was no way to raise a family.

Emma sat beside him, reliving the afternoon that had run well into the evening. He nodded and grunted when he thought appropriate, but the truth was his mind was not on the visit but on Emma. They'd known each other only a few weeks. It was too soon to be thinking the way he was—not only about kissing her, but also about touching her more intimately—or at least asking her if she might feel the way about him that he'd realized he felt about her. He didn't want to scare her off, but he was beginning to feel like if he didn't say something he might explode.

"Max? Are you unwell?" Emma leaned toward him, studying his features in the gathering shadows of twilight.

"I'm okay," he replied. "It's just…"

She hooked her hand through the crook of his arm. "Something is troubling you. You've hardly heard a word I've said since we left the ranch."

He pulled the buggy off the main road and called for the horse to stop. "Let's take a walk," he said.

"Max, it's late and getting dark."

He was already out of the buggy. "A short walk. I

have something I want to ask—tell you." He took the blanket he'd brought along in case the night air was too chilly for her.

"All right," she agreed. "You're being very mysterious." She tried a laugh, but he heard the nerves driving it.

Taking hold of her hand, he led her through the tall grass to the creek that ran past a tall cottonwood. A rising moon made the water sparkle. He spread the blanket on the bank of the creek. "Let's sit for a while," he said.

She did as he asked. He knew she was waiting for some further explanation of his mood and actions. The truth was he didn't know where to begin. Instead, he paced along the creek bank, and when the silence between them grew uncomfortable it was Emma who spoke first.

"Today was lovely," Emma said as she unpinned her hat and laid it aside. She leaned back, supporting herself on her elbows as she gazed up at the moon. "You enjoyed meeting Nick and Grace, didn't you?"

She was trying to help him say whatever it was he meant to tell her. Drawing in a deep breath, he sat next to her and brushed a tendril of her hair away from her cheek. "I like your friends," he said. "I like the way they seem to have life figured out. I like the way they've not wasted time, thinking someday."

"I suspect that had everything to do with the fact that they almost lost each other. I mean, Grace could easily have died in that fire. They'd really only known each other a few months before everything happened."

Nick had told Max the entire story of Grace's stalker

and how she had nearly died in a fire the man had caused, and how when her predator was the one who died, Grace had gone on trial. He'd called himself the luckiest of men to have married her, and Max had seen how very content the man was with the life he'd chosen.

"I'm thinking about leaving the show," he blurted. He felt her tense even though he was not touching her and knew whatever she might have expected him to say, that wasn't it.

Chapter 11

THE ONLY WORD EMMA HEARD WAS *leaving*. MEMORIES of past relationships came rushing forth. Her father's abandonment. The young man who had declared his undying love for her and then chosen the adventure of Mr. Roosevelt's Rough Riders, expecting her to wait—not for weeks or months but possibly years. Even Aidan. Although she had been the one to end that relationship, she'd done so because it became clear to her that Aidan's attraction to her had little to do with romance or passion and a lot to do with a partnership where each of them could make their mark in the Harvey Company.

She swallowed, trying to find her voice in the dryness that had suddenly filled her mouth. "Why?" she managed, silently reprimanding herself for thinking for one minute that Max should consider what his leaving might mean to her. "What would Wolf and Reba and Bert do without you? And Pearl? At her age, she's not likely to be able to find work if the show disbands."

"I expect they'd be upset at first but then find their ways. As for Pearl, Bert will make sure she's all right."

"And then there are all the other actors and crew members, not to mention all those patrons who have purchased tickets to see you perform. You have a responsibility, Max." She realized she was scolding him, sounding for all the world like an old-maid schoolteacher. "I'm sorry. It's hardly my place to say such things."

He stared out at the creek. "You take things like loyalty and responsibility pretty serious, Emmie."

"Don't you? After all, the easiest way to handle the aftermath of Wolf's attack would have been to do what the sheriff wanted, but you wouldn't hear of that."

"This is different."

"Tell me how. I want to understand your thinking, Max. What has brought this on all of a sudden?"

"It's not so sudden, Emmie. I've always known there would come a day when the show wouldn't be enough." He took hold of her hand, stroking her palm with his thumb. "Today was that day. I want more, Emmie. I want what I saw today, and I want that with you."

Emma could not have been more stunned had he said he was thinking of moving to Europe. She opened her mouth to say something, but no words came out.

Max leaned in closer and framed her face with his hands. "Today as I watched Nick and Grace, what I saw was you and me, and I realized that I'm falling in love with you, Emma Elliott."

"You barely know me." *But oh, how I want to believe you.*

"I think I knew from the moment I saw you that first day in the dining room with your Harvey Girls."

He was still cradling her face, his lips only a kiss away. "There was something rare about you—something that drew me to you. At the time, I didn't know where the fascination came from, but today I realized what I saw that day was the woman I had imagined spending my life with—a woman who is beautiful." He kissed her lightly. "A woman who is intelligent." He kissed her again, lingering this time. "A woman who is independent and devoted to her work and her friends."

This time, the kiss was more intimate as he ran the tip of his tongue over her lips.

He pulled back enough to look at her. "I don't know how we'll make it work, Emma. I mean, if you want it to work."

"I do," she whispered.

"I can't ask you to lead the kind of life I've lived these last years—always on the road, moving from one town to the next, never really knowing if the patrons will be there to buy the tickets. That's not what I want for us."

She stroked his cheek, felt the start of the whiskers he would shave in the morning. "What do you want, Max? For us, I mean?"

"I want a home I can come back to at the end of the day. I want kids who come running to greet me. And most of all, I want you next to me every night." He lay her back on the blanket. "You're a woman any man would be blessed to call his own." Now his kisses stole a path down her cheek and onto her throat. His hand lingered over the row of buttons on her shirtwaist. "I want *you*, Emmie, but if this is not what you want, just say so."

Emma felt the stirrings of desire that she'd only known when lying awake alone in her room, imagining being kissed like this, touched like this. She wrapped her arms around his shoulders, tugging him closer. "Yes," she whispered.

For the first time in her life, she understood the kind of passion that knows no barriers. She wanted him, and he wanted her, and that was all that mattered. Even if this was all they would ever have, it would be enough, and she would not waste time on regrets. If there was no tomorrow for them, just this moment with a full moon lighting his features as he slowly unfastened the buttons on her blouse and the music of the creek tumbling over and around rocks nearby, it would be enough.

He spread her shirtwaist open and trailed his forefinger along the edge of her camisole. She was glad she had given up corsets, happy for the freedom he found to touch her. And when he did with his fingers and then his lips, never had she felt so completely out of control. Her body writhed, speaking words she did not have. Everywhere he touched her, she felt as if she were on fire, and when he tugged her undergarment lower and kissed her bare breast, then took her nipple between his lips and laved it with his tongue, she was quite sure she might explode.

She tugged his shirt free of his trousers and ran her hands under it to massage his bare skin, thrilling to the low moan of pleasure her touch elicited. When he sat back on his heels and removed his shirt, he was smiling.

"You're overdressed, Emmie."

He knelt at her feet and removed her shoes and stockings, allowing his hands to run up and under her skirt until he reached the place where she had only imagined being touched. He pressed his hand between her legs and cupped her, then began an agonizing rhythmic massage that had her gasping for breath. She dug her nails into his bare skin and arched her body. She turned to him, covering the length of his body with hers and feeling the hard fullness of his manhood even through the layers of clothing that separated them.

She felt his breath, hot against her throat, and traced the curve of his ear with her tongue. Once again he moved away, but this time he reached for his belt, unfastening it and drawing it through the loops of his trousers like a snake, his eyes never leaving her face, his question as clear as if he had shouted.

Her answer was to reach for the waistband of his trousers and begin unbuttoning the fly. When she placed her hand over his erection, he drew in a breath and swore.

"You're sure, Emmie? Be very sure. No regrets tomorrow."

She hesitated only a moment before pushing away from him and standing. He sighed with what she could only describe as disappointment as he turned away. "Okay," he said softly. "Give me a minute, and we'll head on to town."

Emma quickly removed the rest of her clothes and knelt behind him. "I'm sure," she whispered as she wrapped her arms around him and pressed her bare body to his back. "No regrets," she added. "I promise."

Slowly, he turned, and now he was the one who was speechless. He shed the rest of his clothes, tossing his boots aside in such a way that Emma could not help but laugh. "You'll never find them in the dark," she said.

He grinned and crawled closer like a mountain lion stalking its prey until she had no choice but to lie back. "You'd be amazed what I can find in the dark, Emmie," he said as he gently spread her legs and knelt between them. "Remember, I was a scout long before I was in a show. For example," he whispered as his fingers probed her, teased her to the point of no return.

And then she realized he was no longer touching her with his fingers, but the tip of his erection was pleading for entry. He slid his hands under her hips and lifted her as he slid past the last barrier and filled her. And when she thought he was about to pull away, she urged him back, her hips rising to meet each thrust.

Emma felt tears leak down her cheeks, but these were tears of joy. Whatever might lie ahead for either of them, she would always have this night—this incredible star-filled, moonlit night.

❀❀❀

At first, Max thought it had started to rain, but then he realized Emma was crying. Damn! He'd been too rough. Folding his arms around her, he murmured, "I'm so sorry, Emmie. Please believe me when I say I would never hurt you. I—are you laughing?"

She was.

"Not the reaction I was hoping for," he said, trying hard not to sound hurt. She looked up at him, her cheeks glistening with tears in the moonlight. "You *are* crying."

"And laughing from happiness," she croaked. "Giddy with the pure bliss of what we just shared." She stroked his hair away from his forehead. "I never imagined…never could have known…"

He grinned and hugged her tighter. "Are you cold?"

"Not as long as you hold me," she said softly.

He pulled the edge of the blanket around her shoulders.

"I could stay here forever," she said.

But they both knew that was just another fantasy. They each had responsibilities. "I'm afraid we'll need to get going if I'm to get you back before the clock strikes ten."

"Just a few minutes longer," she pleaded.

He felt her smooth cheek resting against his bare chest, felt her breath fan over his skin, felt his desire stir, and knew a few more minutes—a few more hours—would not be enough.

"Now, Miss Emma, what would it look like if your girls caught you sneaking in past curfew?" He forced his tone to a lightness he didn't feel. What he wanted more than anything was to make love to her again, taking all the time needed to make sure she understood that what they had just shared was only the beginning. He reached around her to get his shirt. "Put this on and go wash up by the creek."

"I don't need…"

He felt himself blush. She was such an innocent, and now he'd been the one to take that innocence from her. "Emmie, there might be a little bleeding," he said softly.

"Oh," she whispered. She turned away from him, letting the blanket fall as she gathered her clothing. "I'll be fine with the blanket," she said, returning his shirt to him.

Max collected his trousers and boots, giving her privacy to stand and wrap herself in the blanket and pad barefoot down to the creek. He heard splashing and then the rustling of clothing as she dressed. By the time she returned, he'd dressed as well and was holding out her shoes to her.

Without a word, she took them and sat on a boulder to put them on, not bothering with the stockings. Together, they walked to the buggy, the silence stretching uncomfortably between them as Max first helped her, then climbed in next to her.

Though he held the reins in one hand, for a moment they sat there, not moving.

"Emmie?"

"It's all right, Max. I don't expect anything more," she said softly, her hand resting on his forearm.

He looked at her. "What if I do?" he asked.

"You're thinking of leaving," she reminded him. "I won't stand in the way of you finding the life you want—and deserve."

He swallowed the words that sprang to his lips. *Come with me*, he wanted to say, but that would be foolhardy. What could he offer her? No, she was better off staying close to her friends and the work she loved. In time, maybe, but it was too soon.

He patted her hand and smiled. "I just said I was thinking about leaving," he reminded her. "I've learned the hard way that dreams can seem simple until you start putting them into action." He touched his fingers to her lips. "We'll find a way, Emmie. It'll take some time, but if you're willing…"

"I think you have the answer to that, Captain Winslow." She snuggled closer to him and rested her head on his shoulder. He snapped the reins, wrapped his arm around her shoulders, and set the horse moving at a slow walk, wanting nothing so much as for it to take as long as possible for them to reach town.

❧

Emma woke to shouting and inched away from Max as he guided the horse and buggy into the yard behind the hotel. Bert was striding toward them and glaring at Max.

"Where the hell have you been?" he demanded.

"You know where," Max said evenly as he climbed down and walked around the buggy to help Emma. "Emma and I were visiting her friend."

"Well, while you were visiting friends, somebody set fire to the chief's camp."

Emma crammed her fist against her mouth to keep at bay the shout of protest she felt building. "Was anyone hurt?" she managed.

"Just scared half to death," Bert replied before turning his attention back to Max. "I put them up in the sleeping cars for the time being, but they've lost everything other than the clothes they were wearing when the fire started." He lowered his voice and stepped closer to Max. "You need to talk to Wolf, Max. He's talking about packing up and leaving for good."

Max's hand still rested on Emma's waist, and she felt him tense as Bert delivered his horrible news. "You should go to Wolf now," she said. "I'll have Tommy take care of returning the horse and buggy."

Max kissed her cheek and took off running in the direction of the livery where Emma knew he'd left Diablo. She turned her attention to Bert. "Why are you here in town and not out at the showgrounds with Wolf and his family?"

"I've been waiting for the sheriff to get back to me with news. He made a big show of rounding up a posse and heading out. I'm pretty sure he already knows who set the fire, but he's playing it close to his vest. I don't intend to let him just walk away from this like he did when Wolf got beat up."

"You think it was the Gilmores?"

"Not the father—he's too smart for that. But the kid is a hothead, and he holds a grudge. I expect he didn't like having to spend even that one night in jail." Bert took a draw on his cigar—lit for once—and blew out the smoke slowly. "Setting up here for the winter might not have been the best idea," he mused.

Emma thought about what Max had said about maybe leaving the show. Now it sounded like the show might be falling apart on its own, no matter what he did. She breathed out a sigh that Bert took for exhaustion.

"Listen to me yammering on when you've had a long day as well." He opened the door to the lobby and waited for her to precede him. "You go on and get your rest, Emma. I'll make sure the horse and buggy get returned."

"Thank you, Bert. I'll see you for breakfast?"

He gave her his showman's smile. "Can't pass up that coffee, now can I?"

Emma waved a farewell as she crossed the lobby and entered the deserted dining room on her way to her office. She had almost reached the kitchen when a sound made her turn.

"Is someone there?" she asked, searching the shadows for signs of an intruder. She saw someone seated in the corner, at the table reserved for Max and the others.

"It's me, Miss Elliott," Trula Goodwin said. "I didn't know...that is, I never thought—" She burst into tears, covering her face with her hands.

Emma struggled to find the empathy the girl undoubtedly sought. Slowly but surely, it seemed as if the fates had aligned to deny her the time she wanted to relive her tryst with Max. And Trula Goodwin had caused her problems in the past. Yet she was obviously in some kind of trouble. Pulling out the chair next to Trula, Emma sat and leaned forward.

"What's happened?" She fished a handkerchief from her pocket and pressed it into the girl's hand.

"What hasn't happened?" Trula moaned dramatically. "Miss Reba hasn't paid me since I started working for her, so I have no resources for leaving, and now the sheriff is going to find out it was me, and I just can't go to jail."

Mentally, Emma sorted through the muddle of information Trula had provided. "Why would the sheriff have the slightest interest in you?"

Trula's hands were shaking badly, and Emma realized whatever had happened, it was serious. She covered Trula's hands with hers and softened her tone. "Just tell me. I can't help if I don't know what we're dealing with."

"He said it was just a prank. He promised no one would get hurt—and no one did," she added, her eyes wide as if she'd just realized this. "I mean, yes, everything they owned was burnt up, but they were all safe. We made sure of that."

Emma's heart hammered. "Trula, are you telling me you and your friend set the fire?"

"Not me," she protested. "All I did was what he asked me to do."

"And what exactly was that?"

"He said since I worked out there, I should be able to figure out when they were away from their tepees, during a show or a rehearsal. But they never were all away at the same time, so he decided to create a diversion."

"And how did he do that exactly?" Emma did not have to ask who *he* was. She had always had reservations when it came to the young man Trula slipped out to see almost nightly during her stint as a Harvey Girl. As it turned out, that young man was the Gilmore son.

"I'm not sure. All I know is I was in Miss Reba's tent brushing her costumes when suddenly everybody started running for the dining tent. It was scary. People were tripping and falling down, and everybody was yelling."

"Did you and Reba run as well?"

"She was still here in town, but I ran. There was a lot of yelling, and all of a sudden a whole bunch of masked men came riding through the grounds, whooping and hollering and shooting off their guns. Some of them were carrying torches."

"And did you recognize any of these men?"

"They wore masks."

"I understand that, but if one of them was the Gilmore boy, surely you would have known." She gave Trula a moment to consider her answer, then pressed her. "Trula, if he was involved, then you might indeed be in trouble as well."

"He was in the lead," Trula whispered. "I thought that's all it would be, scaring everybody half out of their wits, but then we saw the smoke, heard the crackling, and Chief Gray Wolf started running the other way, back toward the tepees. He was limping bad and fell once, but he just kept going." She drew in a labored breath. "What am I going to do?"

"You'll begin by telling the sheriff everything you know about the incident. If you are telling me the whole of your part in it, then you have nothing to worry about for yourself."

"I can't go against RJ. They'll take him to jail, and what will I do then?"

"Trula, I know you believe you love this young man and that he returns those feelings, but think about it. He deliberately put you in a position that might well have ended with *you* going to jail. That isn't love. That's—"

"I'm pregnant," she whispered.

And you think that will make any difference to this scoundrel? Emma wanted to shout the words at Trula but forced herself to remain in control. "That is a different problem, Trula."

Trula gave out a bark of a laugh that held no humor. "I knew you wouldn't understand. How could you? I mean, have you ever been in love?"

"It's your life we're discussing, Trula, not mine. And if you want my help, then you will listen to what I have to say."

Trula sat back and folded her arms over her chest. "All right, but—"

"Listen," Emma repeated.

Trula pressed her lips together.

"Let's address your problems one by one. Once the captain learns Miss Reba is not paying you, he will take care of that. I suggest you tell him as soon as possible."

"She'll fire me, and then where will I be?"

"That brings us to problem number two. Assuming you are pregnant, I doubt Miss Reba will keep you on. She is a woman who puts her needs above those of others, and she will have little sympathy for your situation. That leaves two alternatives, neither ideal."

"I love RJ," Trula said, her voice shaking again with the promise of more tears.

"That is not in question. Does he love you? Enough to marry you and support you and this child?"

The dam burst, and the sobs were heart-wrenching. Emma leaned in and wrapped her arms around Trula's shoulders. "That brings us to your second option. What about your family, Trula? Could you not go home? I met your parents once, and it seemed to me they loved you so much."

"Maybe once," she sputtered. "But now?"

"You are carrying a child—their grandchild. Are you saying they would turn their backs on you both?" Emma had no idea whether Trula's parents would embrace her and her child. She was truly grasping at straws. "Let me put it another way. Imagine this baby inside you is a girl, and years from now, that daughter comes to you and tells you she is unwed and with child. What would you do?"

Trula sniffed back her tears and stared at her folded hands before waving away the question. "There's another way. I think RJ's father likes me. He'll make RJ do the right thing." As suddenly as she'd dissolved into tears, Trula was now all smiles. "Yes. Mr. Gilmore told me himself that I'm good for RJ. That means he likes me, doesn't it? He'll help make this right?"

"Let's say that's true, Trula. Do you really want to spend your life with a man who was forced to marry you?"

"He'll learn to love me," she replied with all the bravado of one who believes she can move mountains. She stood. "I appreciate your listening to me, Miss Elliott, and I apologize for the problems I caused while under your supervision. But I am a grown woman now, a woman in love and expecting a child. If you try to tell the sheriff what I have told you in confidence tonight, I will deny it, and we both know I am an expert at lying." She headed for the door leading to the lobby. "Oh, and I will speak to the captain regarding my wages."

And with that, she walked away, her head high and

shoulders back as if nothing could possibly stop her from achieving whatever she set her mind to doing.

Emma continued to sit at the table, staring out the window, trying to decide what to do. She heard horses coming, several together, and saw Sheriff Bolton ride into town along with a group of men. They headed straight for the saloon and dismounted. It appeared they had no one in custody.

Max would likely not return before morning. No doubt he would spend the night at the showgrounds, trying to make sure Wolf and his people were truly all right. She was sure Max would hate that their leaving would be a victory for the sheriff and those men who had attacked Wolf and most likely set fire to their encampment.

She considered going to the sheriff with the information she'd gotten from Trula. It was the right thing to do, and she could deliver the information without implicating Trula.

Yes, she thought as she stood and ran her palms over her skirt. But as quickly as she'd come to her decision, just as quickly she realized she was in no state to see anyone. The night air combined with the casual way she'd tossed her clothing aside in her haste to make love with Max had left every piece badly in need of pressing. And her hair was also a mess, haphazardly swept up without benefit of a brush or enough pins to hold it firmly. She touched her face where Max's stubble had left its mark. She was glad she had not insisted on lighting a lamp for her talk with Trula.

Bert. She wondered if he'd returned to the hotel or gone back to the showgrounds after returning the horse and buggy. If he was in the hotel, she could tell him what Trula had revealed. After all, this was his business—his and Max's. Let them handle it.

The clock in the lobby struck the hour. Ten o'clock, and the other Harvey Girls would be saying their good nights and hurrying up to their rooms if they weren't already in bed. She went to her office and picked up a stack of papers and tucked her reading glasses on top of her head. She waited until she heard the kitchen door open and close and the muted laughter of two waitresses returning, then shut the door to her office, clutched the papers to her chest, and walked briskly across the kitchen. "That was a close one, ladies," she said as the clock struck its last bell.

"Yes, Miss E," Melba murmured.

"Good night, Miss E," Nan said as the two girls hurried up the stairs without looking at Emma.

She waited at the foot of the steps until she heard their door close, then went to her room and quickly changed into her nightclothes. She would make her rounds, then get dressed again and go down to Bert's room. If he wasn't there, she would write notes to him and Max and slip them under their doors. Bert had said he would be at breakfast, so she could make sure he'd received the news then.

Her plan was working perfectly until the moment she approached Bert's room. Raising her hand to knock, she heard voices coming from inside—Bert's and Reba's, each raised in anger.

"How can you even think of such a thing?" Bert shouted. "After everything Max has put up with from you."

Reba's voice was equally as loud. "Ha! You two would have nothing without me, and you both know it. Max put up with me, as you say, because he needed me. You both needed me to keep this little farce of a show going. Well, I'm done. I refuse to spend one more day in this one-horse outpost of a town. Pawnee Bill's manager has been after me for months now, and I aim to accept his offer."

"If this is your way of getting Max to pay you more, there's no more money in the till, Reba."

"I don't want his money. I want *him*."

"Well, from what I saw tonight, he's made his choice, and it's not you."

"That uptight, prissy waitress? He'll be bored with her within a week."

Embarrassed to be eavesdropping on a private conversation, Emma stepped away from Bert's door and returned to her room. There, she scribbled notes to Max and Bert and crept back down the stairs to slip them under their doors. She had done her duty. She was very good at that.

Chapter 12

MAX FOUND WOLF SITTING ON THE GROUND IN THE burned-out area that had been the encampment. He chanted softly as tears rolled down his sun-burnished cheeks and wisps of smoke rose occasionally from the devastation. Max sat in the dirt next to him and waited. Even after Wolf stopped his chant, they sat in silence for several minutes. Max waited for Wolf to say something, to let him know he was ready to discuss what had happened.

In the distance, a coyote howled, but otherwise all was silent. The full moon spotlighted the wreckage that surrounded them.

"We're leaving, Max." His friend's voice was raspy, and Max figured he'd inhaled a lot of smoke trying to put out the fire.

"I know. Where?"

Wolf shrugged. "North. The border. Maybe cross into Canada, join up with our people there."

Max nodded. "How can I help?" He wouldn't try to stop this. Even though it had been Wolf's idea to add his people to the show, Max knew he'd asked a lot of Wolf and his family already. This was their decision, and the truth was, in their shoes, he'd do the same.

"It is we who will offer help," Wolf said. "The others have agreed to stay until the new moon."

"I appreciate that, but the truth is, coming here and setting up for the winter was probably a mistake." When Wolf said nothing, Max knew his friend agreed. "I thought if we stayed in one place, maybe we could make a difference in how folks thought about the way things came together on the frontier."

"You need to make a choice, Max. Are you a showman or a teacher?"

"Neither. Just a man who loved what this country once was and hates to see it disappearing."

"We can't live in the past," Wolf said. "But we can shape our future."

"By leaving?"

"We're not running away," Wolf muttered.

"No, I'm not saying that. I've been asking myself if maybe leaving is the answer for me as well."

Wolf looked at him for the first time since Max had sat down. "You?"

Max nodded. "The show is in trouble with or without you, Wolf. Maybe it's time we all found other ways." He didn't mention Ed Brunswick's embezzlement of funds, and there was no need to tell Wolf of his own disenchantment with the life he'd chosen.

"There's still wilderness in Canada," Wolf said. "I expect there's a need for an experienced scout as well."

"Canada?" Max shook his head. Again, the two friends let the night and the silence envelop them.

After a while, Max raised the inevitable question. "Who did this, Wolf?"

The chief's laughter evolved into a cough that contorted his upper body. He wrapped his arms around his body, reminding Max his friend was still healing from the stab wounds he'd suffered. After a moment, Wolf stood and looked around. "We both know who did this, Max, and we both know that nothing is likely to be done to make amends. We just have to be thankful that no one was hurt—or killed."

In his younger days, Max would have berated his friend for giving up, for giving in to the system that had destroyed Wolf's way of life in the name of progress. But these days, he understood. Although Bert had told him the sheriff had made a show of organizing a posse and going after the gang who'd done this, Max understood, as did Wolf, that in the end nothing would come of it. In the end Wolf had to do what was best for his family.

So when Max returned to the hotel, looking forward to getting at least a little sleep, and found Emma's note under his door, he laid it aside. Telling the sheriff what Trula had revealed would do little good and possibly incite the Gilmore kid to more mischief, and this time it would surely go beyond damage to property. This time someone might get badly hurt—or killed. Max hated that there would be no justice for Wolf, but that part of the West had not changed.

He suspected Emma would not understand that, but he had other problems to solve, like how to let the cast and crew know the company was bust and they would need to find other work, and like finding some way to reimburse locals who had bought tickets in advance. A loan was out of the question, even if they offered the train and other property as collateral.

Sitting on the side of his bed, he pulled off his boots. He was dead tired, but knew he'd get little sleep. He closed his eyes and tried to think of anything good that had come out of this day.

Emma.

He hadn't set out to make love to her, not that it hadn't been uppermost in his mind for a week or more. But he'd wrestled with the fact that they had only known each other a short time. He'd said as much to Nick when the two of them were alone, riding across the ranch.

Nick had laughed. "Sounds like me and Grace." Then he told Max the story of their first meeting on a train. "I couldn't take my eyes off her," he'd said. "And then once I found out she was a Harvey Girl, I spent more time and money than I could afford having meals at the hotel just to be around her. Pretty soon we were stepping out, and then Jasper Perkins took a shine to her. I reckon that speeded things up some for us. Life is short, Max, and at our age, I don't see wasting time."

"Trouble is, while I know what I'm feeling toward her, I can't be sure she feels that way about me."

Nick had looked at him like he'd suddenly grown another head. "You're joking, right? I mean why the hell do you think Grace wanted you to come out here today and wanted us to go off riding like this?"

"I thought you were just being neighborly."

"To hear Grace tell it, Emma is every bit as on fire

when it comes to you as you seem to be about her. Grace was worried you might not be right for her—being in show business and all."

Max had bristled at the stereotype. "Not everyone in show business is a scoundrel," he said.

"Understood, but when it comes to Emma, my Grace and their friend Lily are like mama bears. They are determined to help her find true happiness but equally as set on making sure she doesn't make a mistake. Seems to me you might be in the running."

"Does that mean you'll tell Grace I have your stamp of approval?"

"That's the plan. The sooner those two females get Emma married and settled, the simpler my life is going to be."

That talk with Nick coupled with seeing the family all together around the table and his natural affinity for kids of all ages had made the day seem just about perfect. He and Emma had stayed long past the hour he'd thought they might, leading to the ride back to town mostly in darkness. Nick's comment regarding not getting any younger had stayed with him, and he realized if he was ever going to have the life he truly longed for, he'd best get started. So he had confided in Emma the idea he'd not admitted to anyone else—even himself. He was thinking of leaving the show. Of course now that was no longer a choice he could make or not. The show was broke—in more ways than just financial. And one way or another, he would need to find a new way of making a living.

He opened his eyes and stared at the shadows

playing across the ceiling. When he'd pulled the buggy off the main road, his intentions had been to deepen the relationship with Emma through a few kisses and some shared hopes and dreams for the future. But things had gone way beyond that, and with everything that had happened since they'd returned to town, he realized he had no idea if she had begun to have second thoughts. He also realized he had nothing to offer her if indeed she still wanted to be with him.

For that matter, he had nothing to offer anyone he cared about. He and Bert had both thought if they stayed in one place for a while, at least they would save on travel expenses. That had certainly helped, but the truth was they could never recoup what Ed Brunswick had embezzled. And now Wolf packing his people up and leaving would create a greater hole. It wasn't so much that they couldn't cover the performances; it was more the roles Wolf's family played behind the scenes—his mother and sister helping out with the cooking, his brothers and nephews tending livestock and repairing harnesses and saddles. And Wolf himself, who was a master at treating injured animals, getting them ready for the next performance.

Max sat on the side of the bed and glanced around the hotel room. Nothing special, but it was costing them every night he spent there. At least he and Bert could be sharing a room. And Reba? She'd have a fit if he suggested she take up a berth on the train. He buried his face in his hands. He felt a complete failure. A life with Emma? Not in the cards. She deserved so much better than he could ever give her. If he loved her—and he did—he'd leave her.

After a sleepless night, Emma stood before Reba's door, holding the actress's breakfast tray, and knocked. Trula answered, and her eyes widened in surprise.

"I'd like to talk to you as soon as it's convenient," Emma said softly as she moved past her and set the tray on the small table near the window. "I'll be in my office."

"Who's there?" Reba moaned from beneath the covers.

"Breakfast time," Emma said in a cheery voice, and then she left.

As she had assumed, Trula came to her office minutes later. "Miss Reba says to tell you she's not ready for breakfast," she said. "She says to tell you she'll let you know."

"Close the door and sit," Emma said, indicating the chair across from her own.

For once, Trula did as she was told.

"I have been thinking about your situation."

Tears formed on the girl's lashes, but she did not permit them to fall. She tossed her head and put on a brave face. "It's really none of your business."

"I understand that, and yet there was a time when you were under my care, and it occurs to me that I may have failed you. I'd like to make amends for that."

"Why would you do that? Why would you care what happens to me?"

"Because I do. Now let's examine the options you have. You could return to your family—"

"RJ loves me. He'll marry me."

"You've discussed it with him then? The baby and marriage?"

"Not yet." She sucked in a breath, and her expression changed from one of doubt to one of determination. "But he owes me. Not only is this his child I'm carrying, but like you said, he put me in danger. I will not shame my family's good name. RJ will marry me. His father won't want the scandal."

Emma could see at least some of what she'd told Trula had sunk in. She noted that Trula was no longer clutching at a straw that RJ's father liked her, but rather she saw the real truth—that RJ's family would not want the scandal. On the other hand, Trula showed no obvious signs of her pregnancy. If she and RJ were to marry soon, there would be no scandal.

"Trula, I am going to make you an offer, but before I do, I need you to be very, very sure marriage to this man is what you want. He does not love you. We both know that. And the chances he will come to love you are, while not impossible, improbable. In marrying him, you are agreeing to a life that could be one filled with unhappiness. But your child will have a father and a family name that means a good deal in these parts. The question is are you willing to sacrifice your happiness for the security of your child?"

Trula had looked down at her folded hands the moment Emma said RJ did not love her, and she had not looked up. Now she sat frozen in place for a long moment. Emma waited, giving her the time she needed to consider the truth of Emma's hard facts. Finally, she raised her eyes.

"What's the offer?"

"I will ask Father O'Meara to speak to RJ's father on your behalf."

Trula's eyes widened, and her lips seemed incapable of forming a single word. This time, the tears fell.

Emma stood. "I will go with Father O'Meara to meet with Mr. Gilmore, and you need to understand that I will make sure he knows that I am well aware of the part his son played in the burning of the encampment."

"Why?" Trula whispered. "I thought you hated me."

"I will admit you caused me no end of worry, Trula, but hate? I felt responsible for you and concerned for your welfare."

"Thank you," Trula whispered through her sobs. "I'm so sorry. I never meant to—"

"That's enough. The past is gone. What we have is this moment and all the ones to follow. Are you sure, Trula?"

The girl nodded.

"Then I will go see Father O'Meara this afternoon. In the meantime, I suggest you go look in on Miss Reba."

To her surprise, Trula stood and embraced her, clinging to her. "I won't let you down," she sobbed.

"You owe me nothing, Trula, but that baby you're carrying? He or she deserves whatever you need to do to secure a future."

She gave Trula a moment to compose herself, then opened the door.

"There you are," George said, addressing Trula.

"Miss Reba has been hollering for you. Best get up there."

With a meekness Emma had never seen, Trula headed up the back stairs. At the landing, she glanced back at Emma and gave her a half smile.

Emma's heart broke for the young woman. After the night she had shared with Max, she wanted everyone to find what she had found—love that could not be questioned. Feeling lighter than she had since they'd returned to hear the news of the fire, Emma hurried off to the dining room, hoping Max would be there.

He wasn't.

❧

Max strode into Sheriff Bolton's office. The sheriff looked up, clearly surprised.

"Look, Captain," he began. "We did what we could to find the gang that attacked—"

"I'm here on a different matter."

Bolton eyed him suspiciously. "And what matter is that?"

"I want you to arrest Ed Brunswick on a charge of embezzlement. I have the proof needed to make the charge."

"You want me to arrest one of your own people?"

"I let Brunswick go shortly after we arrived in town."

"For embezzlement?"

"For cause," Max replied. He might have allowed the embezzlement to slide, given his years of friendship with Ed, but Ed had been behind the attack on Wolf and probably the fire as well. There was more than one way to get justice.

Bolton shrugged. "No skin off my nose if you want to go after one of your own. I'll take care of it." He stared at Max for a moment. "You're letting this other business go then?"

Max felt his entire body go tense with anger. "Would it do any good to pursue it?" he asked quietly, meeting Bolton's gaze.

"Not really," the sheriff admitted. "That is, not unless we get new information."

"Between you and me, Sheriff, we both know who planned and executed that fire. I kept my word when the chief was attacked. The way I see it, you owe me—and the chief."

Bolton chuckled nervously. "You know how these things work, Captain. Seems like you've come up with a plan that will make sure the guilty pay."

"At least one of them," Max muttered as he slammed on his hat and left.

Next, he headed to the Western Union office. They had a telegraph in the office at the showgrounds, but this would be faster.

"Need to send a telegram," he told the woman behind the counter. She pushed a pad of paper and pencil his way and went back to her work. He addressed his message to his former commander, Tyler Newton, at regimental headquarters, Yellowstone National Park.

SENDING YOU THE SCOUT YOU NEED

STOP CHIEF GRAY WOLF STOP BETTER
THAN ME STOP TAKE HIM AND HIS
FAMILY IN STOP YOU WON'T BE SORRY
STOP

He signed it and pushed the pad of paper across the
counter. The woman read through the message and
nodded. "You expecting an answer?"

"Maybe. If one comes, send it out to the
showgrounds."

She frowned. "Not the hotel?"

"No, ma'am."

"I'll get this sent right away." She sat at the telegraph. "And Captain? I won't be saying anything
about the chief and his people leaving. Been enough
gossip already."

"I appreciate that, ma'am." Max tipped his hat to
her and left.

Two tasks down, three to go. Meet with Frank
Tucker and then with Bert and Reba. And finally,
Emma.

Chapter 13

EMMA MET WITH FATHER O'MEARA THAT AFTERNOON. He persuaded her to let him handle the meeting with the Gilmores, assuring her that while he shared her concerns about Trula's future, marrying RJ was indeed the best solution to the situation. He promised to have an answer for her by the following day.

When she returned to the hotel, Aidan followed her to her office.

"Did you know?" he asked.

"Know what?"

"That the captain and Miss Reba and Mr. Gordon were moving out of the hotel?" Her shocked expression must have been answer enough. "Surprised me as well. He didn't offer a reason, just paid the bill in full and left. Miss Reba was not happy."

"I can imagine. Are they leaving town?"

It was evident this thought had not occurred to Aidan. "I don't think so. I mean, folks have bought tickets and expect to see a show. Besides, they've promised extra tickets because of having to postpone performances once the chief got attacked." Aidan chewed his lower lip. "I thought the captain was an honorable man."

"He is. My guess is that with the fire at the show-grounds, Max is simply circling the wagons, so to speak. He's gathering everyone to make sure they are safe."

Aidan bristled. "They are safe in this hotel."

"Of course, but *being* safe and *feeling* safe are not the same thing. Don't take it personally, Aidan. Max has a lot on his mind right now."

"I suppose." He eyed her for a moment. "How was the visit with Grace and Nick?"

She couldn't help smiling. "It was lovely. Nick and Max were like old friends almost from the moment they met, and the children were at their most charming and—"

"You two were gone a long time," Aidan noted.

She ducked her head and pretended to pick some lint from her sleeve. She could feel the blush building, and she did not want Aidan to see. "Grace insisted we stay for supper, and by the time we said our farewells—"

"You're in love with him, aren't you, Emma?"

There was no point lying. She nodded and looked at Aidan. "I am."

Aidan drew in a breath. "And it appears he returns those feelings from everything I've observed, but Emma, he's a wanderer. That's no life for a woman like you."

"That's not for you to decide," she said softly.

"No, but as someone who has always cared for you and had your best interests in mind, even when those interests did not match my hopes for our future, I would be remiss if I didn't speak my piece."

"And now you have. Aidan, I assure you nothing you can say will be anything I haven't already considered. This may not work out for Max and me, but until I know for certain that it won't, I intend to savor every moment we have. It would mean a lot to me to know you are happy for me."

He gave her the boyish smile that had always endeared him to her, then leaned closer and kissed her cheek. "Just make sure the captain understands that if he breaks your heart, he'll have me and George and at least half a dozen Harvey girls to answer to, not to mention Grace and Lily."

Emma laughed. "I'll pass along that warning."

"Oh, I almost forgot. I had a telegram from Mr. Harvey. His son will be here in two weeks. Needless to say, we want to be sure everything is shipshape. We have a lot of work to do."

Emma gave him a salute. "Right, sir. You can count on me."

Aidan's face softened. "I know that, Emma. I've always known that." And with that he left her office, softly closing the door behind him.

Later in the dining room, Emma went through her routine, checking to be sure all was set for the late afternoon train's arrival. She paused when she came to the table Aidan had held in reserve for Max, Bert, and Reba. There was no reason not to set it for six now that Max and the others had left the hotel.

She collected the necessary dishes, flatware, and linens and arranged the extra places. All the while, she thought of Max. No longer could she count on his returning to the hotel for a meal or to spend the night. He would not be crossing the lobby or showing up unexpectedly in the hotel's backyard. The distance between town and the showgrounds was not that great, and yet it seemed as if miles separated them. She felt a loneliness, not unlike the way she'd felt after Lily left on her honeymoon and Grace went home with Nick to their ranch. She understood that this night when she went up to her room, it would feel different. Max would not be nearby, and there was little chance of seeing him with all he had to deal with.

"Miss Emma?"

Tommy stood at the kitchen entrance to the dining room.

"Hello, Tommy. Do you need something?"

He walked forward and handed her a note. "The captain said I should get this to you right soon as you got back from seeing Father O'Meara. He was real disappointed you wasn't here when he came by, but he said it couldn't be helped. Those were his exact words. 'Couldn't be helped.' That's when he…"

While Tommy rambled on, Emma slid her thumbnail under the seal of the envelope and pulled out the single sheet of hotel stationery. The two words scribbled in haste made her heart take wing.

Sunset tonight?

"Yes," she whispered as she put the note in her apron pocket. "That's fine, Tommy. Thank you for being so prompt. The 4:35 is due any time now.

You'd best head for the station so you can direct the passengers here for their supper."

Tommy took off at a run, nearly colliding with Melba and the other girls as they took up their stations.

Sunset, Emma thought and smiled. Never had she been so anxious to feed a trainload of travelers and send them on their way.

❧

Max sat across from Bert in their boxcar office. For once, Bert was speechless.

"We need to face facts, Bert. Even without Wolf and his people, we might have made a go of it, but Reba leaving is a whole other matter. She's the one half the audience comes to see. We both know that."

"She's bluffing," Bert muttered.

"Not this time. Bill Cody made her an offer she'd be a fool to turn down."

"We can make a counter offer."

Max blew out a long breath. "It's done, Bert. *We're* done."

Just saying that out loud made it suddenly seem so real. Now what? What about Pearl and the others? What about Bert? His partner wasn't a young man. Finding work would be hard.

Bert studied him through the smoke rising from his cigar. "You got a plan? 'Cause you always have a plan, Max."

"I reminded Reba she has a contract with us and that I intend to hold her to that for the next two weeks while we put on the performances folks here have already bought tickets to see. Wolf and his people have agreed to stay as well. We'll do the show exactly as it's supposed to be done."

"But what about the mayor and the sheriff? They aren't likely to appreciate you going back on your word."

"Then let them shut us down, and they can explain to ticket-holders why they can't attend the show they paid hard-earned money to see."

Bert knew better than to argue the point. "That'll give us time to maybe find some new acts," he mused. Then, warming to the idea, added, "There's a fella I saw over in Santa Fe who is real handy with throwing an ax and…"

"I'm done, Bert. We need to use the two weeks to do what we can to find work for the others. As soon as we close the last show, we'll hold an auction, get what we can for everything. That money goes to you, Bertie. It was your business to start. I just came along for the ride—got no stake in it. If you've got the sense God gave you, you'll stop playing games, marry Pearl, and buy yourself a little place somewhere you both like being."

"Pearl won't have me. I've tried. Believe me."

"You've tried taking her to your bed, and she's turned you down. Try asking her to marry you. Try making a commitment. I expect that'll turn the tide."

Bert squinted up at him. "You planning on doing that with Emma?"

"Soon as I have something to offer her. Until then…"

Bert held up his hands. "We'll split the money we raise at auction."

"Nope. Won't be enough to give us both a fresh

start. I'm not a kid, but I'm young enough to find work—work that will give me and Emma a chance."

"And she's agreed to all this?"

"Not yet," Max muttered, looking away. The truth was he didn't know how he was going to explain to her that in two weeks, he'd be leaving her. Surely, once she understood he was going off to find some way to build a life for the two of them, she'd be all right with his decision.

He cleared his throat and stood. "So there's the plan. If you've got other ideas, I'm happy to listen, but I've been over and over this, and I'm pretty sure this is the best thing for everybody concerned." He took his hat from the stand by the open door. "I'm going into town for a while. Don't wait up."

Knowing Bert had a good relationship with the managers of the larger shows, he was pretty sure his friend and partner would get busy sending out feelers for jobs the cast and crew might consider. Buffalo Bill was on an extended tour of Europe. It was the smaller companies like theirs that stood no chance, even if Reba or Wolf hadn't decided to leave. Once again, the world was changing, and once again, Max understood he had to accept that fact.

But he didn't have to like it.

❧

Max was waiting for her when Emma climbed the narrow path that led to the overlook. He looked tired and worried, but the minute he saw her, he stepped forward to take her in his arms. He held her close, his chin resting on her hair. "A lousy day just got a lot better," he said softly.

She looked up at him and stroked his cheek with her fingertips. "Tell me," she said. "Aidan says you and the others have moved out of the hotel."

"Figured we should save some money wherever possible."

"It's that dire?"

"Reba's taken an offer with one of the bigger shows, and Wolf's packing up as well." He hesitated.

"There's more, isn't there?"

"Our advance man, Ed Brunswick, has been skimming money for months now. I stopped by Sheriff Bolton's office earlier and turned him in. I hated doing that. Ed was a friend, someone I once trusted with my life. To have things come to this…"

"Come, let's sit and enjoy the last of the sunset," Emma said, taking his hand and leading the way up the path to the outcropping of rocks and boulders they had come to think of as their special place. They sat side by side, their arms around each other, their eyes on the brilliant display of purple, orange, and gold that lit the sky. She knew what the total of the troubles he'd named meant. "The show will be moving on then," she said softly.

There was a beat as if he were trying to decide what to say. Then, "The show will be closing in two weeks, Emma. We'll honor our commitment here in Juniper and then put everything up for sale. Bert is working on finding jobs for the rest of the cast and crew. Reba has no worries, and Wolf and his people will likely return to the reservation."

"And Bert?" *And you*, she wanted to ask.

He chuckled. "Not sure you knew this, but Bert's had a thing for Pearl for years now. Pretty sure she returns his feelings, but the trouble's always been Bert's got a fear of settling down. He'll get whatever we can raise selling off livestock and the train and such, so I told him now's the time."

"Bert and Pearl? I never guessed, but now that you've told me, I can see it was there in the way she watched him that day we were in the dining tent."

"When we travel—when we used to travel," he corrected himself, "the two of them would always sit together. Bert tried to pretend they were just going over the costumes and fabric orders and such, but they didn't fool any of us."

"I thought you and Bert were business partners, so why are you saying he'll get whatever proceeds there are?"

"It's always been his company. He made a place for me, but in the end, it's his. Only fair."

The sun slipped fully behind the mountains, and shadows enveloped them. Max took her hand. "The others will find their way, Emmie. I want to talk about us."

Us!

Her mind raced with possibilities. He might ask her to come with him once he closed the show. Where would they go? What would their life be like? Of course, she'd need some time. She owed Aidan time enough to find a replacement. Would the two weeks the show was still in town be enough? Not with Mr. Ford Harvey coming to visit. It would be unfair to Aidan or whoever replaced her to leave just then. Nan might be a good choice, and if they promoted her right away, there would be the next two weeks to train her while Max was completing his contract to honor the tickets already sold.

"With any luck, I'll find a good-paying job and be back for you before you know I'm gone." He was clutching her hands in his, and she heard his voice crack with uncertainty.

I'm gone. Not *we're gone?*

"Gone?" Her mind sprang to attention, focusing on what he was saying. He was telling her he was leaving. Another man was leaving without her. "Where?"

"Not sure. I just know there's no work here. Nick says the ranches around here have all the hands they need, and besides, that's no life for us, Emmie. Montana might be a good place to look, or Canada. There's still a lot of open country up there."

Montana was hundreds of miles from Juniper. Canada was probably more than a thousand miles away. Slowly, she slid her hands free of his. "You really don't need to worry about me, Max. I mean, I have a good job right here. And I have friends and…"

He cupped her face with his palms. "Emmie, I'm not going for good. I just have to be sure I can find work that will support us—us and a family one day. I love you, Emmie. You stole my heart the minute I walked into that dining room."

Love.

It was the single word she had longed to hear. But did it mean the same for him as it did for her? After all, she and Max lived in different worlds, traveled on parallel tracks. She released a nervous laugh and felt him pull away. Everything in the way his body tensed was an expression of hurt—and doubt. Too late, she realized he thought he'd misread her feelings. And in that instant, she understood what might be lost if she didn't speak up and reassure him. And yet she could not forget the past and the times she had trusted her feelings before.

She reached out to touch him, taking his hand. "I know you care for me, Max, as I care for you, but this is not the time—"

"This is exactly the time," he said, and his voice shook.

"You can't be sure of that, Max. We've barely known each other a month, and what we've shared has been in the midst of a fairy-tale world you and Bert created. The reality is that we are very different people. You are someone who needs to wander. I am someone who needs the security of a place where I know I can take care of myself if need be."

"*I'll* take care of you." He was close to shouting, and he had gotten to his feet and begun to pace the broad, flat surface of the boulder. He stopped suddenly, and she looked up at him. "Is it because of the other night? Because you're having second thoughts about that?"

"It's just that we have to be practical," she said. "So much is happening, especially for you."

"That's not what I asked you, Emma. Are you sorry we…?"

"No!" She felt her chin quiver and realized she was near tears. "No," she repeated more softly. This was not the way she had wanted this evening to go. "I have no regrets," she added, and that seemed to calm him.

He knelt next to her. "Then what is it?"

"I don't want you to go away," she whispered.

He wrapped his arms around her. "I can't stay here, Emmie. There's no work."

"I have a good job," she reminded him.

"A good job that requires you to remain unmarried as long as you have it. Besides, it may be a new century and all, but I draw the line at having my wife support me." He tightened his hold on her and kissed her temple.

Still, the down-to-earth side of her knew that she was not yet his wife, and by the time he left and found work, he could change his mind. It had happened before. What they had, she realized, was this moment. She could choose to mourn the past, second-guess the future, or live this moment.

Choose now. Choose this day—this moment.

She leaned into Max's arms, her back resting against his chest. "Montana, huh?"

She felt the rumble of his laughter. "Or Canada. I could maybe be one of those Mounties."

"Diablo would probably like that. He does like to strut and show off."

And with that moment of casual teasing, she knew they would be all right. Max was not like her father or the man who'd expected her to wait for him. Max Winslow was the man who had walked into the hotel dining room and straight into her heart.

❧

Max felt the tension of the day melt away as he held Emma and relaxed against a smooth rock. As long as he had her, everything would be all right. It was a new feeling for him—one he had no intention of letting go.

As the wind picked up, he pulled off his jacket and

draped it around her like a blanket. "I'm not leaving for good, Emmie," he said. "I'll be back for you or send for you once I'm settled." She was so still that for one panicked moment, he thought perhaps he had misunderstood the depth of her feelings for him.

"I'll be here," she murmured as she kissed him. "In the meantime, we have two weeks." She kissed him again.

"Do you think Aidan might let me stay one more night in the hotel?" he asked.

"Why, Captain Winslow, what are you suggesting?"

He laughed and stood, pulling her to her feet. "You know exactly what I'm suggesting, Miss Elliott. I am through making love to you on the hard ground." When she hesitated, he added, "Or we can wait."

"That's probably best," she said softly.

"If you think so," he said. When she didn't reply, he added, "We should probably go."

They were nearly back to the hotel when she said, "Of course, there's always my room." Her voice was shaking.

He grinned. "Why, Miss Elliott, what would your girls say?"

"They'd be shocked, of course—but delighted."

And she would lose her job if they were caught. Under the circumstances, it was far too risky. "Tell you what," he said, hugging her. "I'll come up with a plan. Bert says I always have a plan."

"Two weeks," she reminded him. "And we both have things we need to do that will take up much of the time we have."

"Just save the nights for me," he said as he kissed her. "We'll find a way."

Chapter 14

BUT IT WAS AS IF EVERYTHING AND EVERYONE CON-
spired to keep them apart. Emma and her girls spent
hours long after the closing of the dining room each
day, polishing silver and checking the inventory of
linens for tears or dishes for chips. Aidan insisted on
rehearsing his plan for the arrival of Mr. Harvey—a plan
that included an entirely new menu. George and his
staff created one new dish after another, and Emma and
her girls were pressed into service as tasters. Once the
menu was set, they were required to practice serving
it to the housekeeping staff. All this was in addition to
serving locals and four trainloads of travelers each day.

And then there was Trula. Father O'Meara had
persuaded the Gilmores to insist their son do the right
thing, and the wedding was set for the Saturday before
everything at the showgrounds was to be auctioned
off. To Emma's shock, Trula had asked her to witness
the small family ceremony on her behalf.

"I have no one else," Trula had argued. "Please."
She stroked the nearly nonexistent bump of her pregnancy for effect.

"Very well," Emma had agreed, not realizing that Trula's understanding of the role differed greatly from her own.

"We'll need to go shopping," Trula announced. "RJ's mother is letting me wear her gown, but it needs a new veil. I thought we could buy fabric from Mr. Tucker and you could make the veil for me. It would be a lovely wedding present."

So Emma had added the making of the veil to her already staggering list as well as attending a tea Mrs. Gilmore had insisted on hosting on Sunday after church. She was doing her best to make sure the coming marriage had all the earmarks of propriety in spite of the fact no one in town doubted for a moment it was being done out of necessity.

Max had not been happy. They had just two Sundays before he would leave, and now one of those would be taken up by the tea. Of course, Max was as tight for time to spend with Emma as she was with him. He was preoccupied with filling holes left by members of the cast and crew who had decided to leave the show before it shut down. Alongside the decimated crew, he took on the work of caring for the livestock and maintaining the grounds to make sure everything was ready for each performance. And then, because those remaining players, including Reba, needed to take on additional roles, Pearl was overwhelmed with costume alterations. Hearing this, Emma offered her help.

"You've got enough to do," Max argued one night as they sat on the veranda after an exhausting day.

"At least I'll get to see you," she replied. "You can bring me the work and pick it up."

"Better than nothing, I suppose," Max grumbled.

Knowing the show was closing, Emma had bargained with Aidan for time for the staff to see a performance—a reward for all the extra work they were doing. Reluctantly, Aidan had agreed.

"But keep in mind, our service to the public and our hotel guests cannot be interrupted."

"We'll manage," Emma assured him, and she divided her staff into teams—one to handle the breakfast and supper shifts and the other the busiest time of day, lunch. She worked out new procedures with George that would make service behind the scenes more efficient. Every night as she climbed the stairs, mentally and physically exhausted, she tried not to count down the days until Max would leave. She longed for one last opportunity to lie in his arms, to inhale his scent, to feel his touch, and store all of it for those lonely days and nights when they would be apart.

But their times together were limited to stolen kisses on the veranda and a quick caress when he came to pick up the alterations she'd finished or drop off work for Pearl. They talked of meeting again at their special place, but there was no time, and she knew Max was every bit as frustrated as she was. Perhaps because of everything that seemed designed to keep them apart, Emma found herself believing they would one day find their way and be together.

On the Sunday of the tea for Trula, Emma dressed for church with special care. Her clothing choice had to be appropriate not only for church but also for an afternoon spent at the Gilmore ranch where she would mingle with men and women who up to now had known her only as one of the waitresses serving them whenever they chose to dine at the hotel. Once she had gotten through the afternoon's events, Max would be waiting for her.

She heard little of the church service, her mind and heart fixated on that moment when she and Max would finally be alone. He did not come to church, and neither did anyone else from the cast or crew. They had already begun to scatter, and Max had told her the showgrounds had taken on the atmosphere of a ghost town, the dining tent more than half-empty these days. Following the service, Trula waited with the Gilmores outside the church. Emma and Father O'Meara had been invited to take the noon meal with them and stay for the afternoon.

When Emma emerged from the church, she saw Trula waving to her. She was dressed in one of Reba's castoffs—a wedding present from the actress. Her husband-to-be stood next to her, looking surly and distracted. For a moment, Emma considered asking Father O'Meara if she might ride to the ranch with him, but then Mrs. Gilmore waved her forward.

"Come along, Emma," she chided. "We have a good deal to do before the guests arrive later this afternoon."

Emma had not fooled herself into thinking she was to be a guest in the same sense as the others who would attend the party. Mrs. Gilmore had made several comments about relying on Emma's expertise when it came to managing such events. Mr. Gilmore helped his wife into their buggy, then climbed in after her. Reluctantly, RJ accepted the hand Trula held out to him and assisted her into the facing seat. When it was clear he was prepared to climb in after her, leaving Emma standing beside the carriage, Mr. Gilmore frowned and muttered something to his son.

RJ looked down at her and, from his seat, extended a hand to pull her aboard. "Didn't realize the hired help expected to ride," he muttered for her ears only as she took her place next to Trula.

"RJ," Trula reprimanded in a whisper.

"Shut up, woman," he snarled and slumped down in his seat, angling his body as far as possible from his future bride.

The elder Gilmores pretended to hear none of this. Mrs. Gilmore smiled brightly at Emma as Mr. Gilmore ordered their driver to move on.

Sunday dinner at the Gilmores was a pretentious affair with Mrs. Gilmore ringing a small bell and a uniformed maid serving each course. Thankfully, Father O'Meara kept the conversation going, discussing plans for a new school with Mr. Gilmore and complimenting Mrs. Gilmore on the meal. Through it all, RJ sulked, and Trula's smile was so artificial and constant, Emma was not sure how she managed to chew the stringy meat served as the main course.

When the meal finally ended, Mrs. Gilmore suggested the gentlemen retire to the veranda with their cigars while the ladies prepared for their guests. So Emma was surprised when RJ sidled up next to her as the group rose from the table and murmured, "This is all your fault. I don't forget a thing like that."

Emma glanced up at RJ, who was a head taller and

as solidly built as his father was. "Is that a threat?" she managed.

His smile was triumphant. "You bet it is." He moved past her, still smiling, and kissed his mother's cheek. "Good grub, Mama."

Mrs. Gilmore tittered with delight. "Oh, you," she said, her expression one of relief and sheer adoration of her only child.

Emma watched as he joined his father and the priest, his demeanor suddenly attentive and respectful as he followed the older men outside. Just before he closed the double doors leading to the courtyard, he caught Emma's eye, glaring at her with a malevolence that made her shiver in spite of the close room and sunny day.

This was the man who had beaten and stabbed Wolf and set fire to the encampment. Once crossed, he was capable of unspeakable actions, and now he'd made it clear he'd set his sights on her.

She jumped at the sound of a crash from the kitchen.

"Emma, dear," Mrs. Gilmore called, her voice shaking. "Could you come, please? I'm afraid we've had a bit of a disaster."

"A bit of a disaster" turned out to be shattered teacups all over the kitchen floor and Trula in tears.

"I never meant... I was just trying to help."

"Clumsy girl," Mrs. Gilmore muttered as she surveyed the mess. "Well, don't just stand there. Get a broom and clean up this mess." This was directed at Emma.

A retort was at the tip of Emma's tongue when she

caught Trula's imploring look. Glancing around, she saw the maid who had served the meal hovering in a corner. "Could you bring a broom please?" she said kindly and then bent to pick up some of the larger shards of china, her mind racing as she tried to come up with some way to salvage the day. "Trula, do you remember the recipe for lemonade we use at the hotel?"

Trula nodded.

"My guests have been invited for *tea*," Mrs. Gilmore reminded them.

"On such a warm day, could not the tea be iced," Emma suggested, "and guests offered a choice of tea or lemonade? After all, you have the finger food they will expect. The cold beverages might be a lovely surprise."

"Oh, Mother Gilmore," Trula trilled as she held a dustpan for the maid who was sweeping up the smaller debris, "just think—everyone will be singing your praises."

"Well, I suppose," the older woman said, tapping her forefinger on her chin as she considered the idea. "Given my husband's standing in the community, it would not be out of the question for me to lead the way in social situations."

Emma and Trula exchanged a look as they got to their feet. "You'll be the talk of the town," Trula assured her. "Now, don't you fret. Miss E and me will take care of everything. Why don't you go lie down for a bit?"

"Yes, a nap will calm me," Mrs. Gilmore agreed, edging toward the door with a last look at the now-cleared floor. "That was my best china," she added.

"RJ and I will replace it," Trula assured her.

Emma watched the exchange and realized that Trula understood the magic of invoking RJ's name.

"Oh no, my dear. We can't have you young people spending your hard-earned money on such trivial things as teacups. RJ will insist, I know, but you must persuade him his money is for the baby—and you, of course."

Just then, RJ stepped into the kitchen. "We heard a crash." His eyes went straight to Emma.

"It was me, darling," Trula said, taking his arm. "I'm afraid I was clumsy and—"

"Nonsense," Mrs. Gilmore declared. "Trula had a brief spell of dizziness. Unfortunately, she was holding a tray of teacups at the time. It's a wonder she wasn't hurt when they shattered. You should take her into the parlor to rest, RJ."

And away they all went—Mrs. Gilmore down the corridor to what Emma assumed were the bedrooms, and Trula, clinging to RJ and feigning weakness, to the parlor. That left Emma and the kitchen maid to figure out a plan for serving guests iced beverages instead of the hot tea they would be expecting. If Emma had held doubts regarding the wisdom of Trula's insistence on joining the Gilmore family, it disappeared with this exchange. It appeared Trula would be just fine.

❧

Max was still waiting to hear from his former commanding officer about a possible job for Wolf. But when he told his friend what he'd done, Wolf rejected the idea.

"I'm going home, Max."

"A reservation isn't home," Max argued. "This is your chance to settle in a place where you and your family will be free."

"Home is where my people are, and right now, they are living on a reservation, which makes that home."

Max shook his head. "Sometimes you have a logic that defies understanding for a man like me."

"And sometimes you have a need to put the hardships of others ahead of your own that is equally as frustrating to me, my friend." Wolf's concern for Max was evident in the furrows lining his brow.

"I'll be all right," Max replied, although he wasn't at all sure he would be. The skills he had did not seem to fit in the more modern world that was already cemented in this new century. These days, there wasn't a lot of call for someone who was good at tracking or handling a six-shooter.

On Sunday, he spent the morning with Bert, going over the books and counting every penny they would need to close out the show. The good news was Bert had managed to line up a number of businessmen interested in the auction. Max's friend, Ford Harvey, had found a buyer for the train.

"We're gonna be able to pay everybody and have some left," Bert reported.

"That money is for you and Pearl to make a fresh start."

Bert blushed. "She got herself a job sewing for that hat shop in town, so I guess we're staying."

"Have you asked her to marry you?"

"I'll get to it," Bert muttered.

Max rolled his eyes.

Bristling, Bert stubbed out his cigar. "You gonna lecture me about what I should be doing? What about you and Miss Emma?"

"None of your business," Max grumbled.

"What's good for the goose, my friend."

"She knows how I feel."

"So does Pearl, but that don't stop you from dogging me about getting down to doing right by her."

Max gritted his teeth. "Emma understands that I need to have the means to give her the life she deserves, Bert."

His friend shrugged. "If you say so." He stood and slapped on his bowler. "I'm going to town to post the notices about the auction and last show. Might sell a few more seats."

Max nodded, then realized Bert was still standing in the open door of the office. "Something else?"

"Yeah. Wanted to say how much I...that is, me and Pearl appreciate what you're trying to do for us. Rest of the players and crew feel the same. You're a good man, Max." Not waiting for Max's response, he hurried down the steps and headed for the corral.

Max sat at his desk, staring at the mounds of paperwork stacked there. He made an attempt at tackling the lineup for the final show, then leaned back in his chair and removed the wire-rimmed glasses he wore. He massaged the bridge of his nose and closed his eyes. The conversation with Bert had struck a nerve. What kind of future did he and Emma have?

Ford Harvey had offered Max a job when the

businessman sent word he'd found a buyer for the train. But sitting in an office—sitting inside anywhere—was not something Max thought he could ever be good at. Just sitting at the desk now, he longed to be outside. But was that being fair to Emma? If he truly loved her—and he did—wouldn't he make sacrifices? Do whatever it took for the two of them to be together?

He pushed himself away from the desk and stood in the open doorway. He knew that right after church, she'd gone to the Gilmore place. He'd tried to persuade her not to go.

"Trula Goodwin has not exactly been nice to you," he pointed out.

"She has no family here. She puts on a good act, but I think she's feeling scared and alone."

That was one of the things he loved most about Emma. She was always looking out for her girls—even the ones who gave her trouble. But he didn't have to like the time she was stealing from them to take care of Trula. He closed the door to the boxcar that housed the office and stood outside looking at what remained of the business that had been his life these past years.

When he saw Reba leaning on the corral fence and feeding her horse a carrot, he decided to join her. They'd been through a lot together, and while his feelings for her were not what she'd hoped for, she was a friend. These days, friends were especially important.

"You all packed?" he asked as he came alongside her.

"I've got a week of shows to perform unless you've decided to let me leave early," she grumbled. She was in one of her moods, so Max knew to tread carefully.

"You've made a good move, joining up with Pawnee Bill's outfit," he said. "They're getting the best and a worthy opponent for Buffalo Bill's Annie Oakley."

She glanced up at him. "You really think so?"

"Yep. I reckon Miss Oakley had best watch out, 'cause there's a new sharpshooter coming."

She gave her horse the rest of the carrot and wiped her hands. "Do you think we'll ever be good enough, Max?"

"You're the best, Reba. We both know that."

"I don't mean performing. I mean good enough for decent folks to accept us with more than a fake smile."

"*We're* decent folks," he said.

She shrugged. "Apparently not decent enough for me to be invited to that fancy party given for Trula today."

Max's heart went out to her. This was hardly the first situation where Reba or another performer had been outwardly embraced and fawned over but deemed not proper enough to be invited into the home of one of the show's backers or a local dignitary.

"Trula's pregnant," she continued. "Pregnant and not married. How does that make her better than me?"

"My understanding is this whole thing today was to cover up that fact until she and the Gilmore kid could be married. Come on, Reebs, you know how this goes. Whirlwind wedding and a baby that comes *early*."

She snorted. "If Trula had the sense God gave a horsefly, she'd come with me and forget all about marrying that man. Have you met him?"

"Not exactly."

"Well, I have. He came to my tent one afternoon after the show pretending to be looking for Trula. But he wasn't at all. He was looking for me. Before I could say Jack Frost, that boy had me backed up against my dressing table with his hands all over me."

"You should have told me."

"I handled it, Max. That's what girls like me learn to do. I gave him a hard knee to the place I knew it would hurt most, and by the time he caught his breath, I had the barrel of my pistol pressed against his forehead."

Max swallowed a chuckle as he envisioned the scene. "What happened?"

"What do you think happened? He slinked off like the wounded rat he was. Never saw him again after that."

"And you wanted to attend a party at his parents' ranch—a party where he would be?"

She grinned. "I thought it might be fun. We have little enough of that, hard as we work, Max. I could just see the look on the mother's face when I showed up. And then there's the mister. He's been less forward, but I've seen him looking at me when we happened to be in the hotel lobby or dining room at the same time. Let's just say like son, like father."

Max laughed and wrapped his arm around her shoulders. "Ah, Reebs, you do keep us all on our toes."

They stood that way in comfortable silence for a moment before Reba said, "I know it would never have worked for you and me, Max, but if you ever need a friend…"

He hugged her a little tighter. "I've got you," he finished. "You've no idea how much that means to me, Reba."

She pulled away and smoothed her hands over her skirt. "Besides, I'm going to be in the money, and if you need a job, maybe I can—"

"Good to know," Max said and kissed her cheek. "Thanks for staying and seeing this through, Reebs."

She stepped back, put her hands on her hips, and gave him a saucy smile. "Are you saying you would have let me out of my contract, Captain?"

"Probably," he replied, laughing. "When it comes to you, I've always been a soft touch."

She patted his cheek. "We're family, Max. Don't forget that. Now, my guess is you were on your way to town to see that waitress when you spotted me out here feeling sorry for myself, so you'd best get going. She has a curfew, you know."

He decided not to mention that Emma had been included in the guest list for Trula's party. Instead, he squeezed his costar's hand and whistled for Diablo to come to him. Reba was right about one thing. Emma would be back eventually, and he intended to be waiting for her.

⚭

By the time she and Father O'Meara left the Gilmores, Emma was more certain than ever that RJ intended to make good on his threat. She considered confiding her fears in the priest, but what could he do? And she couldn't tell Max. He had enough to deal with without worrying about her safety. No, she would just have to be careful never to be alone or away from the hotel after dark.

Everyone knew the show was closing down and that everyone associated with it would move on to other pursuits. Emma suspected RJ would do nothing until he was sure Max was gone. Of course, she could always confide in Aidan—or George.

"Are you unwell, Emma?" Father O'Meara asked, glancing sideways at her as he drove the buggy.

She forced a smile. "It has been a tiring day," she said.

He chuckled. "In more ways than one. I will admit after spending time with those young people, I am having doubts about their future. Still, the important thing is to protect the child."

Emma was not sure she agreed a life with RJ would be best for any child, but clearly the wedding was moving forward and, short of RJ running off, looked likely to occur. "I'll admit to having had concerns about Trula stepping out with that young man from the start. But she's convinced she can change him and that in time he will come to care for her."

"When it comes to matters of the heart, not everyone is as blessed as you and Captain Winslow seem to be." He smiled. "I am happy for you both."

His kindness and support relaxed her, and for the remainder of the ride back to town, Emma put aside thoughts of Trula as well as RJ's threat. Instead, she confided the plans she and Max had made for him to head north seeking work and her hope to follow once he'd found something.

"Until then, I have my work here," she told him.

"Indeed. I'm not sure you appreciate how much you have become a treasured part of the community, Emma. We will be sad to see you leave us when the time comes—sad and pleased for you at the same time." As he pulled the buggy up to the hotel, he patted her hand. "I hope you and the captain will find all the happiness you deserve, Emma."

"Thank you, Father."

"Ah, here is your young man now," the priest said. "I leave you in safe hands, my dear."

His choice of the word *safe* brought back the memory of RJ's threat and the realization that RJ did not always go after his intended target directly. In the case of the fire, he had attacked those people Wolf loved.

Max came toward her, stopping first to shake hands with Father O'Meara and then coming around to help her from the buggy. What if something were to happen to Max because of her? She couldn't bear that.

"You're trembling. Are you cold?" he asked as she took his arm and they walked up the path to the veranda.

"Not with you beside me." She tunneled her hand into the bend of his elbow and moved closer. "I am so happy to see you."

He wrapped his free arm around her. "Bad day?"

"It has been a very long day," she admitted. "But tell me how things are going for you and the others."

"That's my girl, always thinking about somebody else." He kissed her temple as they sat in the rocking chairs they favored on the veranda. "We've got three more shows this coming week and then the auction. I think most everybody still around is ready to move on."

"Are you?"

He was holding her hand and gripped it tighter. "I'm the exception, maybe because I've got a very good reason to not want to leave."

As much as she wanted him to stay and find work closer to Juniper, she understood that would only work in the short term. And as much as she was haunted by previous abandonments by men she had trusted, Max was not either of those men. "You'll find us a place," she assured him. "And once you do, wild horses will not keep me from coming to join you."

"To marry me?" He released her hand and knelt before her, fumbling in the pocket of his vest for a small velvet box he placed in her hand. "Will you marry me, Emmie?"

She opened the hinged lid of the box and saw by the light spilling from the lobby onto the veranda a gold ring with a small turquoise stone. Never in her life had she felt so full of joy. His face was in shadow, but she knew every inch of it. "Yes," she whispered as she removed the ring from its case and slipped it on. The fit was perfect, and that seemed an omen not to be taken lightly. Max got to his feet and drew her up from her chair and into his arms.

"I love you, Emma," he said, his voice raspy with emotion.

"And I, you," she said, her own voice trembling as she was struck by the realization that time was no factor when two people were meant to be together. She and Max may have only known each other for a little over a month, and yet she had never been more certain of anything. "And so the adventure that is us begins," she whispered as much to herself as to him.

"We could go to Father O'Meara tonight and ask him to marry us," Max said.

Never in her life had Emma wanted so much to

stifle her practical nature, but the truth was this was no time to go against reason. "I would have to leave my job," she reminded him.

"And come with me," he said.

"And where would we live and what would I do? You need to find work that will make you happy and provide for our future. If I stay here, I can save my earnings toward helping us settle once you have that."

He released a breath of frustration. "Are you always going to be this sensible?"

"It's my nature, I'm afraid."

He chuckled and hugged her closer. "And it's a good thing one of us has that trait. You'll keep me and our children on the straight and narrow, Emmie."

"Oh, and you will lead them astray?"

"At the moment, the only person I'm interested in leading astray is you." He kissed her—a kiss that held promise and passion. When it ended, he ran his fingers lightly over the features of her face as if he wanted to remember every detail. "Emmie, we have one week before I go."

"A week when both of us will be incredibly busy," she reminded him.

"We'll find time," he promised, kissing her again.

"Yes," she whispered, returning his kiss, opening to him, wanting as much of him as she could gather before he was gone.

"Next Sunday—all night," he murmured.

"Yes," she agreed, knowing in her heart what he was proposing. They would lie together once more before he had to leave.

Chapter
15

EVERY MORNING THAT WEEK, RJ GILMORE TOOK HIS
breakfast at the counter and lingered for some time
over his coffee. He flirted with Nan and Melba, who
smiled politely but found ways to ignore him. Emma
was not fooled by his presence. His intent was to
intimidate her. Well, she would not allow that. She
went about her duties as normal, offering RJ and
the other patrons at the counter her usual courteous
greeting as she passed. And every time she passed, RJ
muttered some comment, meant to be overheard by
those sitting nearby.

"There she goes, the captain's woman" was among
his milder remarks. "Acting all proper, but word has it
she's not so prim when stepping out."

Aidan caught an especially raunchy comment one
morning and confronted Emma. "I'm going to speak
to that young man's father," he declared. "I don't
care how much money and influence they have,
Mr. Harvey's son is on his way here and we cannot
have—"

"I'll handle it," Emma assured him.

"You'll speak to Max? Because we both know he would not tolerate such rudeness."

"I said I would handle it. Max has enough on his hands. Please leave him out of this."

She handled it by staying away from the lobby where the counter was located. She worked in her office and the dining room, seeing the girls in those places if she needed to speak with them. After two days of this, RJ apparently gave up, for Nan reported he was not at the counter on Friday, the day the girls were to attend the show.

Aidan had decided to close the food service at the counter and the dining room after lunch and have the entire staff attend one matinee rather than trying to cover with half a staff. Only one train would be affected, and he'd had the kitchen prepare luxurious boxed meals for those travelers to pick up and take with them as they continued their journeys.

The one thing he required was that all managers be available at the hotel in the event of an emergency. So on Friday after lunch, Emma saw her girls pile into wagons along with the men from the kitchen staff and the women from housekeeping. She waved to them as they left, their excitement evident in their laughter as they drove away. Back inside, the hotel seemed unusually quiet. Most of the guests had gone out for the day, some to the performance and others out shopping.

Emma returned to her office. There were reports to complete and schedules to make. Outside her office door, she heard George preparing the dough for the rolls and bread he would bake the following day. She knew Aidan was probably also working on reports and schedules in his office next to the front desk, ready to spring into action the second a guest came or went.

"Emma?" George knocked on her partially open door and stepped inside. "I need to check the meat in the smokehouse. You'll be all right here?"

Emma laughed. "Why wouldn't I be?"

George frowned. "I don't like the way that Gilmore boy has been hanging around."

"Oh, that." She waved off his concern. "He's a bully, George, and we both know what cowards bullies really are."

"I'll let Aidan know you're back here on your own. I shouldn't be long—maybe half an hour."

"You're making far too much of this, but thank you. I'll be fine."

He didn't look convinced. "How about you lock this door once I leave, and I'll let you know soon as I get back?"

"Now you're the one alarming me, George."

"Better safe than sorry," he replied as he stepped into the kitchen and turned the lock on her door before shutting it and testing it.

Emma was touched by his concern, although she felt perfectly safe in her office. After all, it was the middle of the afternoon. She returned to working on her reports. Once, she heard a sound—the back screen door opening and closing—but thought little of it.

As promised, George returned and knocked to let her know he was back. She stacked her papers and stood, stretching her back before opening her office door. Stepping into the kitchen, she accepted a glass of cold water George offered, then went to the lobby to give the reports to Aidan so he could include them with his. The plaza was quiet, and there was little traffic moving on the street.

"I think I'll go lie down for a bit before the four o'clock train arrives," Emma said.

"George and I can handle the box suppers, Emma," Aidan said. "Take the rest of the day. You've certainly earned the break."

"Thanks," she replied and retraced her steps through the kitchen and up the back stairs to her room.

The door was unlocked.

She was sure she had secured it before she went down for the day. Gently, she pushed it fully open, staying where she was in the hall. "Hello?" she called.

Silence.

She glanced around. With the other girls all away, the hallway was deserted. Gingerly, she entered her room, leaving the door open. Slowly she allowed her gaze to cover the space—her dresser where her brush and comb and other toiletries were lined up properly. Her writing table near the window, the chair pushed back as always. Her bed precisely made.

She gasped. Next to her pillow was the largest, hairiest spider she'd ever seen. The thing stood on several black-and-orange striped legs and seemed to be watching her.

Swallowing a scream, she retreated into the hall and closed the door, then ran down the stairs, almost stumbling in her haste.

"Emma? What on earth?" George looked at her with alarm.

"Spi…spi…" Unable to form the word, she pointed up the stairs.

George, sensing her panic, grabbed a butcher knife and headed up the stairs. "Stay there," he ordered.

She didn't listen but followed him. "It's gigantic," she said, finding her voice at last. "And it's on my bed."

Carefully, he turned the knob on her door and then threw the door wide open, wielding the knife as if expecting an attack.

Emma eased into the room behind him. George motioned her to stay where she was and then glanced around. His eyes finally settled on a chipped vase Emma used when she collected wildflowers on her walks.

George set down the knife and picked up the empty vase. "He's a big guy all right."

"Careful," she warned. "Does he bite?"

"Oh, that he does," George replied, his voice low and soothing as he set the vase gently over the spider. "Tarantula," he murmured as he pressed the vase into the mattress, trapping the spider.

"Now what?" Emma asked.

"Find me something hard and flat—that book might do the trick." He nodded toward the slim book of poetry Emma's mother had sent her for Christmas.

Emma passed George the book. He slid it carefully under the mouth of the vase.

"Okay, move away from the door," George said as he held the trapped spider as far away from his body as possible. Emma was only too happy to oblige.

Slowly, George edged his way to the hall. Emma

shivered as the thing started slowly crawling up the side of the clear vase.

"You're not going to kill it, are you?" Emma asked, suddenly feeling a little sorry for the spider, which obviously hadn't deliberately entered her bedroom.

"Naw. We'll let him go on his way." After they got outside, he carefully set the vase on the ground and lifted it. The tarantula sat for a moment on the poetry book and then scuttled away.

George ran his handkerchief across his forehead and grinned. "No harm done. That fella knows he dodged a bullet. I expect he won't be back this way any time soon."

"Thank you, George. I don't know how on earth the thing got in my room to begin with," she lied. She knew exactly what had happened. The door she'd heard open and close earlier, the spider positioned precisely in the middle of her bed. RJ Gilmore had sent her a message. "Let's keep this little incident between the two of us, all right? I mean, I don't want to upset the other girls."

George nodded and picked up the book and handed it to her, along with the vase. "You'll want to give these a good wipe before you use them again. Tarantulas are poisonous, though never heard of anyone dying from a bite or the venom."

"Thank you again. I don't know what I would have done."

George shrugged. "Good thing he decided to take a nap right on your bed. If you'd sat down on that bed maybe to change your shoes or something, no telling what he mighta done."

She shuddered at the thought. She stepped aside to let George pass.

Back upstairs in her room, Emma crossed to the window and raised it, leaning on the sill as she gulped in air. Then her legs seemed to give out, and she sank onto the chair at her writing table. RJ had made his point.

❦

Max counted down the shows left to perform—just two to go. Today and tomorrow, and then...

The future stretched before him like the vast unknown territory he had explored in his younger years. At an age when most men were settled into their work, many with homes and families, he would be starting over. His refusal to consider making a life for himself in the new modern world had cost him. Now, he'd found everything he'd ever hoped for in Emma, and he had nothing to offer. All this ran through his mind as he went through the motions of performing. He saw the smiles of the crowd, heard their wild applause, even kissed Reba in the finale, but it was all done by rote.

After he and the rest of the cast had lined up outside the performance arena to shake hands with the patrons, he headed back to the show's office. He wanted to see what Bert had to report about interest in the auction and finding work for anyone left who needed it.

"You got a wire," Bert announced the minute he stepped inside the office. "That Newton fella up there in Yellowstone seems to think Wolf's coming to work for him. Wants to know when." He arched an eyebrow. "Thought Wolf turned that down."

"He did. I figured it was all over." Max read through the telegram, and then he grinned. "Wonder if he'd still take me?"

"Be a durned fool not to," Bert replied. "Want me to send the reply?"

"Yeah. Tell him if I'll do, I'll be there by late next week."

Expertly, Bert tapped out the message. "Now what?" Max shrugged. "I guess we wait for his decision."

They didn't have to wait long. Within half an hour, the telegraph started to click. Bert pulled the ribbon slowly out as the words formed. "Says you'll do fine." He waited, but the machine was silent. "That's it."

Max felt as if the weight of a thousand buffalo blankets had been lifted from his shoulders. "I've got a job," he whispered and couldn't seem to stop a grin from spreading across his face. He grabbed Bert and hauled him to his feet, leading him in an impromptu waltz around the office.

"Stop that," Bert protested, shrugging him off and sticking out his hand. "Congratulations, Max. Seems like things are gonna turn out all right for everybody."

"Got to love a happy ending," Max said. "I gotta tell Emma," he announced and gave a whoop of joy that had everybody still on the grounds wondering just what their boss had to be so happy about.

Not wanting to give Diablo extra duty after the show he'd just performed, Max saddled one of the spare horses and took off for town. He pushed the horse hard, anxious to tell Emma the good news.

Yellowstone.

She'd said it had been a dream of hers to visit the

park. He wondered how she might feel about living there. Of course, he had no idea if there would be housing for a married man.

And what about once they had kids?

He had a lot of questions, but somehow it would all work out. He was sure of it. With Emma by his side, he could make anything work. His heart swelled with his love for her. Never could he have imagined such a feeling of happiness and fulfillment. The last few weeks, it had been as if everything was going wrong. He'd felt such a failure, but not tonight. Tonight he believed he'd conquered the world—or at least his little corner of it.

Arriving outside the hotel, he realized he was still in costume, catching the eye of passersby as he hurried up the front path and entered the lobby. Aidan was at his usual post.

"Captain?"

"Where's Emmie?" Max asked, glancing toward the closed double doors of the dining room, then into the reading room.

"I believe she's in her office," Aidan replied, coming around the desk to stand in front of Max. "Are you all right, Captain? You seem quite agitated."

"That's happiness, my friend," Max declared as he clapped the hotel manager on the back and headed for the kitchen and Emma's office.

She was standing in the midst of papers and files. Her hair was coming undone from its usual neat upsweep, a tendril curling close to her lips. When she saw—or more likely heard—his approach, she turned.

"Max, what on earth?"

"How would you feel about going to Yellowstone?" he asked.

"You mean a visit?"

"A life, Emmie," he crowed as he swept her up into his arms and spun around with her. "Our life. Living there, raising our family there."

Her expression shifted from confused to disbelieving and then to the same delight he knew she saw on his face. "Do you mean it?"

"Well, I have a job there. Not sure of the pay, but I expect it'll be enough for us to get a good start. Question is, are you ready for it?"

"Yes," she said happily.

"It won't be like here. It's an army base, not a town, and I'm not even sure they've got a place for a married man to bring his wife and raise a family, but if you're willing—"

"Yes," she repeated and pushed his hat back so she could kiss him.

Behind them, he heard George clear his throat and the titter of a bunch of Harvey Girls drawn down the service stairs by the commotion. Emma saw them as well and broke the kiss as the most becoming pinkish-rose color crept up her neck to her cheeks. "Put me down, Max," she pleaded in a whisper.

"Nope." He turned to face their audience—the girls clustered together in the stairway, George at the sink, and Aidan standing with his arms folded in the doorway that led out to the lobby. "You folks may as well know right now. I've asked Miss Elliott to be my wife, and she's agreed to do just that."

There was a mixed chorus of protest and pleasure

from the girls, and Max held up the hand he had around Emma's back. "Plenty of time for you young ladies to do whatever it is you females think necessary for setting up a wedding. I have to go away for a bit, get things settled in my job and such. I'm sure I can rely on all of you to make sure Emmie here is well looked after while I'm away?" He included George and Aidan in this question.

Everyone nodded.

"See, everybody's on board, Emmie."

"Maxwell," she said sternly, "put me down. Now."

He did as she asked but kept his arm around her waist as her girls hurried forward to offer their best wishes. After a moment, he managed to extricate himself from their midst and stand with George and Aidan.

"You're a lucky man, Captain," George said.

"Damn lucky," Aidan muttered as he left to attend to whoever was repeatedly ringing the bell at the front desk.

❧

Emma could not recall a time when she had felt so happy. Even the incident with the spider could not dampen her sheer joy at the news that one day soon, she and Max would embark on their life together in a place she had always wanted to see. Questions whirled through her brain like a carousel. Where would they live? What would it be like living in a military community? Would there be other wives? Or would she and Max live in a nearby town since he was not a soldier?

At last, the adventure I've dreamed of, she thought, not at all daunted by the fact that she had no idea what lay ahead. What mattered was that she and Max would face the future together. Max would go first and get everything settled while she made sure there was someone properly trained to take her place, and then...

She barely heard the excited chatter of the other waitresses, her gaze meeting Max's as he stood with George, watching her. Melba was going on about the need to organize a party while Nan ruminated about what Emma might wear.

"Ladies, please," Emma said, smiling at them. "There's time for all of that. Right now..."

The girls followed her glance toward Max.

"Of course," Melba announced. "Come on, everybody. Time for us to go upstairs and leave Miss E and the captain alone." She herded the others away, looking back once as they passed Max and giving Emma a knowing wink.

As soon as the Harvey Girls headed upstairs, Max took Emma's hand, and they walked through the lobby and out onto the veranda. He moved their chairs so that they faced each other. After they'd sat down, he leaned forward and took her hands in his. "Happy?" he asked.

"Very much so," she replied. "Oh, Max, I have so many questions."

"Such as?"

"Where will we live? Are any of the other soldiers or officers married? Are there children?"

He caressed her cheek. "I'll find out when I get there."

His answer was a reminder that in just a few days, he would leave and be gone for some time while he made the journey to the park and learned more about the position he'd been offered.

"You'll write me every day?"

"I'll write," he promised, "but some days I might be out in the wild and unable to post the letter."

"But you'll write? I want to know everything— what you see and hear and what the people are like."

"Every detail," he promised. "And as soon as I get settled and find a place for us, I'll send for you, and we'll be married."

"There?" This was an idea she had not considered. She had always thought her wedding would be in Juniper with Grace and Lily attending her and all the people she'd come to know over the years she'd lived in the town celebrating with her.

"We could be married before I leave," he said softly. "Thursday?"

"That's less than a week," she protested. "How can I possibly…?"

He stopped her protest with a gentle kiss. "It's a formality, Emmie. In my mind, we were bound to each other that night after we visited Grace and Nick. Let's make it official and get on with our lives."

When he said it like that, all the fuss and bother that usually came with planning a wedding seemed trivial. "Everyone will be disappointed," she reminded him. "The girls and Grace and, well, this town does love a celebration."

"Grace can attend you, and we can always have a party later. Once we get settled, we can come back, and I'm sure George and your girls would be delighted to throw a real fandango for us." He kissed her again. "What do you say, Emmie? Shall we go talk to Father O'Meara?"

"Yes," she agreed. "Let's go now. He'll just be finishing evening vespers." She grabbed his hand and stood, prepared to hurry down the path and across the plaza to the church.

But although Max stood, he didn't move. Instead, he pulled her into his arms, and this time his kiss held the promise of fidelity no matter what challenges might lie ahead. Other kisses had spoken of his passion and desire—a few had even been teasing and lighthearted. But this was the kiss that she understood offered her his heart, and she returned it in kind.

"We should go talk to Father O'Meara," she said when their lips parted for an instant.

"We should," he agreed before sprinkling light kisses over her cheeks and eyelids and forehead.

"Now," she whispered. "Before he goes to his rooms for the night."

Max released a long sigh, nodded, and took her hand as he led the way to the church.

∞

It was late by the time their meeting with the priest ended. They shared one last kiss before Max left and Emma went up to her room. As she neared the top of the stairs, the memory of the spider and RJ's threat came flooding back, and she dreaded opening the door, even though she knew any danger from the spider had passed. From down the hall, she heard the other waitresses chattering away. They had all gathered in Melba and Nan's room, and she caught snatches of their conversation that told her they were still talking about her wedding plans. Putting off the inevitable need to enter her own room, Emma knocked lightly at the girls' door and opened it.

"I came to say good night," she said.

"Good night," they chimed.

"I also wanted to thank you for being so happy for me. It means a great deal to me."

"We're like family," Nan announced. "And with the Wild West show leaving, we were a little sad, but now, with a wedding to plan…"

"Well, you see," Emma said, taking a seat on one of the beds next to Sarah, "the captain will be leaving on Friday, and we've decided to wed before then—on Thursday."

"That's too soon," Melba announced.

"And it's a workday," Nan added with a pout. "How are we supposed to organize everything in time?"

The mood in the room that had been so festive turned to despair.

"Really, girls, there's no need to make a fuss. The captain and I planned a small, quiet ceremony at the church. Of course, I'd be delighted if you came."

"What will you wear?" Sarah asked.

"I haven't thought about it, but I suppose my Sunday dress will have to do. There's no time to shop, and besides, why would I spend money on something new?"

Three of the girls rolled their eyes, and Melba frowned. "I suppose you have a point," she said.

"Of course I do. The important thing here is that Captain Winslow and I are to be married and I am so very happy."

Frowns turned to smiles as the others gathered closer. "He's so handsome," one remarked.

"And kind," another added.

"A winning combination," Nan announced.

"To Miss E," Melba proclaimed, raising her hand as if holding a glass of champagne.

"To Miss E!"

Emma blushed with pleasure. "Thank you all. And now, tomorrow is also a workday, and we should all get some rest. Good night."

"Good night," they chorused as Emma left the room, closing the door behind her. The minute she did, she heard them whispering excitedly, and that had her smiling all the way back to her room.

But when she opened the door, memories of her earlier fright came flooding back, spoiling the evening she'd shared first with Max and now with her waitresses. She stood for a long moment in the darkened room.

Only you can allow RJ to spoil this happy time, she thought. He had made his point, sent his message. Her response could either be to live in constant fear of what might come next or refuse to permit his vindictiveness to spoil what might just be the happiest day of her life to date.

"I choose happiness," she announced to the shadows as she moved with confidence across the room, lit the lamp, and turned back the covers on her bed. She walked to the wardrobe and took out her Sunday dress.

It would do. She had worn it before, of course, and Max had commented on the color. She doubted he would take notice of what she was wearing when they stood before Father O'Meara.

And after?

She giggled, suddenly self-conscious as she realized that this time on Thursday, she would be Mrs. Maxwell Winslow—a married woman with no reason to try and hide the fact that she and Max would spend the night together.

Where?

Certainly not here in her narrow bed. Once married, she would no longer be a Harvey Girl. Perhaps wherever Max slept at the showgrounds? Did it really matter as long as they spent it together?

"No," she whispered. Nothing mattered. She would find a room at the boardinghouse and take in mending until Max sent for her. Laughing happily, she spun around the room. "Mrs. Maxwell Winslow," she said aloud. "Emma Winslow."

It had a lovely ring to it.

Chapter 16

Late Thursday afternoon, Max stood on the platform outside the railway station and waved as Reba left to join Pawnee Bill's show. Then he walked back to the hotel, where Aidan looked up with a frown.

"You cannot be here," the hotel manager announced.

"I need a room for tonight—for Emmie and me."

"I'll make those arrangements. Now you really must leave, Max." He glanced at the large clock in the lobby. "It's nearly time. You should already be at the church."

Max was used to giving orders rather than following them, but Aidan seemed quite upset by his presence in the hotel, so he left. Making his way across the plaza, he was surprised to realize he was nervous. He'd performed before hundreds of people and never once felt unsure of himself, but suddenly he had doubts. Not about his love for Emmie but rather if he was being fair to her. After all, he had no idea what the work in Yellowstone might entail. He could be away for long periods of time, and she would be on her own among strangers. Of course, in time she would win everyone over, and they would be as devoted to her as were her waitresses and the rest of the staff at the hotel. But that would all take time.

Bert was waiting on the steps of the church. The man had blubbered with happiness when Max asked if he would serve as his best man. As Max approached, Bert tossed aside his stub of a cigar. "You ready to do this?" he asked, his grin as broad as the flashy polka-dotted bow tie he wore.

"You're looking mighty fine, Bert," Max said, ignoring the question.

"And you look like a man who might be having second thoughts," Bert replied with a scowl. "That girl is the best thing ever to happen to you, Max, and if you walk away now—"

"Nobody's walking away," Max grumbled. "It's these fancy duds Pearl insisted I wear. Where is she, by the way?"

"Over at the hotel, helping your bride get ready. Come on. I've got my marching orders. We're to be inside and not watching when Emma shows up."

Inside, Father O'Meara welcomed them and led the way to the small room behind the altar where he kept his vestments. "Might as well sit," he said, indicating a bench. "We've got about half an hour, time enough for me to send one of the altar boys out for a sarsaparilla soda for each of you—unless you'd prefer something stronger."

"Got that covered," Bert said as he removed a flask from his inside pocket and offered it to Max.

"No, thanks. Best keep my wits about me. I'll take that soda though."

The priest nodded and left the room.

"You all right handling the auction on your own?" Max asked.

"That's the third time you've asked, and my answer's the same. Yes." He took a nip of the contents of the flask, capped it, and slid it back in his pocket. Then he pulled an envelope from another pocket and handed it to Max. "Me and Pearl got you a little wedding present," he said and turned away to look out the small window while Max opened the envelope.

Inside was a train ticket to Montana that included passage for Diablo as well. "This is too much, Bert."

"Naw. As Pearl says, the sooner you get there, the sooner you settle in and send for Emma."

Max had noticed that ever since the news broke that they would be closing the show for good, Bert had taken to quoting Pearl often. That told him his partner was spending more time with her. "I'll pay you back," he said.

"It's a gift," Bert muttered. "You've given us plenty. Take it."

Max swallowed a lump of gratitude as he put the ticket in his pocket. "Thanks." A silence stretched between them. "I'm sure gonna miss working with you, Bert," he said softly.

"Pearl and me was talking last night about maybe we might come up that way once you and Emma get settled."

"A wedding trip?"

Bert's cheeks turned a deep mottled red. "Something like that."

Max laughed.

Just then, a young boy opened the door and thrust two open bottles of soda at them. "Father says it's almost time," he reported. "He'll be here to get you in about five minutes."

"Thanks, sonny," Bert said as he raised the bottle to Max. "To you and Emma," he said and took a long swallow.

The cold beverage helped, but Max was still anxious as he stood between the priest and Bert. Several townspeople and most of the hotel staff filled several of the pews. Abigail Chambers, who owned the hat shop in town, sat at the pump organ. She was wearing an outlandish hat, obviously a creation of hers meant to advertise her shop. Pearl occupied one of the pews with Grace and Nick's two children. She was trying to rein them in but not having much success.

Max had never imagined the ceremony would be anything but Emma and him standing along with Bert and Grace as witnesses as the priest led them in repeating their vows. Suddenly, the whole thing had grown into something far more elaborate and formal. Emma had warned him that others had taken charge.

As he ran his forefinger around a collar that was far too stiff and tight for his taste, Father O'Meara nodded, and Abigail struck up a tune that sounded like a fanfare they might have used at the opening of the show. The doors at the back of the sanctuary opened, and Grace Hopkins walked slowly down the center aisle, followed by Nick with Emma on his arm. Max had never seen her looking more beautiful. She wore a forest-green high-necked dress that was trimmed with lace. Her hair was pulled back but fell in curls freely to her shoulders, and she carried a bouquet of wildflowers. She wore no hat or veil, and the late afternoon sun streaming through the tall church windows highlighted the golden streaks of her upswept hair.

As she made her way down the aisle, she kept glancing at him from beneath lowered lashes, and it was only when he smiled at her that she seemed to relax, meet his gaze directly, and return that smile. Before she and Nick reached the altar, Max stepped forward and took Nick's place. "I've got it from here," he said, and Nick grinned and took a seat in the front pew next to Pearl and the children.

"Dearly beloved," Father O'Meara intoned, and those were the last words Max really heard. He knew he played his part, repeating vows dictated by the priest, sliding a thin gold band onto her slender finger, and with the priest's permission, giving his bride a chaste kiss before taking her hand and starting up the aisle. He was aware of women smiling and men clapping him on the shoulder as they passed, but it wasn't until they were outside and he saw Wolf waiting with Diablo hitched to a buggy that had been decorated with evergreens and paper flowers that it really hit him.

"We're married," he said as he stopped on the church steps and looked at Emma.

"I thought that was the plan," she teased.

"Captain and Mrs. Winslow," Wolf called, "your carriage awaits."

Clasping hands, Max and Emma ran lightly down the church steps and climbed into the buggy. Wolf drove twice around the plaza slowly before stopping at the hotel. That gave those attending the ceremony time to walk back. Aidan, George, and the Harvey Girls were lined up to greet them.

"What's all this?" Max asked as he helped Emma from the buggy.

"I tried to stop them," Emma said, "but the girls and kitchen staff insisted on a wedding supper, and Aidan says he has a special surprise for us. That's all I know, honestly."

Once inside the lobby, their escorts led the way to the dining room, which had been magically transformed into a garden of more greens and paper flowers and a candle centerpiece on every table. Nick and Grace as well as Bert and Pearl were already seated at a head table to either side of two empty places for the newlyweds. A long serving table lined one side of the room with a buffet of meats and fruits and side dishes.

"Oh, Max, they thought of everything," Emma said as they took their places. "No one needs to serve—we can all serve ourselves." Crystal wineglasses bubbled with champagne at each place.

Max watched as the waitresses, housekeeping, and kitchen staff took their seats at tables around the room. Several of the townspeople had been invited as well, and soon the room was alive with chatter as the guests lined up at the buffet. Pearl and Grace insisted on preparing plates for Max and Emma. "You are the guests of honor," Grace reminded them. "Just sit back and enjoy."

Once they had finished the main course, everyone pitched in to clear away the dishes and reset the places with dessert forks and coffee cups. Then George entered the dining room pushing a cart on which sat a three-tiered decorated cake.

"The frosting is white," Max heard Grace tell Emma, "but rest assured the cake is chocolate. Someone told us that's Max's favorite."

As soon as the cake was sliced and served and pots of coffee and tea had been added to each table, Aidan stood and lightly tapped his cup with a fork. "Ladies and gentlemen," he said, calling for attention. "I have a telegram of congratulations I'd like to read the newlyweds. It is from Emma's dear friends Lily and Cody Daniels, who could not join us on such short notice." He cleared his throat. "Sending congratulations and best wishes to the happy couple. Stop. Please accept our gift of a night's stay in the hotel's grandest suite. Stop."

The buzz in the room was increasing to the point of nearly drowning out the rest, but Aidan held up his hand and waved a second sheet of paper. "There's more," he shouted. "The Harveys have set aside one of their usual requirements that Harvey Girls remain single and granted my request that Miss Elliott—I mean, Mrs. Winslow—be allowed to remain in her quarters and at her post until such time as she leaves us to join Max in Montana."

A huge cheer resounded through the room.

Max looked at Emma to see how she might be taking this news. They really had not talked about what she might do while he was away. Every time he'd broached the topic, assuring her she had no need to worry about paying for a room in the hotel or anything else, she had waved off any such discussion.

"I've been on my own for years, Max. I can take care of myself until you send for me."

But now he saw tears of happiness glistening in her eyes and knew this news was a relief. Beneath the table, he covered her hand and squeezed it.

"To Max and Emma!" Aidan lifted his cup, and everyone rose to their feet and did the same, repeating the toast.

Max was unused to being on this side of any show or celebration. He was usually the one making the speeches or offering the toasts for a show well done or in celebration of a company member's wedding or the birth of a child. He glanced around the room, studying each happy face. He and Bert had brought the show to Juniper because of its location and mild weather. He'd not once thought of the people he might meet there—the friends he might find, not to mention the woman he would fall in love with. He stood and raised his cup in return. "To the good people of Juniper," he said, his voice cracking with emotion, "and to the friendships and memories Emmie and I will take with us wherever we go. Thank you one and all." He took Emma's hand and urged her to stand with him as once again he raised his cup, this time to her. "To my beautiful bride," he said. "Today, I count myself the luckiest man alive."

Instead of drinking from his raised cup, he leaned forward and kissed her, and everyone cheered.

⚬⚬⚬

Emma would not have believed it possible that she could be any happier than she'd been when Max proposed. But she was. Her heart pounded with sheer joy whenever she looked at him or he at her. She was only vaguely aware of the others around her. From the moment he'd stepped forward to take her hand in the church, there had been only Max and her. And when he stood and toasted her and then kissed her, she thought her heart would surely explode.

Now it was Grace who was tapping her fork on a china cup. "Ladies and gentlemen," she said once she had their attention. "Since Emma and Max will be spending the wedding night right here in the hotel, we have arranged that they will leave here now and take one more ride around the plaza, giving you all the chance to see them off, as it were. Please join us in the lobby."

Some guests started for the double doors while others gobbled down the last bite of cake and hastily wiped their mouths before rising. Meanwhile, Grace continued to orchestrate the finale. "You and Max wait here until everyone is gathered on the veranda," she instructed. "Then Chief Gray Wolf will be waiting with Diablo and the buggy. I'll warn you, there may be a bit of a gauntlet to endure before you are safely aboard, but it's all in good fun."

She kissed Emma's cheek and then Max's and hurried away. They were truly alone together for the first time all day.

"Well, Mrs. Winslow," Max said as he tucked a tendril of hair behind her ear. "Are you happy?"

"Happy is too small a word for what I'm feeling, Captain Winslow. Perhaps overjoyed or ecstatic are better. What I know for certain is that I am very delighted to be your wife."

He wrapped his arms around her. "The honor and delight are all mine, Emmie. You are without a doubt the single thing that has been missing in my life. To have found you and now married you?" He shook his head as if words failed him.

Emma raised herself on tiptoe and kissed him. He tightened his embrace and deepened the kiss.

"Excuse me, but everyone is waiting," they heard Pearl announce. Reluctantly, Max pulled away without releasing Emma.

"Tell them to keep their shirts on," he grumbled and turned back to Emma.

She pressed her fingers to his lips. "We should go," she said softly. "The sooner we go, the sooner they leave and we can…"

Max grinned. "I like the way your mind works, Emmie. Lead the way, Pearl," he said as he tucked Emma's hand in the crook of his elbow and together they crossed the dining room.

"Once I open these doors," Pearl said, her hand on the knobs of the double dining room doors, "I suggest you make a run for the buggy outside."

"Why?" Max asked.

"You'll find out," Pearl replied with a wicked smile. Then she threw open the doors, and they heard Bert shout, "Ladies and gentlemen, the happy couple."

The guests had lined the route from the dining room through the lobby onto the veranda and all the way down the front path to where Wolf waited with the buggy. As Emma and Max started down the makeshift aisle, they realized they were being pelted with rice.

"What on earth?" Max shouted as he pulled Emma closer to protect her from the storm.

"It's good luck," someone shouted.

"A sign of prosperity," someone else called out.

"And fertility." That comment set off a wave of laughter and a final downpour of rice as they reached the buggy.

"Drive," Max ordered, and Wolf snapped the reins.

But as they moved forward, Emma and Max were both smiling and waving. They continued to look back at the hotel until they saw everyone leave or go back inside. As Wolf turned the corner, they settled into their seats, and Emma picked rice kernels from Max's thick hair, then rested her head on his shoulder, lulled by the gentle rocking of the buggy as Wolf guided it slowly around the plaza. By the time they reached the front of the hotel, everyone was gone, and the sun was just about to set.

Wolf turned to face them. "Well, here you are. I'll take care of Diablo and meet you tomorrow morning for the train," he said, his eyes on Max.

Emma knew the chief and his family would also leave the following morning, but their journey would be by wagon and on foot. She sat forward and touched his arm. "I wish you and your family the best," she said. "Promise you'll write and let us know once you are settled."

He patted her hand. "I will. And you take care of yourself, Emma. Not sure what this guy would do if something were to happen to you."

An unexpected chill ran through Emma's body. Had George told Wolf about the spider? Had he surmised it was no accident but a threat? Surely not. Wolf was just being kind. She smiled. "I'll be fine," she assured him.

Max and Wolf climbed down and shook hands. "Thanks for everything," Emma heard Max say. Wolf nodded. Then Max was holding his arms out to lift her down from the buggy. "Mrs. Winslow," he said, "I believe we have a room reserved at this Harvey House, if that suits."

"It suits just fine," she said.

They stood on the veranda waving to Wolf as he walked Diablo and the buggy down the street to the livery. When they entered the lobby, for the first time Emma could recall Aidan was not at the front desk. Instead, his assistant presented Max with a key and wished them both a good night, treating them with the same deference given to any guest of the hotel.

The room they'd been assigned was at the opposite end of the hall from the rooms where Max, Bert, and Reba had stayed. Max fitted the key and opened the door. Gas lighting softened the shadows, and she saw that it was really two rooms in one with a sitting area and a large four-poster bed. There was even a private bathroom—small to be sure, but they would not need to walk down the hall.

"Leave it to Lily," Emma murmured. She had no doubt that her dear friend had made sure she and Max would have the very best the hotel could offer. On a round table near the windows sat a silver bucket filled with ice and a bottle of champagne, as well as two glasses and a plate of the special candies Mr. Tucker carried in his mercantile. Max lifted the bottle.

"Shall I open it?" he asked.

"I'd rather have a nice glass of water," Emma admitted.

Max grinned and scooped ice from the bucket into each glass before stepping into the bathroom to fill them.

On the bed was the most beautiful nightgown Emma had ever seen and a note.

From Lily and Grace with joy that all three of us have found our true loves!

Max came up behind her and handed her the water. "Your friends have excellent taste," he said. "Can't wait to see you try that on." He faked a yawn. "Come to think of it, it's been a long day."

Emma laughed. One of the things she loved most about this man was his ability to put her at ease and make her smile. She knew he was deliberately trying to make this night as memorable as possible—a night they would cherish for years to come.

"I agree," she said as she picked up the nightgown and went to the bathroom. "I won't be long," she promised and closed the door.

Her hands shook as she unfastened the buttons on her dress and stepped out of it, folded it, and set it on the edge of the sink, then did the same for her under-garments. Naked, she picked up the gown that was made of a cream-colored closely woven batiste, light as air. It would not leave much to the imagination, she was sure. It had an exquisite wide lace collar that fell away from the round neckline and the ribbons that closed the front of the garment. Similar lace formed the sleeves from the elbow to her wrists. The rest of the gown was unadorned.

Barefoot, she turned to catch a look at herself in the oval mirror above the sink. She removed the combs that held her hair back and arranged it over her shoulders. She bit her lips and pinched her cheeks, trying to add some color.

"Emmie?" Max knocked lightly at the door. "Are you all right?"

"Yes. Coming," she called and took one more look at herself before drawing in a deep breath and opening the door.

He'd lowered the lights and turned back the covers on the bed. He was barefoot and naked to the waist, the top button of his trousers undone.

"Oh, Emmie," he whispered when he saw her.

She knew the streetlamp outside the window cast a glow behind her, exposing her silhouette beneath the thin fabric of the gown. She was tempted to cover herself by wrapping the folds of fabric closer to her body, but when she saw the way Max was looking at her, she realized that to him she was indeed beautiful—desirable.

They moved toward each other until she could feel his breath warm against her skin as he untied the first ribbon, and then the second. It seemed an eternity but was only seconds before he pushed the fabric away to expose her shoulders. He kissed her throat, her collarbone, her bare shoulder, and used his teeth to pull the gown lower until he'd uncovered one breast. He cupped her with his hand, his thumb teasing her nipple as his mouth covered hers in a kiss so filled with passion Emma thought she might faint.

She clung to him, pressing herself to him until she felt the swell of his desire. He trailed kisses down her neck to her breast, suckling her as he dispensed with the nightgown, letting it fall to the floor in a pool at her feet. Then he lifted her, urging her to wrap her bare legs around his waist as he carried her to the bed. He lay her against the pile of pillows and quickly finished undressing before lying down next to her.

She reached for him, but he stopped her by kneeling next to her and planting a trail of kisses from the hollow of her neck to the juncture of her thighs. She felt a jolt of pleasure like none she'd ever imagined when he massaged her inner thighs. Spontaneously, she lifted her hips to meet his touch, wanting more. He obliged by slipping his fingers inside her, stroking her until she thought she might go mad with her need for him to enter her. She clutched at his hips and back, her nails scraping over his skin as she urged him to fill her.

In an instant, he lifted and turned her so that she was astride him. "I don't know what to do," she said, her voice shaking with emotion.

"Yes, you do, love. We're one—two parts of a whole," he whispered as he positioned her so that he could slide inside.

And as if she'd been born to it, she moved with him, joining him in this lover's dance where no one led and no one followed, but they were as a single body moving together toward a pinnacle only the two of them could reach. And Emma understood that the sheer bliss of that moment would stay with her for all the days of her life.

Through the night, they dozed and woke to make love again. Too soon, Emma saw the dawn creeping in to scatter the shadows. Too soon, she knew Max would have to rise and dress—and leave.

Too soon, she would be alone.

❧

Max stood on the platform, his saddlebags slung over one shoulder, his free arm around Emma's waist as they watched a railway worker load Diablo. He had known leaving would be hard but could never have imagined the way his heart raced with a kind of panic—a feeling something was not right.

Earlier as they lay in bed watching the sun brighten the large room, they had talked about the future—their future. How he would get to Yellowstone and assess the situation, find them a place to live, and send for her as soon as possible. He was anxious for them to start their life together and impatient with the very idea of this necessary delay.

But Emma had assured him they would both be so busy with work, the time would fly by. "It's important we get off to the best possible start. We'll have years to share," she'd said, snuggling more closely against him as she stroked his face as if trying to memorize each feature.

"All aboard!" The conductor paced the platform as he shouted his command.

Max set his saddlebags down and wrapped both arms around Emma. "I have to go," he said unnecessarily.

"I know," she replied, her eyes glistening with tears he knew she would not allow to fall. "Wire me the minute you arrive so I know you are there and safe," she said.

Max kissed her. "You'll write me?"

"Every day," she promised.

The train whistle let out a long, shrill blast.

They were the only two people left on the platform. The conductor stood on the metal stairs of a passenger car. "Come on, buddy. Kiss her and let's go."

Max didn't need permission. Emma was his wife. He could kiss her anywhere, anytime.

The train let out a belch of steam and started to slowly roll forward.

"Go," Emma urged. "Let's begin this adventure."

Max grabbed his saddlebags and dashed for the train, catching hold of the stair railing in time to pull himself aboard as the train picked up speed. The conductor shook his head and entered the passenger car, but Max stayed where he was. He was determined to keep Emma in sight for as long as possible. She hurried along the length of the platform, waving and smiling. "I love you," she shouted, although her words were lost in the noise of the moving train.

Max was smiling as he took his seat by a window. *This adventure,* she had called it, and that was exactly what it was. There had been nothing ordinary about their meeting or brief courtship. Some would say they had rushed into a marriage neither of them could possibly guarantee would last. And yet Max had never been more certain of anything in his entire life as he was that he and Emma had been destined to find each other and build a life together.

Still smiling, he leaned his head against the window and felt sleep about to overtake him. He chuckled as he realized a good long nap was exactly what was called for. After all, neither he nor Emma had gotten much sleep the night before.

∞

Emma stayed on the platform until the last car of the train had disappeared, then walked slowly back to the hotel. The hour was early, and the shops had not yet opened. The plaza was deserted. The quiet was an appropriate backdrop to her melancholy now that Max was gone.

Work!

That was the answer. She would throw her heart and soul into helping Aidan choose her replacement and training the person. In the meantime, she would make sure every file and report were up-to-date, and because they were still shorthanded since Trula's position had never been filled, she would go back to being a regular Harvey Girl, serving customers wherever she was needed. It would set a good example for the others.

Drawing in a deep breath, she bypassed the front entrance to the hotel and crossed the veranda, running her fingers lightly over the rocking chairs where she and Max had so often sat. At the kitchen entrance, George looked up.

"He's gone?"

She nodded and bit her lower lip. Hearing the words spoken aloud somehow added to the reality of her situation. "I'll just go change," she murmured and fled up the back stairs. She stopped at the second floor and hurried down the hall to the suite where she and Max had spent their first night as man and wife.

She closed the door and stood with her back to it, surveying the rumpled covers of the bed, and saw the nightgown puddled on the floor. That made her smile and then giggle. She certainly hadn't gotten much wear out of the garment. But there would be other nights—a lifetime of nights.

She picked up the gown and folded it carefully. Then she removed the case from the pillow Max had slept on and folded that as well. She pressed the fabric to her nose, inhaling his scent. She would cover the pillow in her room on the third floor with the case, and in some small way it would be as if he were there with her.

Checking to be sure neither she nor Max had left anything behind, she left the room and hurried up to the third floor. On her door was a note, and she recognized the handwriting as Aidan's.

Please come to my office as soon as possible once Max is gone. Aidan

Ford Harvey was due to arrive any day now, and Emma suspected Aidan's nerves were getting the better of him. She hurried to wash and change out of her wedding clothes and into her uniform. Expertly, she swept her hair up and secured it with hairpins and the white bow all the waitresses wore. As she reached around to tie the sash of her apron, she heard the other girls come down the hall. With a last check of her appearance, she opened her door.

"Good morning, ladies," she said brightly and had to work hard to keep from laughing at their shocked faces.

"Miss E, what on earth?" Melba demanded.

"We thought you and the captain," Nan began, then blushed scarlet. "You know."

"I have just come from seeing the captain off," Emma said as she led the way downstairs. "And now it's time for work. Mr. Campbell wants to see me, so I'll trust you ladies to get everything ready for the breakfast service."

Melba released a long breath of pure frustration. "And that's it? Nothing has changed?"

Emma patted the girl's cheek. "Oh, Melba, a good deal has changed," she said softly and then winked as she went to find Aidan. Behind her, she heard the girls giggling and chattering as they went about their morning tasks.

Chapter 17

AIDAN WAS IN HIS OFFICE, STANDING AT THE WINDOW, when Emma knocked and then entered the immaculate room. "Aidan?"

He turned to face her, and she realized he looked haggard and exhausted. "What is it?" she said, crossing the room and taking his hand. Aidan was her friend, and she hated to see him so obviously distraught. "Has something happened?"

"I didn't want to say anything until I had done everything possible to prevent this." He held up a letter she hadn't realized he was clutching. "They are shutting us down—closing the hotel."

Emma could not believe what Aidan was telling her. "But where will everyone go? What will happen to George and the girls—and you, Aidan?"

He sighed and, with a gesture, invited her to sit. "The confirmation came two days ago. It's the reason the Harveys agreed you could stay on. I didn't want to spoil your happiness, so I waited until now. But time is of the essence. George and I have been offered our same positions at a new hotel being opened in Colorado. The kitchen and housekeeping staffs will be offered positions by the new owners here. The Harvey Girls will have jobs in other Harvey establishments should they choose to accept, or they can stay. The Harveys have made sure this is all part of the terms of sale."

"I don't understand. We've been successful here, have we not?"

"The railway is changing its schedule and cutting two passenger trains from stopping here each day. The freight business will continue as usual. I had hoped I could get Mr. Harvey or his son to visit—to see for themselves what a success we've made of this place. I saw no need to alarm everyone, and I was so sure…" He shook his head as he dropped the letter in the wastebasket.

Emma's mouth went dry. Although Max had assured her they would be fine—financially speaking—she had counted on her earnings as head waitress to provide a stake that would get them started while he settled into his new job. *A nest egg for our future*, Emma had thought.

Aidan must have seen her fear, for his sour expression softened. "We have until the end of the month, Emma, and the truth is by then Max will probably have sent for you. Nevertheless, I'll do my best to be sure you receive the full month's wages."

She understood there was nothing to be done. The decision had already been made. "How do you want to give the news to the rest of the staff?" she asked.

"Earlier this morning, I spoke to George and Tilly in housekeeping." He handed her a sheaf of papers. "Here's a list of current openings for waitresses in the organization. Share this with your girls—young women," he corrected himself. "As you will see, some positions are open now, meaning they need to be filled as soon as possible, while others are becoming available later in the month."

Emma accepted the packet of papers. "I'll meet with them tonight."

Aidan nodded. "I'm really sorry, Emma."

"It's hardly your fault. We'll just have to do our best. After all, that's the Harvey Way." She smiled and was relieved to see Aidan smile in return. "And now, because we are already shorthanded thanks to Trula's position being left unfilled, I need to get to work."

She started for the door but stopped when Aidan cleared his throat, signaling he had something more he wanted to discuss.

"I'm sorry things did not work out for us, Emma—I mean personally. However, from what I saw yesterday, you have never been happier—or more radiant. I am so very pleased for you."

Emma retraced her steps and kissed his cheek. "You've no idea how much that means to me, Aidan, and no matter where we are, know that I will always think of you as my dear friend."

"We'll stay in touch," Aidan replied, his voice raspy with emotion. Then he chuckled. "It's been quite a journey we've shared."

Emma laughed. "Indeed it has," she said and felt a good deal of the lightness she'd felt earlier return. "And together we will close down Mr. Harvey's establishment here with the style and refinement we both know he expects."

Aidan gave her a sharp salute, and she was still smiling as she left his office and headed for the dining room. Of course, that was all before she realized RJ Gilmore was sitting in the lobby, his gaze riveted on her and a wicked smile on his face.

"Mrs. Winslow," he said without rising to his feet as any gentleman would in addressing a lady. "Looks like you and the captain beat me and Trula to the altar." His eyes widened in mock surprise as he added in a volume meant for all passing through the lobby or seated at the counter to hear, "You ain't by any chance in a family way, are you?"

He had caught the attention of a trio of local women, including Abigail Chambers, a renowned gossip. Emma could see her whispering to the others as she glanced Emma's way and shook her head with condemnation.

Emma moved closer to RJ and put on her best Harvey Girl smile. "So it is your plan to ruin my reputation?" She kept her smile in place even as she lowered her voice for his ears only.

He smirked. "I reckon I don't have an actual plan, but when opportunity presents itself?" He shrugged and strode across the lobby, tipping his hat to the women as he left.

Emma was aware that Melba and Nan, working the counter, had seen and heard everything.

"Back to work, ladies," she murmured as she returned to the kitchen.

But later, after their long hours of work had finally ended, the two waitresses knocked at Emma's door. She was exhausted but had never once refused to listen when any of the young women came to talk. She invited them inside her room and shut the door.

"I was just coming to call a meeting," she said.

"We heard the Harveys have sold the hotel." Melba maintained her place by the door while Nan took up a position at the foot of Emma's bed.

"To Mr. Gilmore," Sarah added.

It was a piece of news Aidan had failed to share. "Yes," Emma admitted. "That is the purpose of the meeting. I'm sorry you heard about the change before I had the chance to tell you."

"This is terrible news." Nan moaned and plopped down on the bed, her head in her hands. "I mean, what will we do?"

"Come on," Emma said, taking hold of Nan's arm. "It's best if I speak to everyone at once. The good news is you ladies have several options from which to choose."

Melba looked doubtful but opened the door and led the way back to the room she and Nan shared. "Meeting!" she called out as they passed the other rooms.

Once all the girls had crowded around, Emma cleared her throat. "I can see you have all heard the news," she said and was not surprised to see them looking miserable. "As you know, the Harveys are fair employers, and they have made certain you have opportunities." She handed out the list of open positions within the Harvey Company. "Or they have arranged for you to continue your employment right here for the new owners."

"Or we can leave," Melba added. She was a natural

leader, and although she had tested Emma's strict rules more than once, Emma was glad to have her.

"That's true," Emma agreed. "Sarah, I know you have been looking forward to returning to Ohio. Something about a young man who is about to receive his medical license waiting there for you?" Her teasing made Sarah blush and the others smile. "The truth is, it is a new century, and young women like you have opportunities your mothers never dreamed possible. Juniper is thriving and there are other possibilities right here—working in one of the shops, for example."

"Or opening a shop of our own," Nan suggested.

The mood in the room shifted from downhearted to optimistic as the girls chattered on about what the future might hold. "In any case," Emma said, speaking louder to gain their attention, "you will always be a Harvey Girl, and that, my dear ones, is worth a great deal."

She stayed for another hour, speaking with each waitress individually as they considered the available openings. For some of them, staying in Juniper was more desirable. They had become part of the community and more often than not had a beau who worked for the railroad or on one of the neighboring ranches.

It was nearly midnight when she finally said good night and returned to her room. She still wanted to write Max. She wondered if he might have delayed leaving if he'd known about the sale of the hotel. By now, his train would be well on its way to Montana and the northern entrance to the park where the regiment was stationed. She tried to picture him there—tried to imagine them both there.

A light knock at her door startled her from her reverie. "Yes?" she called.

"Miss E?"

Trula?

Emma crossed the room and opened the door. "Trula, what's happened?" She was not an alarmist, but it was after midnight, and Trula looked as if she'd gotten caught in a storm, her hair undone and tangled, her dress ripped, and her breath coming in ragged gasps.

Emma gently led her to the bed, kicking the door shut. "Sit down." She poured a glass of water and handed it to the girl, who drank it down.

Emma took the glass from Trula, setting it on the small table next to her bed before sitting next to her. "Who did this to you, Trula?" But she was sure she knew.

"He didn't mean it," Trula protested. "He just gets so mad sometimes."

"RJ."

Trula nodded. "It was my fault, really. I have this habit of provoking him. I don't mean to. I don't even know I'm doing it, but then he gets upset, and I can see it's all because of me."

"It is not your fault," Emma assured her. "That young man has a temper. Did he strike you?" She gently lifted Trula's chin and brushed her lank hair away from her face. The answer was there for all to see.

"He didn't mean it. I mean, whenever he gets this upset, he's always sorry and so very sweet the next day. Tomorrow, you'll see, he'll be right as rain."

Emma sucked in her breath. "Are you telling me he has done this before?" She thought of a time when she had reprimanded Trula for wearing rouge and now realized perhaps she'd been concealing another blow.

"He just can't help it," Trula said.

Emma could see there would be no reasoning with Trula tonight, so she poured water into the bowl on her washstand and handed Trula a washcloth and piece of soap. "Clean yourself up and then get out of those clothes. You'll stay here tonight. I'll mend your dress, and tomorrow—"

"I won't turn him in." Suddenly, Trula was quite adamant. "RJ says you've got it in for him because of what he did to the chief. If you go to his father or the sheriff, I'll deny everything."

Emma could not recall a time when she'd been more frustrated or exhausted. "Then why come to me now?" she asked.

Trula stared at her. "Because I'm a Harvey Girl—or I was—and I had no place else with Miss Reba gone, and you always told us once a Harvey Girl, always—"

"A Harvey Girl," Emma finished softly. "Wash up and undress. You can sleep in my bed."

Trula smiled for the first time since entering the room. "Yes, Miss E," she said softly and began unbuttoning her dress while Emma turned back the covers on the bed, removing the pillow covered in the case that Max had slept on. There were some things she would not do for her girls.

❧

Max made his way to the dining car as the train continued its journey north. He'd had a restless night, his mind going over and over the plan he and Emma had adopted. Why leave her behind? There was bound to be a way they could be together, even if it meant her staying in one of the small towns just outside the park. They'd had just one night together as man and wife. What if something happened to him—to her? What if that was all they ever got?

At dinner that evening, he heard two men mention Fred Harvey, and his ears perked up. Something about the Harveys selling off hotels in the smaller towns due to changes in the railway company's schedule.

"Excuse me," he said. "I couldn't help overhearing. Do you know which hotels are being sold?"

One of the men rattled off the names of three towns—including Juniper. "You thinkin' of buying one of the hotels?" he asked.

"No. Just curious. Enjoy your supper."

He ate without tasting although the food was good and there was plenty of it. But as the metal wheels clicked off the miles taking him farther and farther from Emma, Max came to a decision. He looked up at the tall, thin, gray-haired black man who served him a dessert of bread pudding. "Is there a telegraph on this train?" he asked.

"Yes, sir."

"I need to send a wire. Can you help me with that?"

The man grinned. "Yes, sir. I'll be right back." He was gone for only a moment before returning with a pencil and pad of paper. "If you'll write out your message and its destination, I'll see it goes out right away."

Before he could change his mind, Max pushed his dishes aside and scribbled a message to Colonel Newton.

```
CHANGE OF PLANS STOP WILL ARRIVE
IN A WEEK WITH MY WIFE STOP RELY-
ING ON YOU TO UNDERSTAND STOP
```

He hesitated a moment, then handed the paper to the waiter. "What's your name?" he asked as he placed his future in the man's hands.

"Jonah, Captain Winslow."

Max chuckled. "Have we met?"

"I've not had the pleasure, but I have seen the posters for your show, sir. That's a fine-looking horse you own."

Diablo. Diablo was on the train. No need to arrange for a return ticket. He had a ride.

"What's our next stop, Jonah?"

"Garden City. Should be pulling in around ten tonight." He held up the paper Max had given him. "I'll get this sent right away."

"If there's an answer…"

"I'll get it to you," Jonah assured him as he hurried away.

Max finished his coffee and dessert and left a large tip for Jonah next to his cup. With a nod to the men at the next table, he headed back to his seat.

Later as the conductor moved from car to car, calling out the next station, Jonah hustled down the aisle and handed Max a telegram. "Got an answer for you," he said.

Max opened the paper.

```
WIFE? STOP MRS NEWTON DELIGHTED
STOP ONE WEEK STOP NO MORE STOP
```

Max grinned. "Jonah, can you make sure my horse is unloaded here?"

"Yes, sir."

As soon as the train pulled into the station, Max gathered his saddlebags and left the car, preferring to wait on the metal platform joining the cars, the wind on his face, the promise of a reunion with Emma in the air. He'd decided not to send her a wire. It would be more fun to surprise her. Max leaned into the rush of wind and let out a whoop of sheer joy.

❧

Once Trula had fallen asleep, Emma mended her dress and finished a letter to Max. Then she laid her head on her folded arms on top of the writing table, intending to doze for a bit before writing up her report for Aidan regarding which Harvey Girl wanted to apply for which position.

The first rays of daylight and a stiff back woke her. She glanced at the bed where Trula snored softly and decided to let her sleep. As quietly as possible, she washed herself, dressed in a fresh uniform, and slipped from the room.

Downstairs, George looked up and scowled. "One of your girls left the kitchen door unlocked," he said.

"My girls were all in their rooms well before curfew. Trula came in much later though, so I suppose—"

"Trula? She's back working here? I thought she and that Gilmore boy were planning on marrying."

"They are. They had a...lover's quarrel. Trula came here seeking solace. I let her stay."

"Well, that explains one thing." George jerked his

head toward the lobby. "He's out there now, questioning Aidan and insisting she came here last night and is now missing."

Emma sighed. "She's hardly missing," she muttered as she headed for the lobby. "Mr. Gilmore," she said as she crossed to the desk. "Trula spent the night with me. She came to me fairly late—and quite upset. I felt it was in her best interests to let her stay."

"And not let anybody know?" RJ demanded. He took a step toward Emma, and Aidan came out from behind the desk to intervene.

"No harm done, Mr. Gilmore. Your fiancée is safe, and I'm sure Miss Elliott...Mrs. Winslow will be happy to let her know you've come to call on her."

Emma was aware of Nan and Melba taking their places at the counter, preparing to serve the morning customers—and hearing every word. She saw them whispering behind their hands and shot them a look.

"No harm?" RJ scoffed. "This woman has filled Trula's head with all manner of lies about me. I demand—"

Emma had had enough. She stepped around Aidan and addressed RJ directly in a low voice meant for his ears only, although Aidan obviously heard every word. "What is it you demand, young man? What is it you want from me? What have I ever done to you to warrant your threats and vile attempts to frighten me?" With every word, she could see RJ's fury building. "Will you strike me, sir? As you have struck Trula?"

RJ's eyes widened, and he actually took a step back from her. "I never. If she told you that, she's lying. She fell."

Once again, Aidan stepped between them. "Emma, please go and let Trula know Mr. Gilmore is here. If she chooses to come down, that is her business and none of ours."

"And if not?" Emma replied, her eyes still on RJ.

Aidan turned his attention to RJ. "Then I would suggest she needs a bit more time. Meanwhile, Mr. Gilmore, why don't you come to the counter and have a cup of coffee? Anyone can see you've had a stressful night." He took the young man's arm and led him away, looking back to send Emma a pleading look.

With a sigh, she went to wake Trula.

"I told you," she squealed when Emma reported RJ waiting for her downstairs. She leapt from the bed and began dressing. She studied her reflection in the mirror above the washstand, pinching her cheeks and finger-combing her hair to lie over her shoulders and conceal the mark on her cheek. "How do I look?"

Emma was beyond any ability to reason with the young woman. "You look like a woman who has been struck by a man she claims to love," she said. "You are carrying a child, Trula. What happens when he hurts your baby?"

"He would never," Trula protested, cradling her stomach protectively.

"I hope you're right," Emma said wearily and opened the door. "He's at the counter."

Trula practically flew from the room, and her footsteps could be heard tripping lightly down the tile stairs to the second floor where Emma assumed she continued down the guest room corridor to the main staircase. If the girl had learned anything from Reba, it was how to make an entrance.

Unable to stop herself, Emma followed, waiting at the top of the curved staircase that led to the lobby, hoping Trula might come to her senses. But when Trula walked slowly down the stairs, tossing her head like a proud—and angry—filly, RJ stood and wiped his mouth on his napkin before coming to her. The man actually bowed his head in shame as he took Trula's hand in his, touched her injured cheek tenderly, and murmured words to her. Emma saw Trula offer forgiveness by cupping RJ's face in her hands and whispering something back to him. Then smiling, they clasped hands and left the hotel.

Emma thought she might be sick.

For the rest of the day, Emma and the other waitresses spent every spare moment preparing an inventory for the Harvey Company that included searching for seldom-used cookware and silver serving pieces that no one seemed to be able to locate. They rummaged through every cupboard and closet in the hotel, occasionally finding success when a piece turned up behind a pile of linens. All this was in addition to their regular duties. And for Emma, all this was in addition to working shifts as a waitress while finalizing arrangements for her staff to either accept a position with the Gilmore company and stay on or secure one of the open positions at a Harvey establishment.

Exhausted, she still kept her appointment at the Gilmore ranch, pinning and altering Trula's wedding gown and listening to Mrs. Gilmore prattle on about who all was coming for the ceremony on Sunday.

"Mr. Fred Harvey is sending his son," she confided. "He and my husband will finalize the sale of the hotel," she added. "And then RJ and Trula will manage it. RJ has never been one for ranching—he's too fine for such a rough life. The hotel is our wedding present to the happy couple—a secure future in a town that is booming."

"Oh, Mother Gilmore," Trula gushed, "you are far too kind."

Emma was relieved to see that Trula's bruise was well hidden by her hair, and she saw no evidence of further injury. For her part, Trula acted as if RJ were her knight in shining armor.

It was after dark by the time Emma climbed into her rented buggy for the return trip to town. She felt a sense of pure relief that by this time tomorrow, she would no longer have need to interact with Trula or the Gilmores. That thought gave her such pleasure that even seeing RJ leaning against the gate as she passed through the entrance to the ranch on her way back to town did not rattle her.

It was only when he tipped his fingers to his hat that she felt a shiver of apprehension. The final alterations had taken longer than usual, and she'd already climbed into the buggy when Trula called her back to the house. It would be after nine before she reached town. Earlier she'd refused George's suggestion to send someone with her to the ranch—one of his staff.

"It's perfectly safe," she had insisted. "No one is going to bother me in broad daylight."

But the sun had set, and the road ahead was deserted. She snapped the reins, urging the horse to a brisk trot, all the while listening for hoofbeats coming upon her from behind. The fact that none came made her twice as aware of her surroundings, pockets of shadows where she imagined friends of RJ's might be lying in wait. Then she wondered if he'd perhaps put another spider or a snake in the buggy and even now the thing was inching toward her.

Oh, why had she not insisted on going to Montana with Max? Why stay on? Duty? Loyalty? Did a few weeks matter? Lily had often accused her of putting the well-being of others before her own. Grace had pointed out her dedication to her work as something that was keeping her from finding the true happiness she deserved.

Well, Max was gone, and here she was, on a deserted road at night, her heart racing, her hands shaking. Again, it struck her that what they'd shared on their wedding night might be all they got. What if everything they'd dreamed of as they lay together—a home, children, years of happy times—never came to be?

She brushed away a tear with the back of one hand and straightened in the seat. "No," she whispered through gritted teeth. Whatever RJ had planned for her, she would not allow him to win. Keeping her eyes on the road ahead, she pushed the horse harder until at last she saw the glow on the horizon that meant the town was in sight.

As she made her way to Main Street, she slowed the horse to a calmer pace, determined to ride through town and to the hotel as if nothing was amiss. But when she saw Aidan and the sheriff standing at the hotel entrance and when they started down the path toward her as she reined the horse to a halt, she understood something was definitely not right.

"What's happened?" she asked, accepting the helping hand Aidan extended but looking at the sheriff.

"Mind if I have a look in your bag there, ma'am?" he said, already reaching to relieve her of the cloth bag she used to carry her sewing supplies to and from the ranch. Clearly, he did not expect an answer.

"Aidan?"

"The sheriff had a wire from the Gilmore ranch. Seems a valuable piece of Mrs. Gilmore's jewelry has gone missing." Aidan turned his attention to the sheriff. "Surely, Sheriff Bolton, you can't think Emma would ever—"

The sheriff removed a large jeweled brooch from Emma's bag and held it up to the light. "What do you reckon we've got here?"

Emma was about to say she'd never seen the jewelry before in her life but then realized she had seen it. Mrs. Gilmore had been wearing it the day of the tea. Suddenly, the memory of RJ standing at the gate, tipping his fingers to his hat, came back to her. He hadn't needed to follow her or have his friends lie in wait. He had already done what he intended.

"I'm waiting, miss," Sheriff Bolton said. "You got any idea how this ended up in your sewing bag?"

Instead of addressing the sheriff, she turned to Aidan. "Mr. Campbell, if you would be so kind as to ask Mr. McCoy to come to the jail as soon as it would be convenient."

Jacob McCoy had recently opened a law practice

in town, yet another sign that Juniper was a growing community on the rise.

She took the bag from the sheriff and handed it to Aidan. "Ask Melba to put this in my room and take charge of the schedule for tomorrow." Then she turned to Sheriff Bolton, who was still holding the brooch. "I assume you wish to arrest me, Sheriff, so shall we get on with it?"

She could see the sheriff did not like her taking charge. "Come on," he grumbled and took a none-too-gentle hold on her elbow, steering her toward the plaza.

"I'll wire the captain," Aidan called after her.

"You'll do no such thing," Emma replied as she hurried to keep up with the sheriff's long strides. "Have Tommy return the horse and buggy, please," she added. "And send word to Mr. McCoy."

The jail was exactly as it had been when Grace had been arrested years earlier. The iron cot bolted to the wall, the slop bucket in a corner. A thin, stained mattress and rough, threadbare blanket. Emma marched straight to the open cell and entered. She stood with her back to the door until she heard it clang shut and the sheriff turned the key in the lock.

She removed her hat, then spread her shawl over the mattress and sat. She was aware of the sheriff at his desk, watching her. "Why do something so foolish?" he asked. "You were bound to get caught. Of course, I suppose you thought you'd be off to Montana by the time the Gilmores realized the jewelry was missing."

She let him rattle on, refusing to engage in the discussion. Clearly, he did not like that. "I'm talking to you, girlie," he said.

"I hear you," she replied. "I am not talking back."

He slammed back his chair and was standing at the cell bars seconds later. "You Harvey gals think you're special, do you? Well, you're about to find out the law don't care what fancy airs you give yourself. You're about to learn some hard lessons, girlie."

The front door opened, and Aidan stepped inside with a man Emma recognized as the attorney. He was shorter than Aidan and wore a pair of spectacles with thick lenses that reminded Emma of the bottles holding the cream at the hotel.

"I'd like a few minutes with my client, sheriff," he said politely.

Without opening the cell, Sheriff Bolton returned to his desk. "Ten minutes," he muttered.

Mr. McCoy pulled a three-legged stool closer to the cell and sat, his back to the sheriff. Aidan stood behind him. "Tell me what happened, Mrs. Winslow. Start with when you arrived at the Gilmore ranch earlier today."

While he took notes, Emma relayed the details of her time at the ranch.

"And was your bag ever out of your sight?"

"No. I carry all my sewing supplies in it and—" But then she remembered. "Wait. I was just leaving and had placed the bag in the buggy when Trula called me back to the house. Something about how she didn't think the veil I'd made matched the fabric of the gown. I took it as nerves and did my best to reassure her, then left."

And suddenly, she knew exactly what had happened. Once again, RJ had persuaded Trula to be his accomplice. That was why he'd been standing at the gate, looking so smug. She was in the process of telling the lawyer—and Aidan—about the spider and the threats when the jailhouse door banged open and her former roommate, Lily Travis Daniels, marched right past the sheriff and said, "I do not understand how it is that you and Grace are the ones who end up in jail when everyone knows I'm the renegade in this trio." She turned to look at her husband. "Cody, perhaps you and the sheriff can find some common ground that will not have Emma staying here for the night?"

Emma reached through the bars to embrace her dear friend. "What are you doing here?" she asked.

"All Grace's idea. A kind of reunion, and since you rushed to the altar without giving me proper notice, here I am. After all, we had to find a time before you leave to live off the land in that wilderness you've always dreamed of." She shuddered at the thought. "Not my cup of tea, but to each her own. Now, what's this all about?" This she directed to Mr. McCoy, who meekly handed her his notes. "Cody? Do you remember the Gilmore boy?"

Cody grimaced. "Yes. Kid was trouble—nothing serious enough to get him arrested, but always around whenever something went wrong." He glanced at the sheriff. "Can't think he's changed much."

The sheriff had gotten to his feet the minute he saw Cody—a rare sign of respect on his part, Emma realized. Cody had held the sheriff's position before becoming territorial representative.

"RJ's not changed," Bolton admitted. "Just gotten smarter about the way he does his mischief."

"You call setting fire to Chief Gray Wolf's encampment and endangering the lives of his people 'mischief'?" Emma clutched the bars, her knuckles white.

"No proof of that," Bolton griped.

"And if I have a witness?" Emma demanded, knowing the likelihood that Trula would testify against her betrothed was a long shot at best.

The sheriff tried explaining to Cody why RJ was not his problem while Aidan quizzed Emma on why she had not told him about the spider.

Lily clapped her hands sharply to gain everyone's attention. "People! One thing at a time." She strolled over to the sheriff's desk, her Harvey Girl smile firmly in place. "Now, Sheriff Bolton, what will it take to release our friend?"

Emma saw that the sheriff had recovered some of his bluster. "Security," he replied, squinting at Lily. "Bail."

"Bail has not been set," Mr. McCoy objected.

"True," Bolton replied with a slight smile. "And it could take a couple of days to get word to the judge up in Santa Fe and go through all that paperwork. Or maybe we could work something out—just between us. It's just, the Gilmores are pretty powerful people around these parts, and you folks are asking me to put my position as sheriff in jeopardy and—"

"How much?" Aidan interrupted.

The sheriff named a figure that left everyone—even Lily—stunned into silence.

"You cannot be serious," she finally managed.

"Yes, ma'am. Now I'm going to ask politely for you folks to leave. If you come up with the money, you're welcome to come back. I'll be here all night—and so, it appears, will Mrs. Winslow."

Emma saw Cody nod to Lily, and after clasping Emma's hands through the bars, she said, "We'll be back. Don't worry. This isn't over." This last she directed to the sheriff as Cody ushered her out the door.

"You two need to go as well," the sheriff told Aidan and Mr. McCoy. "You've had more than your ten minutes."

"Go," Emma urged, knowing there was little they could accomplish by staying. "I'll be fine." She bit her lower lip to keep them from seeing how very frightened she was.

She must have dozed, because she jerked awake when someone started pounding on the outer door. Grumbling, the sheriff stumbled from his room, hooking his suspenders over his shoulders as he opened the door. "What now?" he demanded.

Emma got up and moved closer to the corner of her cell so she could see what was happening. Led by Lily, Melba, Nan, and Sarah stepped into the office.

"Here," Lily said, handing the sheriff a fat envelope. "Now let her go."

"There's the matter of paperwork," the sheriff said as he thumbed through the money.

"There's the matter of an officer of the law accepting a bribe," Melba countered, and when the others looked at her in surprise, she added, "My father is the mayor of our town back in Wisconsin, and my uncle is the chief of police."

"Well?" Nan demanded.

The sheriff tossed her the keys. "If she runs…"

"She's not running," Sarah informed him. "She's got no cause."

Ignoring the sheriff, the four Harvey Girls hurried to unlock the cell and surround Emma, Melba and Lily each taking hold of one arm as they escorted her outside with Nan and Sarah making a show of slamming the door before following.

The fresh, clear night air hit Emma like a tonic. She realized she could breathe freely again. And raise questions. "Where on earth did you manage to get that amount of money?" she asked.

"Never mind," Lily said. "The important thing is to make this Gilmore boy confess."

"That'll never happen," Emma told her. "Unless…"

The others all stopped when she did.

"Well?" Lily demanded.

"What if we turn the tables on him? His tactics often include humiliating his intended targets. What if we keep the wedding from happening?"

"We could stage a protest," Melba announced. "You know, like those women who march around trying to close up the saloons and such."

"I saw them in action once," Nan said. "They lined up in front of the saloon door and linked arms, and who was going to try and break through?"

"We could say the wedding can't happen until RJ admits what he did," Sarah added.

"He'll never do that," Emma said, chewing her lower lip. "On the other hand, his mother might demand that the charges be dropped in order to avoid the embarrassment."

"Would that be enough, Emma?" Lily asked. "The point is to clear your good name."

"If they drop the charges," Melba said.

"No one believes the charges," Nan fumed. "My guess is Mr. and Mrs. Gilmore don't really believe the charges."

"I wish there were some way we could save Trula from this marriage," Emma said.

"How can you say that?" Melba demanded. "She's been helping him."

Emma shrugged. "She deserves better—her child deserves better."

Lily rolled her eyes. "All right, ladies. Our mission is to stop the wedding at least until Emma's been cleared of all charges. Beyond that…" She threw up her hands.

"Come on, Nan, Sarah," Melba shouted as she took off running for the back hotel entrance. "Let's get the others organized."

"Full uniforms, ladies," Lily called after them. Then she linked arms with Emma and walked up the front path. "This is going to be like old times. We need to send word to Grace."

❧

By the time Max reached Juniper, he was falling asleep in the saddle, and he'd driven Diablo so hard the horse's hide was slick with lather. The first thing he noticed as he rode into town was that it seemed to be deserted—unusual for a Saturday. He was close to the livery, and Diablo needed a good rubdown and rest.

The blacksmith was fitting a new shoe to a horse.

"Hello, Mick," Max said as he dismounted and led Diablo into the shelter of the stables.

"Captain? Thought you left."

"Change of plans. Can you take care of Diablo for a day or so?"

Mick left his work and moved closer. "Looks like he's been rode hard. For that matter, so do you. Guessing you heard about your missus getting herself arrested."

"Emma? Arrested? On what charge?"

"Taking some piece of fancy jewelry from Mrs. Gilmore. Nobody believes a word of it—nobody except the Gilmores, that is."

Max was sure he must have heard wrong. The very idea that Emma would covet anything the Gilmore woman wore was ridiculous, not to mention her strict moral code had no place for thievery. "Mrs. Gilmore is accusing her?" He pulled the saddle from Diablo and set it on a sawhorse.

"No need. Sheriff found the jewelry in her bag after she came back from sewing up the Goodwin girl's wedding dress." Mick led Diablo through the stables out to the back. "She'll sure be glad to see you back, so I'll take care of getting Diablo here cooled down and fed."

"Thanks." In spite of being dead tired, Max took off running through town. As he approached the railway station where the midmorning train had just arrived, he saw the kid—Tommy—on the platform, watching the travelers step down from the long row of cars.

"Tommy!" Max shouted as he changed course and stopped in front of the boy.

"Got no time, Captain. Mr. Campbell says I'm to get Mr. Harvey and bring him straight on to the church." He jerked his hand toward the far end of the plaza where Max saw an unusually large crowd of people gathered outside the church.

"Is Emma—Mrs. Winslow—still in jail?"

Tommy rolled his eyes. "No, sir. Everybody's at the church. Miss E and her girls are blocking the entrance so the wedding can't happen. She says RJ Gilmore is a lyin' coward—them was her very words. Never seen her so mad at anybody before."

"Max?"

Max turned at the call of his name. Ford Harvey was walking down the platform toward him, a huge smile on his face. "It's been a long time, Max," Harvey said, extending his hand and gripping Max's firmly.

"Too long," Max agreed. "I heard you might be paying a visit."

"More than a visit," Ford replied. "Father and I have sold this establishment to a local businessman. I've come to finalize the deal." He grinned and clapped Max on the back. "I understand you've stolen my best head waitress, married her before I could put her in charge of the new hotel we're building in Colorado."

Max realized it had been only two short days since he'd boarded the train for Montana, and yet everything in Juniper seemed to have changed. "We're going to live in Montana. I'll be working for the national park up there."

"Congratulations." Harvey turned his attention to Tommy, who ducked his head and fidgeted nervously as he delivered the message that he was to escort Mr. Harvey to the church.

"Oh yes. The wedding." Ford rolled his eyes. "The things I do for this business, Max." He handed Tommy a coin. "Thomas," he instructed, "please see to my luggage."

"Yes, sir," Tommy muttered and took off at a run to where the railway workers were unloading the luggage.

As the two friends walked across the plaza, Max filled Ford in on what he knew so far. When they reached the back of the large crowd gathered outside the church, they stopped.

"Oh my," Ford murmured, "what have we here?"

Max hesitated as he took in the scene.

The Harvey Girls, in full uniform, stood shoulder to shoulder, arms linked, at the entrance to the church. Emma was at the center of the lineup. Grace Hopkins was on her left and a woman Max didn't recognize was on her right, all three also in uniform. Sheriff Bolton stood before them, shouting out threats to arrest the whole lot of them. Off to one side sat the bride, her face blotched with either fury or misery or both. Father O'Meara stood between McCoy, the local lawyer, and Mr. Gilmore, trying without much success to get them to lower their voices. And instead of consoling his bride, whose day had clearly been ruined, RJ stood with his arms around his mother— and his eyes fixed on Emma. Max started making his way through the crowd.

"Wait, Max," Aidan called, stopping him. "Let them alone. This just might work."

"Mr. Campbell," Ford said, "please explain why employees of the Harvey Company are staging what appears to be a protest outside a church of all places."

"It was all their idea," Aidan said, gesturing toward the waitresses. "Emma's really—along with Grace and Lily, of course."

"Who's Lily?" Max asked.

Aidan pointed to the woman standing to Emma's right. "She's married to Cody Daniels over there. He was the former sheriff here before Bolton took over. Now he's the territorial representative."

Daniels was standing with Nick, and both men were smiling as they watched their wives. Max felt his temper rise. This wasn't some show. This was *his* wife, accused of a crime she did not commit and about to pay a price for that. He strode over to the two men. "What's so funny?" he asked, directing his question to Nick.

"Max! You're back, and none too soon," Nick said. He ignored Max's question and introduced him to Cody Daniels.

Cody shook his hand then turned his attention back to the women. "Magnificent, aren't they? It's a new world, my friends, one where our ladies will no longer be content to step aside and allow the men to fight their battles. I've seen hints of this in Washington and on my travels but never thought I would see it here in Juniper."

Max realized the smile he had taken for humor was in fact pride. "Still," he said, "Emma needs help, and I aim to be the one who gives it."

He took a step forward but was stopped when Daniels and Nick blocked his way. "Big mistake," Nick told him. "Look at your wife, Captain."

He realized Emma had been so caught up in the drama playing out on the church steps, she had yet to realize he was there. But he also saw her head raised in defiance. Her eyes were bright with the certainty that she was in the right. He felt a smile tug at his mouth.

Just then, Frank Tucker approached Emma and the other women. "Ladies, perhaps you could tell us what it might take to end this standoff and allow these young people to get on with their wedding."

The crowd stilled and leaned forward to catch every word.

Emma turned her head and fixed her gaze on RJ. "An admission of truth," she said.

"And an apology," Grace added.

Cody's wife, Lily, stepped forward. "Does anyone here who knows Emma Elliott think for one minute she would ever take something not hers? Does anyone here think for one moment she would be caught dead wearing that gaudy piece of paste jewelry?"

Mrs. Gilmore's head snapped up. "The stones in that brooch are real," she shouted. "Tell them, Seymour."

Suddenly, the bride stood and marched forward. "It was RJ," she said, standing toe-to-toe with the sheriff. "He told me to make some excuse to call Miss E back to the house as she was leaving. I did as he asked." She glared at her intended. "As I have always done, but no more."

RJ grabbed her roughly by the upper arm.

"Are you going to hit me again?" she said, tossing her head. "Because with all these people watching, it would be hard to say I fell."

RJ hesitated just long enough for Trula to wrest herself from his grip. She turned and walked to the lineup of Harvey Girls, standing before Emma. "He'll never apologize," she said, her voice shaking, "but I will. I am so very sorry."

Max saw Emma unlink her arm from Grace's and make room for Trula to join their ranks.

RJ's parents stepped forward. His father's face was bloated with anger. "Young lady, that is my grand-child you are carrying." He ignored the shocked gasp that came from several onlookers, but Mrs. Gilmore grasped his forearm tightly.

"Seymour, not here," she said.

"Not according to your son," Trula replied. "He says it's not his. Go on. Ask him."

But RJ was already striding away, pushing his way through the crowd as he headed for the saloon.

Mr. Gilmore, however, was far from done. He turned his focus to the others. "Some of you young ladies might have had an opportunity to continue working here, but no longer. You are dismissed."

Quietly, Ford Harvey moved to stand in front of the line of Harvey Girls, facing Gilmore. From an inner coat pocket, he removed a packet of official-looking documents.

"Mr. Gilmore, I am Ford Harvey, Fred Harvey's son and representative. I would respectfully remind you that none of these young women presently work for you until our deal goes through. If that happens."

"If? What do you mean, *if*?"

"While I do not yet know all the facts, it would appear that we have credible testimony that this young woman is blameless in the matter of your wife's missing jewelry. I believe you—and your son—owe her an apology."

"Never," Gilmore blustered. "I never apologize to hired help."

Without another word, Ford Harvey tore the papers in half and handed one part to Gilmore. "Perhaps you might wish to sleep on that refusal, sir. Should you—and your son—make the appropriate amends to restore this lady's good name and reputation, we can talk. Until then, that hotel over there will remain a Harvey establishment."

Max watched as Gilmore threw the papers on the ground and stalked away. "I don't need your hotel or anything else connected to you. Millicent!" He shouted to his wife, and she hurried to his side.

"Ladies and gentlemen," Father O'Meara announced, addressing the crowd, "I do believe the crisis has passed. May I suggest we move inside for morning mass?"

As the crowd dispersed, Max watched the Harvey Girls gather around Emma to celebrate what had clearly been a victory for them all. He felt a swell of pride in his chest that surprised him. Emma was a woman who could handle anything—and apparently anyone. He stepped forward and knew the exact moment she realized he was there.

"Max!" she shouted and ran to him.

He caught her up in his arms and kissed her full on the lips, not caring whether those gathered would approve.

"You came back," she said, her smile a sunburst of pure joy.

"Yeah. I realized I forgot something important."

Her smile turned to a frown. "Bert already sold everything at auction. He and Pearl—"

"Not the show, Emma. *You.* I forgot you. I realized the worst idea I ever had was thinking I could go off and start a new chapter in my life without you right by my side."

"But—"

"No buts, Emmie. Remember what I said? We're two halves of a whole. I bought some time before we need to report to the colonel. How soon can you be ready to leave?"

"Is tomorrow soon enough?"

He grinned. "I reckon that'll work just fine."

Once again he spun around with her, and when he stopped, Grace and Lily were grinning at them.

"So this is the good-lookin' cowboy who stole Emma's heart in record time," Lily said. "Not bad," she murmured with a smile. Then she winked at Emma. "Not bad at all."

"Come on, Lily," Daniels said, taking his wife's hand. "Let's give these two some privacy."

"But," Lily protested, "they'll leave tomorrow and…"

She was still talking as Cody led her back to the hotel.

While Emma accepted congratulations from Mayor Tucker and others, Grace leaned in and kissed Max's cheek. "Thanks for changing your mind and coming back," she said. "How about I have Nick see Aidan about getting a room for you two for tonight while I get Lily to help me pack Emma's things?"

"Thanks—for everything," Max said and hugged her.

"What's this?" Emma demanded, hands on her slim hips. "I turn my back for one minute and one of my two best friends is in your arms?"

"Emmie…"

"She's teasing you," Grace said. "Best get used to it. Our Emma has a wicked sense of humor." She waved as she walked to the hotel, leaving Max and Emma alone for the first time since he'd arrived.

"You need a bath," Emma said, but instead of moving away from him, she wrapped her arm around his waist. "There's this room in the hotel—has its own private bath and everything."

"Sounds nice."

"And later, I might just find a need to put on that lovely nightgown Grace and Lily gave me."

Max chuckled and drew her closer. "And maybe three or four minutes after that," he said, his voice husky, "I expect I'll find a need to remove it for you."

He nuzzled her cheek, nibbling at her ear.

"Captain Winslow," he heard a familiar voice say. "I must remind you that such a public display of affection is not the Harvey way."

Max chuckled as he and Emma turned to face Ford Harvey, who grinned at them.

"Ah, but Mr. Harvey," Emma said sweetly, "it *is* the Winslow way." And before Max could stop her, she wrapped her arms around her husband's neck and kissed him.

There was something to be said for these modern times, he thought—at least these modern women.

Author's Note

Dear Readers,

Thank you for reading my story—I hope you enjoyed the adventures of these true pioneers of the Old West! In both *Trailblazer* and *Renegade* I gave you recipes from actual Harvey establishments. This time, I thought it would be fun to share one of my recipes. Fair warning: because my life is full to the brim (like a cup of Fred Harvey coffee!), I take the easiest possible route to turn out good food. Hope you enjoy my recipe for chili!

All best,
Anna

Anna's Easy Chicken Chili

- 1 store-prepared rotisserie chicken, deboned and skinned. You can also use ground beef or another meat or *no* meat in place of chicken.
- 1 large onion, chopped
- 1 cup celery, chopped
- 1 can chopped tomatoes
- 1 jar salsa (medium, or hot if you prefer a stronger kick)
- 1 jar spaghetti sauce (I use one flavored with herbs)
- 1 can dark kidney beans, drained
- ½ cup elbow macaroni
- 1–2 cups Bloody Mary mix
- OPTIONAL: mushrooms, salt, pepper, herbs such as oregano, parsley, cilantro; one cup Merlot wine

In a large stew pot, sauté the onion and celery in butter or cooking spray; cut or pull chicken into small pieces; mix everything in with onions and celery. Simmer on low; as sauce thickens, add more Bloody Mary mix.

Serve with a thick crusty bread—or cornbread. Makes a large pot and it's even better the second day. Enjoy!